MARVEL

CAPTAIN AMERICA: STEVE ROGERS

DECLASSIFIED

Notes, Interviews, and Files from the Avengers' Archives

Dayton Ward & Kevin Dilmore

SMART POP

Smart Pop Books
An Imprint of BenBella Books, Inc.
Dallas, TX

© 2024 MARVEL

Smart Pop is an imprint of BenBella Books, Inc.
10440 N. Central Expressway
Suite 800
Dallas, TX 75231
smartpopbooks.com | benbellabooks.com
Send feedback to feedback@benbellabooks.com

BenBella and *Smart Pop* are federally registered trademarks.

Printed in the United States of America
10 9 8 7 6 5 4 3 2 1

Library of Congress Control Number: 2024003770
ISBN 9781637743461 (trade paperback)
ISBN 9781637743478 (ebook)

Editing by Elizabeth Smith
Copyediting by James Fraleigh
Proofreading by Sarah Vostok
Text design and composition by Kit Sweeney
Additional image support by Aaron Edmiston
Cover design by Morgan Carr
Cover image © Shutterstock / Oleh11 [photo border]
Printed by Lake Book Manufacturing

MARVEL PUBLISHING
Jeff Youngquist, VP, Production and Special Projects
Sarah Singer, Editor, Special Projects
Jeremy West, Manager, Licensed Publishing
Sven Larsen, VP, Licensed Publishing
David Gabriel, SVP Print, Sales & Marketing
C.B. Cebulski, Editor in Chief
Special thanks to Markus Raymond, Stuart Vandal, and the Official Handbook of
    the Marvel Universe team.

Special discounts for bulk sales are available.
Please contact bulkorders@benbellabooks.com.

CONTENTS

Foreword ... v

I. Recovery ... 1

II. Reckoning ... 29

III. Reassessment ... 63

IV. Recompense ... 103

V. Reconstruction ... 137

VI. Requiem ... 183

VII. Reborn ... 203

VIII. Redemptions ... 223

IX. Reconnection ... 249

Afterword ... 265

Acknowledgments ... 267

About the Authors ... 271

FOREWORD

The American Dream.

Across the nation and around the world, people visualize this decades-old concept in no uncertain terms: liberty, equality, inalienable rights, representative democracy . . . and, above them all, freedom. The freedom to do, the freedom to be. Uncounted persons have aspired to these concepts, but over generations, only one of them is regarded as the living embodiment of this intangible, perhaps even unattainable Dream.

That person is Steve Rogers. And to acknowledge and celebrate the anniversary of his miraculous return to duty decades after he was believed killed in action during World War II, I set out to find him.

No, he is not hidden among the masses or shying from the spotlight of scrutiny. Far from it. He not only represents these ideals, he literally fights for them. He protects and preserves them against any threat--domestic or galactic--that would strip them from us. He has died for these ideals.

For Steve Rogers is Captain America--and I want you to know them both.

Despite the stories and tales that have defined Captain America for generations, you don't know Steve Rogers. I assuredly did not, until I asked him whether he would be willing to sit with me--not unlike how his fellow Avenger Tony Stark had before him--to share not simply the stories of his heroic life but also what he had learned. I wanted to know about who he was in the past and who he is now. I wanted to know as much about how he had shaped his country as I did about how his country has shaped him.

Unsurprisingly, and definitely unlike Tony Stark,
Captain Rogers agreed to do so with no reservations
(at least none he voiced to me). Why was he so eager?
Because, he said, Americans are owed these insights,
and he felt duty bound to share them.

As I did with Mr. Stark, I began my research
with a series of Freedom of Information Act requests
from the Departments of Defense, the Army, and
Veterans Affairs. This provided me with as complete
a picture of Captain Rogers' military service as
one could hope to assemble. Despite the fragmentary
nature of such information about those who served
before and during World War II, it did not surprise
me to learn that his records had been diligently
preserved. (Naturally, they had been updated after
his remarkable discovery in suspended animation by
the Avengers.) Those departments, along with the
Strategic Homeland Intervention, Enforcement, and
Logistics Division (S.H.I.E.L.D.), began keeping their
own copious records of Captain Rogers' activities
following his revival, and nearly all of these
documents were made available to me.

These files chronicle the facts of what happened
and Captain Rogers' role as the events of his "second
life" unfolded. His viewpoint and thoughts on such
matters are represented in the form of post-action
reports, debriefing transcripts, and interviews with
various government agencies and media outlets. Seeing
these documents together granted me new appreciation
for his thoughts and feelings about the incredible
experiences he had endured, either working alone
or with the Avengers. I've presented excerpts
here from a number of those official records and
other documents.

Another aspect to the story of Steve Rogers exists beyond the man himself, in the lives he has affected: family, friends, comrades in arms, and even those he has loved. In many cases, their words can be found here too. Every bit of this information proved vital to my research, but what it ultimately fails to do--at least to a significant degree--is provide us insight into the man who continues to serve not just the country of his birth but indeed the entire world as Captain America. Only his own words can do that.

The interviews forming the core of this work, primarily conducted over several sessions and a considerable span, address a broad range of topics. Certainly I was curious about the challenge of reintegrating into a society not only radically different from the one he last experienced but also not always capable of understanding the true toll military service--particularly during wartime--can impose on a person's psyche. With Steve Rogers, we have a living and vital representative of World War II, the repercussions of which continue to be felt globally to this day.

Undertaking this effort, I imagined Steve Rogers as a man out of time; someone whose mind and body had been revived into our world of today while his heart and spirit very well might have remained in the war-torn world of decades ago. I approached him as the super hero he has become to Americans as well as the Super-Soldier he remained to himself. I wondered whether Steve Rogers believed he belonged in the world of today. I wondered whether I myself believed it.

The answers might surprise you.

I. RECOVERY

It is at once fascinating and surreal to sit down with someone who lived a life decades before you were born, and for whom the memories of that life are less distant than those of your own childhood. This was my initial thought upon meeting Steve Rogers. I walked into our first session with my guard up against the mystery surrounding this man, but I need not have worried, for he ended up being more open and accommodating than I ever could have hoped.

Born into a world most of us know only through history books and perhaps far too many films and television shows (which typically sacrifice accuracy for spectacle), Steve Rogers was like many young men of his generation. The son of poor immigrants who traveled from Ireland to find new opportunities in the United States, he along with his parents and countless other families endured the hardship of the Great Depression. Despite such challenges, they still believed in the potential of life in America and worked hard to attain their dream. But early childhood saw Steve face the death of his father, a tragedy compounded by his mother's succumbing to pneumonia while he was still a teenager.

Less than two decades after the end of the First World War, patriotism was running strong among the young men and women watching the steady wave of fascism and tyranny wash over Europe. Believing it inevitable that the United States would once again become embroiled in a global conflict, many offered themselves to the growing effort to prepare for that day.

That is where Steven Rogers' story begins. Our journey with him, however, begins differently.

INTERVIEWER: *Thank you for agreeing to meet with me, Captain Rogers. It's a genuine pleasure to sit with you.*

STEVE ROGERS: Please, call me Steve. I've honestly never been very comfortable with the "Captain Rogers" bit.

They did promote you.

Retroactively, and even then it still took me a while to get over drawing a sort of mental line between Private Rogers and Captain America. I guess it doesn't matter anymore now that everyone knows who I am, but old habits are hard to break.

Duly noted, Steve.

I've read an early version of the interviews you conducted with Tony. I figured you'd be doing the same thing with me, going all the way back to the beginning with my life before the Army and Captain America.

As it's the celebration of your return to the world of today that brought us together, I'd prefer instead to start with your being found in the ocean. You can fill us in on your previous life as you see fit along the way.

I understand what you mean, but please understand *me*. What you see from your point of view as a "previous life" is simply part of my whole life. Decades spent sleeping doesn't change a guy.

DAILY 🎺 BUGLE

NEW YORK'S FINEST DAILY NEWSPAPER

$1.00 DAILY
$1.50 SUNDAYS

GIRL! But—
m where? p.3

W CAN THE TRUE
PTAIN AMERICA
LL BE SO YOUNG?
OR IS CURIOUS.

details on page 9

TAND BACK!
'LL GET HIM!

CAPTAIN AMERICA IS ALIVE

World War II Hero Found Frozen in Ice, Revived by Avengers

AVENGERS MANSION, NEW YORK—Iron Man himself took the podium before a pool of reporters to make a stunning announcement earlier this afternoon. While on a mission aboard their specially designed submarine, Iron Man and other Avengers discovered the body of Captain America, the legendary hero of the Second World War, entombed in a melting block of ice.

Using the advanced equipment at their disposal, the Avengers completed the process of thawing the Super-Soldier from his bizarre tomb, only to be further surprised to learn he was not dead but instead existing in a state of deep hibernation.

"Suspended animation," explained Iron Man. "We believe his unique physiology and the special enhancements he was given to make him Captain America all those years ago

The legendary Captain America with the Avengers: Iron Man, the Wasp, Giant-Man, and Thor.

is what kept him alive, and he hasn't aged a single day. It's a truly amazing turn of events, not just for him but all of us."

Of course, Steve. This is your story and I want your perspective.

The whole bit of my traveling through time was good shorthand for the papers trying to explain this to readers, but it's not the best illustration of what happened. I didn't just skip over chapters in the history books. In my book, those chapters were ripped out and what remained was pasted together. I did no traveling. I simply woke up.

Captain America
and Bucky, during
World War II

What were your first memories upon awakening?

For the most part, it was as though no time had passed. One minute I'm falling from the sky after we sabotaged that Nazi plane, thinking my friend, Bucky Barnes, had been killed. Then I hit the water, and I remember how cold the ocean was. I remember the water in my lungs. I remember drowning. Then the next minute, I'm awake and surrounded by this . . . group of people in strange costumes. A robot, a giant, a tiny flying woman I called "Tinkerbell," and this escapee from a circus carrying a hammer.

The Avengers can be a bit to take in, even in a world where costumed heroes are a far more frequent sight. You were still coming to terms with the reality of your ordeal.

It's not like I got a lot of time to do that either. No sooner are we docked in New York than my first impromptu mission is to help rescue my own saviors, who'd been turned into stone statues by : . . an alien. That's right, my first day in this strange new world was something else.

And yet, you wasted no time rescuing them.

With the help of an unexpected friend, Rick Jones, who I at first mistook for Bucky. That was pretty awkward for us both, but he took it in stride. He didn't believe me when I told him who I was, and it didn't help that I was sure it was all a crazy dream.

But you eventually convinced each other, and you helped him rescue the Avengers.

After which, Iron Man and the others invited me to join their team.

It wasn't an offer you accepted, at least not initially.

I blame Stark, even though it wasn't really his fault. He mentioned Reed Richards and his work to perfect time travel, and I was sure that was my ticket back to my own time and a chance to save Bucky from what happened to him. Stark tried to explain the danger. I didn't understand a lot of the mumbo-jumbo about temporal paradoxes. It took the president of the United States himself to set me straight.

You met with the president, and he told you he couldn't allow you to risk altering history. How did you take that?

I saluted and acknowledged his orders, but that didn't do anything for how I felt. After I'd had a chance to acclimate a bit, I started researching whatever I could about me and Bucky. I contacted the Department of the Army, Veterans Affairs, even organizations like the American Legion and the Veterans of Foreign Wars and research specialists at a few different World War II museums.

And I'm guessing you didn't find anything.

Our Army personnel files either had been classified or destroyed, and our supposed deaths during the war were covered up. I learned they found other soldiers to wear Captain America and Bucky uniforms, pretending we were still alive and fighting overseas, to keep the illusion going in order to maintain support back home.

How did you react to that?

Personally, I couldn't have cared less. In my mind, that was enough to justify my hanging up my shield and returning to something resembling a normal life. If that couldn't be in my own time, then I guess I'd have to make a new life in the here and now.

But you were angry about Bucky.

He gave his life for this country and was never publicly acknowledged for his heroism. At least, not at the time and never for the person he was behind his mask. Eventually, when they gave up the idea of there still being a Captain America and Bucky, they put up those statues of us at Arlington, but James Buchanan Barnes himself? (*he shakes his head*) He was one of the bravest young men I'd ever known, and so far as the world was concerned, he never existed.

Memorial statues of Captain America and Bucky, Arlington National Cemetery, Arlington, Virginia

It's fair to say you struggled with assimilating into modern society.

Stark warned me about your gift for understatement.

You destroyed your own statue at Arlington.

Statues are for honoring the dead. I don't qualify. Not yet, anyway.

I understand the shock of awakening from hibernation did affect your long-term memory, at least for a time.

That's right. My memories were scattershot. I could recall bits and pieces of detail about other friendships, or events that took place when I was much younger, but there was no real cohesion, at least at first. Looking through what few older photographs still survived, or reading press releases and other documents from the war, helped a bit. Memories would return of their own accord, without warning. A familiar song, or smell, or even an offhand remark someone said might trigger something. I'd wake up from dreaming, and a memory I didn't even realize I'd forgotten would be there to greet me. (*shakes head*) It was an interesting time, rediscovering my identity and my past.

On a related note, I imagine facing the challenge of learning about decades of history and technological advancement that occurred while you slept had to be daunting.

(*laughs*) I carried around a notebook, this little memorandum book, similar to ones we used in the Army back in my day, with a green cover and pages of lined paper. At first, that book was where I scribbled notes for my recon reports to my commanding officer, General Jacob Simon in Army Intelligence. Later, when I reconnected with General Simon in person, he took me through the history that Tony Stark had glossed over. I made lists of the things I decided I wanted or needed to learn from him. Whenever I crossed something off, I usually ended up adding two or three new things. I finally gave that up once Stark and Rick Jones showed me how to use a computer.

What are one or two of your favorite things that happened during the years you skipped?

The Moon landings. (*he shakes his head*) What an amazing feat. When I was a kid, it was Buck Rogers and Flash Gordon who flew in space. I used to go and watch those movie serials every week, and I read stories by Wells and Verne. It was all so fantastic to dream about, and now we have satellites and space stations and unmanned probes surveying the other planets. Incredible.

Anything else?

Microwave popcorn.

FOR IMMEDIATE RELEASE

PRIORITY

AVENGERS RECRUIT CAPTAIN AMERICA TO JOIN THEIR RANKS

It is with great pleasure and pride that the Avengers welcome their newest member, Captain America.

Already a living legend thanks to his service to this great nation during the darkest days of the Second World War, the man known to many as "the Sentinel of Liberty" was believed to have given his life while fighting Nazi oppression during the closing days of the war in Europe. For decades, he has been the subject of books, films, history lessons, and memorials across the United States.

In a miraculous twist of fate, Captain America did not perish on that fateful day, but instead was entombed in ice that slowed his body functions almost to a stop, perfectly preserving him. It was only by fortunate happenstance that we, the Avengers, found him still interred in what for any normal man would have been an icy grave. The wondrous enhancements his body underwent back in 1941 and that turned him into America's first Super-Soldier were also the key to his ultimate salvation: once we thawed him from the ice, he returned to consciousness without having aged a single day.

Despite his understandable confusion about what happened to him, we are pleased to report that Captain America has wasted no time adjusting to the new world in which he finds himself. His physical abilities and his leadership expertise, to say nothing of his fierce love for the country he served during one of the darkest times in recent history, make him an ideal addition to our team. Captain America will make the Avengers an even more effective force for good, and we're very fortunate that he has chosen to join our ranks.

Despite your initial reluctance, you not only joined the Avengers but quickly became someone the others looked to for leadership.

It's not as though I had trouble fitting in. (*he gestures to a nearby closet, where I can see his uniform and the shield*) I came to the party with my own costume, after all.

I know it's been quite a few years since your reawakening, but do you recall your initial impression of your fellow Avengers after they revived you?

I guess we have to start with Stark, don't we? There's no denying he's brilliant. (*shakes head*) He sheds skin cells that are smarter than most of us. The trouble with Tony is that he *knows* he's the smartest guy in any room he enters. That has a tendency to rub some people the wrong way, but he backs up that arrogance with an intelligence and passion you simply can't ignore. He's definitely someone you want at your side when things go wrong.

STARK,
ANTHONY EDWARD
KNOWN ALIASES/ALTER EGOS:
Iron Man

High praise, coming from you.

We're alike in more ways than either of us would rather admit. It took a while, but I came to view him like a brother. (*smiles*) The older brother who never lets you forget you're the younger one, but a brother just the same.

And like brothers, you sometimes disagreed, and sometimes you even fought.

Oh, yeah. We certainly did.

I suspect that will be its own topic of conversation before we're finished, so let's table that for now. Tell me about Thor.

ODINSON, THOR
KNOWN ALIASES/ALTER EGOS:
Donald Blake

He may have been the one who was hardest to believe, at least at first. I mean, he's a god. At least, there are those who view him that way. I knew of the Norse and Greek gods from school, of course, but the God I knew, I learned about in church and Sunday school. Can Thor be an alien from another world and at the same time the personification of Norse mythology? It sure seems like it. But I admit it was a bit hard to swallow at first.

Are you saying you struggled in reconciling Thor with your religious upbringing?

There's no denying his abilities border on the sorts of things you'd expect from a god. I certainly see him as someone who is compassionate and generous while also being fully capable of unleashing righteous fury in the right circumstances. (*smiles*) I remember thinking at the time that if this really was *the* Thor, appearing in physical form before us mere mortals, then perhaps the God I learned about might one day appear, as well. That'd be something to see, wouldn't it?

I think it would. What about Hank Pym?

Dr. Pym was perhaps one of the most intelligent people I'm ever liable to meet, Stark and Dr. Erskine included.

Dr. Erskine being the scientist who created the Super-Soldier serum.

PYM, HENRY JONATHAN
("HANK")--Deceased
KNOWN ALIASES/ALTER EGOS:
Hank Pym, Giant-Man, Ant-Man,
Yellowjacket, Ultron

VAN DYNE, JANET
KNOWN ALIASES/ALTER EGOS:
Janet Pym, Wasp

Right. I know Dr. Pym never fully shook the feeling of being ostracized from the rest of the scientific community, who didn't respect his research and experiments.

His work doesn't receive nearly the recognition it deserves.

(*looks away for a moment before replying*) I'm no scientist so I'll never fully grasp what he discovered about our universe, but I respected his passion and desire to better understand our place in it. I think I could've learned a lot from him.

I wish I'd had the chance to meet him. What do you recall from your first meetings with Janet Van Dyne?

Stark told me how they found each other, and it didn't take long for me to see how she gave him a run for his money in the brains department. In the time I got to watch them together, it was obvious they complemented each other wonderfully. They each brought something that the other seemed to be missing, whether it was a different outlook on life or simply learning to see past their own perceived limitations. A soulmate can do that . . . if you're lucky enough to find one.

INTERVIEWER'S NOTE: Rogers paused at this point, his gaze turning toward the nearby open window and the sounds of the city drifting through it to us. Though I felt tempted to lean into his last comment and see where—and to whom—it took us, I opted to save that topic for a more appropriate time.

Though the public record shows you adapting to your new situation without too much trouble, my conversations with Mr. Stark indicate it wasn't all smooth sailing.

Oh, there were a lot of settling-in adjustments. The Avengers did what they thought they could to help me, but it was a lot to take in all at once. I suppose it helped that they wasted no time putting me to work, by having me help them against the Sub-Mariner. Once that situation calmed down, I was left with time on my hands and a head full of runaway thoughts.

I understand Stark took you back to your old neighborhood in Manhattan.

That was definitely one of the larger shocks to my system. We went to where Ebbets Field used to be and the Dodgers once played. They were long gone, of course, having moved to Los Angeles more than a decade after the war ended and I went into the ice. An apartment complex was built on the site years and years ago, but someone thought enough of the old place to put a commemorative plaque on the fence encircling the apartments. Seeing the dates on the plaque—1957, 1960—really drove home for the first time just how long I'd been asleep and just how far the world had moved on during all those years.

You would encounter other reminders, of course.

Not a day goes by that something doesn't trigger a memory of my old life, or simply reminds me that I'm still largely out of step with this world. I've just gotten better at handling it.

Unidentified photographs
recovered from Steve Rogers's
personal possessions at the
time of his purported death

You leaned on your fellow Avengers a lot in those early days.

Talk about throwing yourself into your work. (*smiles*) Being an Avenger is a lot like being in the Army. There's a lot of waiting around for something to happen, so you fill those hours with training or—in my case—my continuing education so far as everything I missed, but all of that gets set aside when a mission comes along. I applied what I knew in both types of situations, but at the time, I much preferred the missions because they didn't give me time to be alone with my own thoughts.

Much has been written about your revival, but it seems many of these chronicles overlook a key element: For you, the passage of time was instantaneous. As you mentioned earlier, your last memories are of your final mission during the war.

And Bucky.

JONES, RICHARD MILLHOUSE ("RICK")
KNOWN ALIASES/ALTER EGOS:
Bucky, A-Bomb, Whisperer

I can only imagine trying to cope with his loss was one of the greater challenges you faced.

You're not wrong. Growing up, I never had a brother, but that changed once I joined the Army. With my parents gone, Bucky was the closest thing to family I'd ever have. I think that's why I took such an early shine to Rick Jones. He reminded me of Bucky in so many ways, at least when I first met him.

He'd been with the Avengers almost from the beginning.

Largely due to his friendship with Bruce Banner, who saved him in the gamma bomb accident that made Banner into the Hulk. I remember thinking at the time that Rick reminded me of me in a few ways. We're both orphans, and neither of us let any perceived personal limitations stop us from trying to do the right thing. In that regard, he was also a lot like Bucky. He even looked a bit like Bucky.

It's fair to say that resemblance contributed to your willingness to mentor him. He even served alongside you as Bucky, at least for a time.

It certainly wasn't my idea. As soon as I saw him injured, albeit accidentally by Banner as the Hulk, I immediately thought of Bucky and how my carelessness caused his death. I couldn't stand the thought of something like that happening to Rick. It came to a head when Rick found Bucky's old uniform and tried it on. He was an uncanny match for Bucky, especially with the mask, but I quickly realized Rick didn't have Bucky's training or experience.

Seeing Mr. Jones in your friend's old costume must have come as quite the shock. I've seen photos of him in the costume and I have to tell you, the resemblance to Mr. Barnes was uncanny.

You're telling me. The first time I saw him, it stopped me dead in my tracks.

He seemed as determined to be your partner as Mr. Barnes once was.

(*nods*) Again with the understatement. I couldn't fault Rick for his passion. That, and the simple fact I still wasn't over losing Bucky and feeling guilty for believing I was responsible for his death, was enough to push

Captain America with Rick Jones as Bucky

me toward giving Rick a chance. It meant so much to him, and despite my initial concern that he might get hurt—or worse—while wearing Bucky's costume, I liked the idea of having a partner again, someone who could watch my back.

But he wasn't ready, was he?

No. There's no other way to say it. Rick wasn't Bucky. He had the drive, of course. He was in good shape, better than a lot of men his age, but his training tended toward athletic pursuits, rather than preparing for actual combat. Bucky had a lot to learn when he started out as my partner, and the learning curve was steep, considering he was right there with me as we fought Nazis and everything else.

Mr. Jones was almost the same age as Mr. Barnes was when he first became your partner during the war, but he lacked that same sort of real-world experience visited upon you both at far too young an age.

(*another nod, this one with more conviction*) Yes, that's it. I tried to train Rick, but his youthful exuberance—I hesitate to call it "immaturity" because that sounds like criticism and that's not really fair to him—was working against him. At least that's how I felt about it at the time.

Obviously, Mr. Jones felt differently.

Yes, and while his reaction can be explained if not excused by his youth, I could've handled things better. I was still dealing with memories of the war and Bucky's death, and I just couldn't stand the idea of losing another partner that way. Thankfully, Rick eventually understood where I was coming from, and we became friends.

You've mentioned before that your new teammates had gone out of their way to help you feel welcome in this new time, and that they were not alone.

And I'll always be grateful for that. Early on, it was easy for me to feel pretty overwhelmed by the technological marvels that Tony could create seemingly off the top of his head. One of the first gizmos he made for me was a set of miniaturized transistors he installed in my shield that communicated with a set of magnets on my glove to return it to me no matter how hard I'd thrown it. He and the other Avengers also shared with me cards and letters sent from across the country, even from around the world, by people expressing their gratitude for my return to life and to duty.

That had to help put your mind at ease.

In some ways, sure. I also was struggling with a sometimes debilitating and demoralizing case of survivor's guilt. Bucky was never far from my thoughts, and neither was my driving need to learn who was responsible for his death. I never would have imagined how close I was to uncovering the truth.

You're speaking of your first clash with the so-called Masters of Evil.

Yeah. Catchy, huh? Each member of the group was chosen because each carried a personal vendetta against a member of the Avengers, including me.

AMORA
KNOWN ALIASES/ALTER EGOS:
Enchantress

HORGAN, BRUNO
KNOWN ALIASES/ALTER EGOS: Melter

CHEN LU
KNOWN ALIASES/ALTER EGOS:
Radioactive Man

SKURGE
KNOWN ALIASES/ALTER EGOS:
Skurge the Executioner

GARRET, NATHAN
KNOWN ALIASES/ALTER EGOS:
Black Knight

ZEMO, HEINRICH

KNOWN ALIASES/ALTER EGOS:
Baron Zemo the 12th

Your sworn enemy was Baron Zemo.

Baron Heinrich Zemo, specifically, the twelfth member of his family to carry the title. He blamed me for a disfiguring accident that occurred decades before, when I encountered him working as a scientist for Hitler. Zemo'd created a substance he called Adhesive X that he intended to weaponize for the Wehrmacht. A toss of my shield shattered the vessel containing Zemo's concoction, which struck the baron and saturated the fabric hood he used to cover his face from public view.

I can imagine that was a life-changing accident for him.

The fabric adhered to his face with an unbreakable bond. I certainly regret what happened to Zemo. I don't regret stopping him from perfecting a chemical agent that, in Hitler's hands, would have wreaked who knows what level of havoc on the world. But that turn of events was . . . unfortunate.

You met Baron Zemo in person for the first time in our time after the rest of the Avengers had incapacitated the other Masters of Evil.

That's right. Zemo's plan to channel the hate and aggression each of his villainous partners held toward the individual Avengers got upended when we surprised them by trading our adversaries. Black Knight didn't anticipate a challenge from Thor, nor did Radioactive Man expect to take on Iron Man and Giant-Man. Zemo also didn't expect to learn that the Avengers had come up with a counteragent that would dissolve the bonds of his Adhesive X.

Something from the mind of Tony Stark?

Not this time. Our own Wasp suggested we contact Peter Petruski, who at the time was serving a sentence for his criminal activities as Paste-Pot Pete. Petruski was a research scientist whose work involved all manner of multi-polymer adhesives, and in exchange for a reduced sentence, he revealed to us the existence of what he called a super-dissolver. Once we knew it worked successfully to render Adhesive X useless, Rick Jones secretly exchanged the dissolver for canisters of Adhesive X, which the Masters of Evil sprayed around the city and effectively undid their own plan.

That couldn't have worked out better.

The only downside was Petruski ending up on the street again. He had no intention of reforming his ways and continues to operate as a criminal today. When Zemo learned of this super-dissolver's effect on Adhesive X, he became obsessed with getting his hands on it. That's when I took him on hand-to-hand. Zemo's fighting skills were remarkable, I'll grant him that. What gave me the upper hand was my passion to fight for freedom. That fight wasn't about stopping Zemo from spraying adhesive. It was about preventing him from devising his next plan—and his next and his next—to crush our democratic system and subject us all to his brand of tyranny. (*pauses*) This idea that we could lose everything—it's a load of hokum to you.

INTERVIEWER'S NOTE: *My expression must have given me away—and I couldn't admit in that moment that he was right. As his accusation hung between us, Captain Rogers had a look of what I read as disappointment . . . and I sensed that disappointment was in me. I thought I'd blown this interview and perhaps this whole story.*

Pardon?

Hokum, what you'd call bull.

I know what hokum is but I . . .

I get it. I can't fault you for it. You're a part of this place and this time, and because you've known a world of heroes who protect you from danger, who've prevented catastrophe on global and even cosmic scales, the thought of our way of life still being at risk today doesn't seem possible. Does it?

I suppose not.

But it is. There are demagogues and autocrats, bad actors and conspirators, forces of oppression and authoritarianism. The players change but the threat against this nation—and what it was founded to be—remains. I saw it in the Nazis and I see it now, and I believe what we have is worth fighting for with my life. I'd use words that sound less alarming to people today, but those words are the right ones. This is a reality I feel to the core of my being, even when I sense in a moment that I'm alone in feeling it.

I've heard people speak of the responsibility you feel for what you represent. I knew coming in to expect sincerity in your words. But your . . . authenticity. I feel it from you in a way I couldn't anticipate. I've met no one more genuine than you.

Okay. (*pauses*) I'll take that. You're saying I'm starting to grow on you.

(laughing) Yeah. Yes, you are, Steve.

Stark said you'd grow on me too.

That's unexpected praise.

He didn't say that you grew on him.

Well, that's more like him.

So, where were we?

Baron Zemo.

Exactly. After our first go-round, I focused on Zemo once I'd determined he was who I'd been seeking since my return. Zemo was responsible for Bucky's death, and I knew I would stop at nothing to bring him to justice. I tracked him to the Amazon jungle and pursued him back to American soil only to be stopped from exacting revenge by the Executioner, who by that time was in league with the Masters of Evil. When we next took on the group, we were distracted by the arrival of a costumed fighter who introduced himself as Wonder Man.

Wonder Man (at center) with Amora, Skurge, and Zemo

Wonder Man

POST-ACTION_REPORT_-__
AVENGERS_INTERNAL_USE_ONLY

Contact_and_interaction_with_subject_known_as_
Wonder_Man_as_reported_by_Dr._Henry_Pym_
(transcript of oral report)

I and other members of the Avengers responded to a
hotline alarm reporting a bank robbery in progress.
On our arrival, we encountered Baron Zemo as well as
the banished Asgardians known as the Enchantress and
the Executioner. We engaged them in combat and shortly
after were joined by a man in a cowl and colorful
costume who introduced himself as Wonder Man.

The costumed man exhibited multiple superhuman
powers including greatly increased strength and speed.
He seemingly outmatched the three perpetrators on his
own, prompting them to flee and escape apprehension.
After the skirmish, Wonder Man told us he was from the
heart of the Amazon jungles and had waited a long time
to find us with the hope of joining the Avengers. He
later shared that he'd been vacationing in the jungle
when he was captured by a scientist named Zemo, who
had forced Wonder Man to act as an experimental subject
before he escaped captivity. I recall Captain America
initially casting doubt on Wonder Man's story, but then
Cap had an apparent change of heart, saying that Wonder
Man's true motivation for finding the Avengers was that
he was dying of a rare disease and hoped the Avengers
might find a cure.

I joined Tony and Don in researching possible
cures for what threatened Wonder Man's life, but our
efforts were in vain as we could find no biochemical,
surgical, or technological relief for our new ally.

A few days had passed when Wonder Man contacted
the Avengers by radio to say he'd been recaptured
by Baron Zemo in the Amazon jungle. On our arrival
to Zemo's jungle hideaway, Wonder Man surprised and
attacked us. He had the upper hand from the start
and ultimately beat each of us into unconsciousness.
We awakened to see Zemo and the Enchantress fleeing
the scene but were unable to apprehend them as a
blast charge apparently set by Zemo prevented us from
reaching them.

When we reached Wonder Man, he'd collapsed and his
condition was deteriorating. It was clear to us that
the only way we'd survived our vulnerable, unconscious
state was a defense Wonder Man had put up. When Tony

asked Wonder Man why he saved us at this risk of his own life, Wonder Man said he'd dreamed of performing one noble act in his life, and that was it. He then died of an affliction placed upon him by Zemo, who'd withheld an antidote capable of curing Wonder Man's condition.

I must admit my regret at losing Wonder Man as a potential ally. I only can ponder on what he might have accomplished during a much longer career as an Avenger.

(transcript ends)

The death of Wonder Man

That was your first encounter with Simon Williams.

We certainly had no way of knowing it wouldn't be our last.

And as for Baron Zemo?

It wasn't long before he lashed out at us again. By dumb luck, I glanced up from putting a letter in a mailbox to see Enchantress and the Executioner in a chauffeured car, so I was able to assemble the rest of the Avengers and warn them. Together, we witnessed Rick Jones' kidnapping by a passing jet plane. Somehow, the craft was able to generate some unseen force to draw him from the ground and into the plane as it flew overhead.

WILLIAMS, SIMON
KNOWN ALIASES/ALTER EGOS:
Wonder Man

This was part of Zemo's plot?

Not that we knew it at the time, but yes. We attempted to track the jet in Tony Stark's XL-750 rocket plane but were attacked by Melter and the Black Knight, who we learned later had been broken out of prison by Enchantress. As the Avengers jumped into the fight against the four Masters of Evil, I stayed at the controls of the rocket plane. I then chose to do what a soldier would do. I took the fight directly to Zemo in his Amazon compound.

On your own?

Yes. My mind couldn't let go of the idea that Zemo would harm Rick Jones or, worse, end his life as he did Bucky's. I met with enemy fire as soon as I approached the area and returned fire from my aircraft. As I strafed the compound, I saw the unimaginable. It was Rick in a glass-domed trap being elevated directly into my craft's line of fire.

Your nightmare come true.

In that moment, I recognized Zemo's madness. I knew his goal was to force me into killing Rick, which nearly happened. But my rocket fire managed to break the glass without harming Rick, and I made it to his side before Zemo's forces could reach us.

You must have been very thankful for that.

Zemo's hatred of me had consumed him, and I'd separated him from his fighting men. He took aim at me with his disintegrator pistol just as I was able to position my shield with the sun to reflect its rays into his eyes. Zemo fired wildly, triggering a rockslide that unfortunately took his life. In that moment, I felt that justice had been served and that Bucky's death had been avenged. That feeling was fleeting however. As I dug Zemo's grave in his jungle refuge, an act I'd performed for soldiers who'd given their lives for truly noble causes, I felt no sense of victory or elation. I felt. . . numb and empty, ill at ease. This chance to bring closure to Bucky's story felt like a closure of my own in some way. But now my battlefront had changed.

The grave of Zemo

Changed in what new direction?

I had no sense of that, at least not until Rick and I returned to American soil and Tony's mansion, only to be greeted by a crowd of people gathered on the front lawn. I learned that in our absence, the other Avengers had voted in three additional members. Rick and I were introduced to the Scarlet Witch, Quicksilver, and Hawkeye. Iron Man then gave me the even more startling news that he, Giant-Man, and the Wasp would be taking leave of the team. We arrived as their decisions were being made public.

MAXIMOFF, WANDA
KNOWN ALIASES/ALTER EGOS:
Scarlet Witch

**MAXIMOFF,
PIETRO**
KNOWN ALIASES/ALTER EGOS:
Quicksilver

BARTON, CLINTON
KNOWN ALIASES/ALTER
EGOS: Hawkeye, Golden
Archer, Goliath, Ronin,
Captain America

Press photo of Captain America arriving at
Tony Stark's East Side Mansion

Audio recording transcript of Avengers membership-announcement press conference held in Avengers Headquarters auditorium

IRON MAN: Ladies and gentlemen of the press, we called this meeting to announce a change in the official Avengers lineup. We felt that a direct statement would be better than having the public confused by guesses and unconfirmed rumors. And now, it gives me great pleasure to announce the first new Avenger replacement in many months. I take pride in presenting the man known as Hawkeye. Hawkeye has successfully passed our rigorous series of qualification tests, and has been thoroughly investigated and approved by the Federal Security Agency at our request.

UNIDENTIFIED REPORTER: Iron Man! You used the word "replacement." Does that mean some Avengers are resigning?

UNIDENTIFIED REPORTER 2: Say, that's right! Is that the reason Thor and Captain America aren't with you?

IRON MAN: I'm afraid that any information about our two missing Avengers is restricted for the present. But I can tell you this much. We are in the process of interviewing other applicants for membership and will announce their acceptance as soon as it is final. That's all for now, ladies and gentlemen. Thank you for attending.

(transcript ends)

UNCLASSIFIED

Television broadcast transcript of Avengers membership announcement press conference held outside Avengers Headquarters at Tony Stark's mansion

IRON MAN: Ladies and gentlemen, may I have your attention? I'd like to put a stop to the wild rumors and speculation that seem to be going around. I've been asked to announce that there will be a new lineup in the ranks of the Avengers until further notice. Effective immediately, Captain America, having seniority over the others, will be the spokesman for the group, which includes Hawkeye, Quicksilver, and the Scarlet Witch. They will appear in person to confirm what I have said in a very few minutes. Thank you.

(Crowd cheers)

CROWD VOICE: Here they come! It's the new Avengers!

CROWD VOICE 2: Say it, Cap! Let's hear it just once more!

CAPTAIN AMERICA: All right, this is for you. Avengers assemble!

(Crowd cheers)

(transcript ends)

BREAKING NEWS 7:03 *LIVE*

IRON MAN MAKES AN ANNOUNCEMENT

Is that turn of events something you had any reason to suspect?

Not at all. Remember, this was when we weren't as transparent with each other. We hadn't even shared our identities, apart from our heroic personas. Well, at least none of them had. Everyone knew who I was.

How did that feel, Steve?

I never questioned it. That intelligence is on a need-to-know basis and at that point I didn't need to know. I was more taken by the fact that their departures meant I was the senior member of the Avengers and would serve as their leader and spokesman. Iron Man left me with this new team and a single directive: Find the Hulk and make him an Avenger once again.

The Hulk? Okay, no pressure.

Exactly.

II.
RECKONING

At this point, I was beginning to understand how Captain Rogers accounted for himself in this bizarre new world of his. Out of duty to our country first, then to others, and only lastly to himself, he assumed roles and responsibilities that he'd had thrust upon him more than he'd sought him. When his country needed him to be, he was a hero. When his comrades needed him to be, he was a leader. But what he wanted to be was a soldier--the kind of soldier he had been in his life before now. Does the nation need that from him, I wondered--and had he ever questioned that himself?

INTERVIEWER: *So, with a team of heroes new to you and new to each other, you set your sights on allying with the Hulk.*

STEVE ROGERS: I'm going to be honest with you here.

You haven't been honest before now?

Heh. I'll rephrase and say I'm going to be candid here. Iron Man's ideas for what makes the Avengers work aren't always in line with mine. I took the mission, but not for the reasons he envisioned. His hope was that the Hulk would add his seemingly limitless brute strength to the team's benefit. I couldn't imagine a conflict or an emergency situation in which an enraged Hulk would take commands from me as a team leader. He's an unpredictable force of nature. However, I could see in Iron Man's purpose a path toward building loyalty and teamwork among the new members. They weren't ready to follow me instinctively. They didn't view me as a strong leader. They didn't want me around.

What makes you say that?

Hawkeye was hot-headed and unused to taking direction from anyone, let alone someone with a military background. I felt he was in the Avengers more for his own ego than for the cause. Quicksilver said to my face that he believed Tony Stark to be a better guiding genius behind the Avengers after seeing the technology available to us in our mansion headquarters. Scarlet Witch questioned Stark's role in things altogether. She seemed to find it hard to believe that the powerful Iron Man would be employed by Stark and wondered whether it secretly might be the other way around. So I didn't worry about being successful in bringing the Hulk into the team—because I knew the Hulk would not make us a team. We only could succeed as Avengers once we learned each other's capabilities and character, and knew that we could depend on each other in battle. Tracking and engaging the Hulk would forge this new team in fire.

I can't argue that.

I knew it from experience, with my then former teammates, and it was these experiences that also motivated me to tighten the new team into a fighting unit as fast as I possibly could. Hulk or no Hulk, I needed these new Avengers at their best to take on who I viewed as our—and Earth's—next greatest threat. We needed to be ready for Kang the Conqueror.

KANG THE CONQUEROR

KNOWN ALIASES/ALTER EGOS:
Nathaniel Richards,
Iron Lad, Kid Immortus,
Scarlet Centurion

The time traveler from the year 3000.

As best anyone can tell, yes. I'm not even sure we can call him part of our reality, but he certainly wants to force us into his. The first time we encountered Kang, he drew us into his spacecraft and managed to immobilize us with his advanced technology of another time. Rick Jones and the Wasp hatched a plan to distract Kang and rescue us. We attacked with our strength and a solvent cartridge from Giant-Man's labs in an attempt to damage Kang's technology-based suit, but he still managed to escape to his craft and elude us in the timestream.

How do you fight someone able to navigate in time like Kang?

Our wits. Our grit. Our knowing that any tyrant convinced of his infallibility always will underestimate the determination in the hearts of those of us who fight for freedom and personal liberty. Kang got a sample of this when he attacked us using a robot duplicate of Spider-Man, which we defeated thanks to the help of the real McCoy. He came after us from the future again with a robot duplicate of the Hulk, so I got a taste of what it's like to go toe-to-toe with that savage. Ultimately, Kang located a time at which he perceived we were at our weakest, which was while Thor was on his way to Asgard with Sindri, King of the Dwarves, to be judged by Odin for his offenses on Earth. Kang transported us to his time using a device of his own making, believing it would catch us off our game. He attacked us with forceful technology while Iron Man covertly destroyed his solar power source. Just as we thought we had defeated him, Kang got the drop on us by throwing the four of us directly back into the timestream using the same device that drew us to him.

You entered the timestream . . . without a destination?

Somehow, we were borne back to the point from which he had taken us. It was an unsettling experience to be sure, one filled with visions of unknown origins that may never fully leave my mind.

Such as, Steve?

I'm not at liberty to discuss it.

I won't force you to but in full disclosure, I do have your report.

POST-ACTION_REPORT_-__
AVENGERS_INTERNAL_USE_ONLY

Observations_during_timestream_transit_between_
unknown_origin_point_and_present_time_as_reported_by_
Steve_Rogers_during_activities_as_Captain_America
(transcript of oral report)

Following our engagement with an army of Lava Men
led by Sindri, King of the Dwarves, Iron Man, Giant-
Man, the Wasp, and myself were taken from our time
by an unknown force to what appeared to be a command
center or laboratory run by Kang the Conqueror. As we
struggled to free ourselves from captivity, Iron Man
engineered our escape by destroying the source of power
for Kang's equipment. Kang responded by activating some
sort of floor panel, which transported all of us into a
dimension beyond my understanding.

As we tumbled head over heels, blown about by
winds through a seemingly endless void, each of us
witnessed visions of no clear source. Perhaps they
were glimpses into our futures, or maybe flashes of
different realities, or even detailed
illusions created by Kang himself.
I've chosen to make this report now,
shortly following our safe return to
our own time and place, before the
memories of what I saw fade from my
mind, in case this information can
prove useful to us Avengers or other
heroes at a later time.

First, we saw a group of what
I believed were Avengers combating
some breed of lizard men. Among the
fighters appeared to be versions of
Thor, Iron Man, and Hulk battling
alongside a pair of Black women,
one of whom was wearing a variation
of my own uniform while carrying a
shield similar to the very first
shield I took into combat.

Next, we saw a number of
costumed fighters entering battle
against a colossal human being,
one who was magnitudes greater in
size than the largest height I've
ever seen Giant-Man achieve. In the
moment, I was struck by a sense

of the purple-clad giant radiating what felt to me like pure . . . _evil_. Among the giant's attackers, I recognized only one, Ben Grimm of the Fantastic Four, which led me to assume the costumed fighters were allies of good.

As we spun faster and more out of control, some of us were gripped by feelings of fear. We witnessed Thor leading the charge of an army of Avengers by the score, many of whom I did not recognize. Somehow, I knew this was an army of reinforcements in the battle against the purple giant.

In an attempt to tighten my grip on our rightful place in the universe, I tried to focus my mind on people and events I knew to be true. I found myself with Iron Man, Thor, and a caped red-faced man aboard what seemed to be a large spacecraft populated by bizarre and menacing green gremlin-like creatures.

I could see that the others were having greater difficulty processing these visions. I called out instructions for them to close their eyes and focus on their memories of themselves and of us as Avengers. "Whoever these people are, they are not us," I remember saying. "I'm haunted by my ghosts, Bucky and all the others, but I know who I am!"

With that, we found ourselves returned to this time and place, and thankfully so.

(transcript ends)

Well, so I see.

Your report of your unexpected travels through time is pretty matter-of-fact.

I just wanted to record what I had observed. Those details might have offered the right clue to the right person sometime in the future, whether it was three days or thirty years from that point.

I get that. But beyond the mere details, what did you gain from the experience yourself?

What did I gain? Well . . . confidence.

I'm intrigued.

My teammates were witnessing events of a time beyond their under-standing. They were unnerved and unsure of how to react. I'll borrow a line from a movie you'll know: "Welcome to the party, pals." That's how I've felt since I was rescued from the ice. So, I instructed them to focus internally, which had helped me cope uncounted times as I acclimated to this world. I may not know the world around me but I'll always know myself.

The tourist in time became the tour guide.

(laughs) Please keep your hands and feet inside the anomaly at all times.

You led from experience and from example.

Thank you. I'd like to believe so.

Did this strategy work on everyone else? Did these new Avengers become the team you had hoped they would?

Certainly not at first, and I shoulder the responsibility for that. As their leader, my head was not in the game. I carried an unhealthy focus on myself that made me feel I was failing them. No, that's not true. I felt I was failing all of America because I was failing myself.

Um, help me follow you here.

The more time I spent as a resident of Avengers Headquarters, accepting Tony Stark's food and shelter, the more I regarded myself solely as the ramrod of a fighting team. I had no private life to call my own. I did appre-ciate my being accepted by millions as a living symbol of our nation, but to myself I was a frustrated anachronism. I wanted to find my rightful place in this new world, my own identity. What I wanted was to be appointed to Nick Fury's counterintelligence unit.

I'm sure he would have accepted you in a heartbeat.

I could not yet bring myself to desert the Avengers. Iron Man, Thor, Giant-Man, and Wasp placed the torch in my hands to light the way for this new team. I needed to remain. I accepted missions I believed would raise my visibility to Fury, some of which were beyond the scope of crimefighting these new Avengers wanted to tackle. They pushed against my leadership, particularly Hawkeye. I don't say this with pride, but our dysfunction as a team reached a low point after a rough run against public opinion.

Transcript of opinion segment broadcast by commentator Steven Salbus on WXYZ-AM Radio, New York City.

Time for "What's the Word?" with your pal Steven Salbus, and today's word is "Stop"! That word goes to the Avengers or, as we in the news biz call them, Cap's Kooky Quartet. I'm not talking about the Avengers you might be used to, friends, but some new tights-wearers with everything but old-fashioned heroing on their minds. We've got the speedster Quicksilver, the wild Scarlet Witch, the hothead Hawkeye, and leading the pack is Captain America himself. Oh, you heard me, all right. Captain America!

Heroic hijinks are one thing but lately this group is doing more harm than a Hulk on ten pots of coffee! They show up to Sutton Place and rip apart a city block—blowing up cars, bringing down buildings brick by brick, fracturing the street. When New York's Finest arrived to put a stop to it all, according to officers on the scene, these yo-yos blamed everything on a thirty-foot monster that no one could see but them!

The next day, they apparently thought sabotaging a set of subway tracks would be a barrel of laughs—and what's more, Hawkeye used a trick arrow of his to explode an empty railcar! Some trick, right? Again, our men in blue asked for an explanation, but all the Avengers had was that they were investigating a plot. Plot against who? The people of New York? Seems to me the only plotters we should be worried about are the Avengers!

Your pal Steven has another word today, and that's "Action"! And I mean action taken by the city council to keep the Avengers from taking the law into their own hands. This kooky quartet is hardly made up of heroes. They are public menaces. If the council knows what's good for us all, they will seek a court order to keep these creeps off the streets and disband these so-called Avengers for good.

I'm Steven Salbus and that's the word.

That's what happened, isn't it, Steve?

When I took command, the Avengers were at the height of their power. But certainly not after this defeat. I let it get to me. I wondered whether the flesh-and-blood Steve Rogers could live up to the legend that Captain America had become in my absence. I thought I deserved to have stayed lost in the past.

But it was you who cracked the whole case. You discovered how Enchantress and the villain Power Man had conspired to use her illusions to lure you into being blamed for each incident.

I caught a lucky break.

Was it just luck that you tape-recorded enough of Power Man's confession to help exonerate the team and return you to full standing with the city and law enforcement?

Well, no.

Power Man and Enchantress

And after all that, you walked off the team.

An apology from the city council didn't erase my realization that the citizens of my country expect more from me, and they will not respond with understanding when I fail to deliver. I needed time to center myself. I needed to understand what this world needs from me. I escaped by taking a job as a trainer for a champion boxer upstate. What I didn't realize at the time was how my departure had put the whole team in jeopardy. Just as Kang had attacked the previous lineup of Avengers when he sensed a liability, he did so again when I left and captured the three teammates I left behind.

You could not have known.

Had I been at my best, of course I could have known. Kang pulled the same battle strategy with us twice in a row. I was too turned inward to recognize how I had left them vulnerable. I woke up to my error only when I had heard a radio report of their kidnapping. I retrieved a Time Reversal Ray from Avengers Headquarters and used it to call out Kang as the criminal responsible for the kidnapping.

B5A02. 50/20

Item No. 0105—Time Reversal Ray

Also known as the Recreator, this chronographic viewing device is capable of taking readings of a living being or inanimate object and then projecting images from the past of actions involving that being or object. Dr. Calvin Zabo, also known as the criminal Mr. Hyde, invented the Time Reversal Ray and used it in an unsuccessful plan to exact revenge on Thor. This device was confiscated by the Avengers following the arrest of Dr. Zabo.

You goaded Kang into helping you rescue your teammates.

Another predictable aspect of Kang as an opponent is his arrogance. I had a feeling he would not be able to resist bringing me forward to his time to challenge me personally. Kang transported me to a small kingdom thriving in that future of his. At first he managed to get the upper hand, but then, as soon as the four of us Avengers were reunited against him, he sicced his legions of armed soldiers against our kingdom refuge and escaped to the safety of his spacecraft. We then learned a new vulnerability of Kang's. This entire conflict against the kingdom had grown from his quest for the heart of its princess, Ravonna.

Kang was smitten?

Smitten and scorned by Ravonna, which drove Kang to rage. Hawkeye, Scarlet Witch, and I were captured as the kingdom fell, but Quicksilver was nowhere to be found. While we were imprisoned, Kang's heart dared to show mercy on Ravonna's conquered father. This turned his own elite guard against him as they perceived his mercy as his first sign of weakness. In his desperation, Kang recruited us Avengers to quell the insurrection and save the lives of Ravonna and the royal family.

He knew you to be true heroes. Kang knew you would not refuse his request.

I guess that makes me predictable too. Kang broke away to his master control complex and made quick work of the situation. He of course knew every weakness of his own legions and exploited them by focusing high-frequency waves in a counteroffensive that destroyed every armored vehicle and piece of artillery they possessed. True to his word, once we shared in this victory, Kang returned us to our rightful time. We only could wonder whether we would face him as a foe the next time we met.

It feels safe to say that when such a time came, your Avengers would be ready.

They would be, and in our subsequent adventures they proved themselves repeatedly. They did so well that, once again, thoughts of leaving the Avengers returned to me. At first, I had believed they did not want me around. Then, I was convinced they didn't need me around. Hank Pym returned in the guise of Goliath, combining his powers of giant-sized strength and the mastery of the insect world. So, believing my obligation had been fulfilled—as I did, after all, keep the Avengers together until one of its original members returned to the roster—I left the team. However, I did not leave them wanting for a capable fighter in my absence.

How so?

My battle for justice brought me into contact with the brave and powerful King T'Challa of Wakanda, known as the hero Black Panther. After fighting alongside him to unmask a would-be successor to Baron Zemo, I asked T'Challa whether he would succeed me as a member of the Avengers, and he agreed. It did not take long for him to win the trust of my former teammates and be invited to full membership.

T'CHALLA

KNOWN ALIASES/ALTER EGOS:
Black Panther

And that allowed you freely to pursue your goal of working with Nick Fury.

It did, yes.

STRATEGIC HAZARD INTERVENTION ESPIONAGE LOGISTICS DIRECTORATE

TOP SECRET—EYES ONLY

FROM: Fury, Nicholas J.
TO: Distribution List Alpha Omega 3955-P
SUBJECT: Establishing the valid identity of Rogers,
         Steven Grant

It's Christmas morning, people.

I know there are those of you among S.H.I.E.L.D.'s upper echelon who have cast understandable doubts as to veracity of reports from Stark and his fellow Avengers that they retrieved the actual living and breathing Captain America from the ocean. When I first heard the news, to say I was skeptical is selling short my inherent cynicism. However, now that I've met the man face-to-face and looked him in the eye? I have no doubt we've been graced with the return of one of the greatest heroes this country has ever produced.

Even so, I still had him tested.

That's to say I had our people take samples of his blood and test them, and in each case the results came back with the same conclusions: His blood matches the samples taken from Steve Rogers in 1941. They also include the unmistakable markers of the formula developed by Professor Joseph Reinstein, the German scientist whose death we faked before bringing him to the States to continue his work of creating Super-Soldiers in anticipation of having to square off against Hitler and his army. As we all know, Reinstein was killed shortly after administering to Rogers the serum he developed, and the secrets of that formula died with him. Reinstein's previous attempts at developing the protocol, as well as all subsequent efforts to replicate what he produced with Rogers, have proven unsuccessful to varying degrees, but identifying it has always been easy.

The man the Avengers recovered is who he claims to be: Steve Rogers, alias "Captain America."

I know that to you, he's a name from history books or newsreels, or even those low-budget movies they did back when war films were all the rage. For me, he's someone who put his back against mine as we took on all comers. There's not an atom in his body that doesn't love this country. He put it all on the line before any of you were born, and he'll do it again without hesitation. Steve Rogers is more than just an enhanced soldier; he's the personification of an ideal. You can imagine his acclimating to a world that left him behind decades ago presents a challenge, but he's already stepped up on that front, and despite some bumps in the road, he's already made himself an invaluable asset to the Avengers. I highly suggest that we not squander this extraordinary gift that has been dropped in our laps.

—Fury

page 2/2

Despite your decision to leave the Avengers, you found other means of contributing your skills and desire to help defend the country—and even the world, in many respects—against various threats.

This country made me what I am today. I still feel the same call I did the first time I tried to join the Army and they turned me away.

In what I'm sure you had to consider an odd quirk of fate, that same U.S. Army ended up providing one of the very few connections to your previous life, in the form of Nick Fury.

You know, if there was anyone I figured might survive the war and somehow manage to still be kicking around today, it'd be Fury.

The reports and stories I've read about Fury and his "Howling Commandos" are quite hair-raisng.

During the war, he and his unit had had several successes in Africa and Italy. Then when the Allies invaded France, the team was given a broad range of increasingly dangerous missions. They often worked deep behind

First Attack Squad, Able Company,
U.S. Army Rangers—June 1944

KNOWN ALIASES/ALTER EGOS: "The Howling Commandos"

German lines where they were sent to gather intelligence, rescue high-value individuals or capture important enemy targets, or retrieve weapons and other technology the Nazis were developing.

For all their effectiveness on the battlefield, they weren't exactly posterboard soldiers.

There's an old saying: "No combat-ready unit ever passed inspection, and no inspection-ready unit ever passed combat." Fury and his Howlers exemplified the former part of that statement, in the best possible way. They may not have looked pretty, but they knew how to get the job done.

I understand you fought alongside him a few times. Is it true you two didn't get along at first?

(*laughs*) We may have butted heads here and there, but when it counted, we knew we could trust each other with our lives. There aren't many people I'd rather have next to me when the bullets started flying.

Did you ever imagine Fury still fighting all the wars that took place while you were asleep?

And working for an organization Tony Stark's father founded during the Cold War. How's that for a small world?

My understanding is that the world became even smaller for you, so far as connections to your past life. I'm speaking of the S.H.I.E.L.D. operative you initially knew as Agent 13.

CARTER, SHARON
KNOWN ALIASES/ALTER EGOS:
Agent 13

(*nods*) Sharon.

I suppose we should get the obvious part out of the way first. Yes, she bore an uncanny resemblance to Peggy Carter, who I knew during the war. We'd . . . worked together.

My understanding is that there was more to your relationship with Peggy Carter than the purely professional.

(*looks away, smiling as though recalling a pleasant memory*) Yes, that's right. Our romance was one of the many memories I . . . revised after my awakening.

"Revised"? Tell me about that.

They say all is fair in love and war. I will tell you that war is horribly unfair to love. The events of the war threw us together and pulled us apart, again and again. Heh. (*chuckles*) Peggy once said to me that every time we were together felt to her like it would be the last time. I told her that I always felt it was the first time.

That's sweet, Steve.

She called me a sap.

From the journal of
Margaret "Peggy" Carter, circa 1943

Even though I've never seen the face behind the mask, with or without the guise of Captain America, in my heart I know there could be no disguising his bravery, his courage, his intelligence.

And one of these days, we will meet. Quite by accident, probably, and we will know each other face-to-face. And then there will be no disguising ourselves or our feelings. Captain America is an invaluable member of the Resistance, but we could—and would—go on without him.

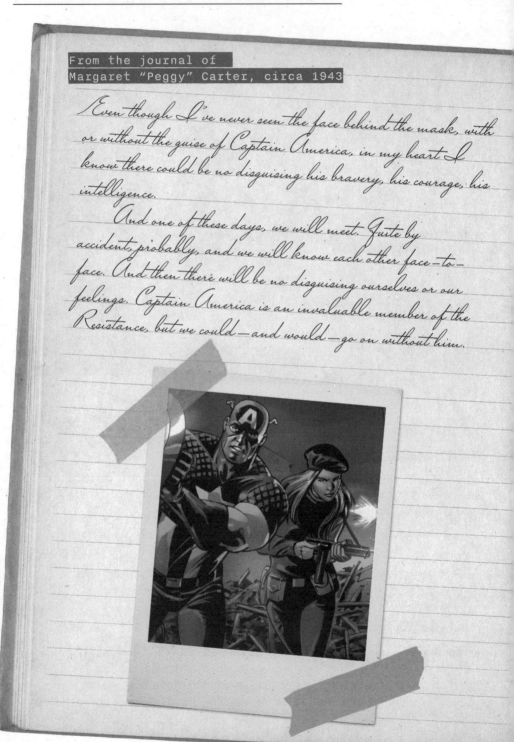

From the journal of Margaret
"Peggy" Carter, circa 1945.

But I'm not sure I could. Or would.

That time never did come. We had another year of struggle and subterfuge. Another year of sneaking around . . . hiding our faces. More of the worst . . . and the best that we could do. Sometimes together. More often apart.

And then it was over. And I never saw him again. Not that I know of.

She wrote "not that I know of." Did you see her again?

No. And it's not just that our connection, for Peggy, ended in 1945 when I was reported killed. After we last met in person, Peggy suffered a head injury while in the custody of the Gestapo. For a time she didn't know herself, much less me. Not that I knew this at the time. Then, I believed she had given up on us—or worse, had been killed. Now, as I said, I've revised my memories.

And your feelings for her have changed.

Given the specifics of my loss and return, and the events of her life, complications have led to an understanding. Out of respect for Peggy, that's all I have to say.

And out of respect for Sharon Carter?

Did you go into this level of . . . relational detail with Tony?

I was restricted by my publisher to keep my writings within one volume.

Okay, you just bought yourself another question.

You did eventually develop similar feelings for Peggy's niece, Sharon.

I don't know that I'd call it "eventual." I admit when I first realized who Sharon was, she reminded me so much of Peggy. I simply couldn't shake it. Yes, I even proposed to Sharon, once, but at the time she was focused on her work with S.H.I.E.L.D. I'd like to think the relationship she and I eventually developed was an honest, natural outgrowth of our working together and bonding over time.

As well as over similar high-risk and high-pressure situations not unlike wartime.

That's a keen observation. I guess I have a type.

STRATEGIC HAZARD INTERVENTION ESPIONAGE LOGISTICS DIRECTORATE

Excerpt from transcript of after-action debriefing .
interview conducted by S.H.I.E.L.D. Director Nicholas
Fury with Sharon Carter, official designation
"Agent 13."

DIRECTOR FURY: Agent 13. It's good to see you. How are
you feeling?

AGENT 13: Better now, thanks. The doctors say I'll make
a full recovery.

DIR: As first missions go, this one was pretty
colorful.

A13: In more ways than one.

DIR: Walk me through what happened.

A13: It was supposed to be a simple exchange. You sent
me to pick up a package, which I was then supposed to
transport back to S.H.I.E.L.D. Headquarters.

DIR: What was the package?

A13: Don't you already know all of this?

DIR: For the report, Agent 13.

A13: According to my pre-mission briefing, the package
was a cylinder containing a sample of an experimental
chemical explosive designated Inferno-42.

DIR: What do you know of this explosive?

A13: I was informed the cylinder I was sent to retrieve carried enough destructive power to level a city the size of Manhattan. Given it was actually in Manhattan, that definitely weighed on my mind.

DIR: Describe what happened during the pickup.

A13: Everything was going according to plan, until it wasn't. I was carrying a fake package identical to the one I was sent to retrieve, and I met my contact on the street as instructed. We did the whole clumsy-people dance, with him bumping him into me and me dropping my cylinder onto the sidewalk. He makes the big show of apologizing and bending down to retrieve it while making the sly switch with the real package, which he handed to me. Piece of cake, right?

DIR: Except . . .

A13: Except this guy saw the whole thing. He tried to warn me about what he thought had happened, and I tried to convince him he didn't see what he saw. It was like a 1970s sitcom, for a minute there.

DIR: You watch 1970s sitcoms?

A13: Sometimes I can't fall asleep. Sue me. Anyway, I thought I was in the clear, but then this other clown shows up.

DIR: Batroc the Leaper.

A13: He attacked me right there on the street. I managed to get a shot off, but he was on me too fast. I know I've been trained in unarmed combat, but he was no slouch. Did you know Batroc talks about himself in the third person?—

DIR: Maybe he's planning a run for office. So, that's when Captain America showed up.

A13: Out of the blue. In the blue. Whatever. Yeah, he showed up, and then everything went sideways . . .

(transcript ends)

Good thing you chose that day to take a stroll through the city.

I'd been in my own head a lot at that time, still adjusting to this new life I'd been given, and what I wanted from it versus what was expected of me. Was I Steve Rogers or Captain America? To be honest, I still have that conversation with myself, even after all this time.

So, you see this Batroc character attacking Ms. Carter...

And instinct along with my training kicked in. He's quite the skilled fighter, trained in *savate*, a French form of kickboxing. He's also very strong, but I still managed to get the upper hand. I also got him talking, which ended up being a good thing.

What did he reveal?

That during our scuffle, Sharon had gotten away with the package that contained the Inferno-42 explosive. I had knocked it out of his hands, and Batroc said if my move had cracked the cylinder's outer casing, we now had about thirty minutes to find it and Sharon or else it would level the city.

You managed to find her.

Just in time too. She'd been overcome by the effects of the cracked canister, which was glowing just as Batroc warned. While I was worried about

BATROC, GEORGES
KNOWN ALIASES/ALTER EGOS:
Monsieur Lapin, the Leaper

her, Batroc found us and grabbed the cylinder. I followed him to the people paying him to retrieve it. I wasn't able to get it back from them and Batroc got away, but by then I was too worried about Sharon.

You didn't even know who she was at this point.

And I wouldn't learn her real identity for a while yet. At the time, she was simply "Agent 13."

The same code designation her great-aunt used during the war.

Which is even more bizarre when you realize I didn't even know Peggy's name at the time we worked together. (*laughs*) Talk about history repeating itself.

And it was Sharon who led you to S.H.I.E.L.D. and Director Fury.

I was wondering when we'd circle back around to him.

I'd been trying to make contact with him once I learned he was still alive and kicking. Of course he found me first. He was always good at that sort of thing.

That must've been quite the first meeting, after all these years.

We each had our own reactions. To him, I looked the same as I did the last time he saw me during the war. I hadn't aged a day, but I still think I had the bigger shock, seeing him much younger than he had any right to be given how long since the war we're talking.

The Infinity Formula.

At the time it seemed incredible if not unbelievable, but I've seen enough wild things by now that Fury doesn't even move the needle anymore.

He came seeking your help.

Yes. He showed me a miniature model of a human brain grown in a lab by scientists working for a secret organization known only as "THEM." Fury told me he believed it was part of a larger plan for engineering artificial beings to be used for all sorts of nefarious purposes.

You don't really hear people using words like "nefarious" anymore.

It does sort of date me, doesn't it?

I think it gives you a certain charm.

Don't tell Stark you said that. I'll never hear the end of it.

Chemical Android, as created and deployed by THEM

Speaking of nefarious plans, THEM sent one of their "artificial beings" after you and Fury.

They must've tracked Fury to me at the Avengers Mansion and sent this thing after us. We managed to defeat it, but it basically self-destructed, breaking down to its most basic form, and leaving nothing behind for us to examine.

It was after finally meeting Fury that you decided against leaving the Avengers to work for S.H.I.E.L.D.

I decided I'd made a commitment to Stark and the others. If not for them, I might still be frozen in ice somewhere. I may not always agree with their methods—or Fury's, or S.H.I.E.L.D.'s, for that matter—but I know their intentions are noble.

Given what you learned from Fury about THEM, it seemed prudent for the two groups to work together.

Exactly. We later learned THEM was a spin-off of Hydra, which I thought I'd seen the last of during the war. And we eventually learned THEM was actually a group calling itself Advanced Idea Mechanics. A.I.M.

Working hand in hand with another group, the so-called Secret Empire.

Right. While THEM—and now A.I.M.—has always been focused on developing or acquiring technology to allow them to overthrow the world's governments, the Secret Empire's primary mission is to distract S.H.I.E.L.D. and similar organizations.

And they employ a rather vast array of schemes and weapons to do just that.

That's putting it lightly. There seems to be no limit on what they might do to achieve their goals, even if that means courting pure evil.

You're talking about the Red Skull.

Boy, am I ever. His was an evil I believed I had left behind long ago.

SCHMIDT, JOHANN
KNOWN ALIASES/ALTER EGOS:
Red Skull

Excerpt from after-action report
submitted by Nicholas J. Fury,
Sergeant, U.S. Army

POST-ACTION REPORT—
OFFICE OF STRATEGIC SERVICES

INTERNAL USE ONLY—30 MARCH 1945

One of these days, I'm going to learn to say no when
you ask me to do something crazy like charge into
Berlin while it's still crawling with Nazis.

Sure, the RAF was dropping bombs left and
right, so the Jerries are on their last gasp and a
lot of the low-rank, fuzz-faced grunts are running
for the hills. But a bunch of the top brass are
still there, hiding in bunkers and wherever else
cockroaches go when you kick on the lights.

That said, despite the best efforts of me and
the Howlers, the little man with the mustache hasn't
turned up yet, but I figure he's getting desperate.
The whole thing's falling apart around him, if you
ask me. The scuttlebutt I've heard is the Russkis
are planning something big. With them rolling into
town, this thing might be over in a month or so.

Anyway, you sent us in there to track Captain
America's movements while he hunted the Red Skull.
We lost him when he entered the underground bunker
system, then another bombing run from the RAF let go
with one of their giant blockbuster bombs near his
last known position. I don't know how he survived
that, but he did, and according to the report he
gave me, the bunker where he found the Skull took
an almost direct hit. Cap said he was separated
from the Skull when the ceiling started coming down
around them, so he hot-footed it out of there. He's
pretty certain the Skull was buried in the rubble.

·U.S. ARMY
SPECIAL ADVISORY GROUP

Turns out he didn't die back then, but instead somehow managed to survive the bunker's collapse in a section that was protected. Some kind of experimental gas was released into pockets like his, and it made him go to sleep, a lot like I did. He apparently remained in suspended animation while his wounds healed until he was found many years later by THEM.

It's a surreal bit of symmetry, the two of you surviving to fight each other once again.

(*laughs, but there's no humor*) I guess I shouldn't be surprised that a world able to produce someone like me and keep me alive after all those years and battles would also find a way to preserve something like the Skull. There's probably a joke about balancing the universe in there somewhere, but I'm not smart enough to make it.

I could ask Mr. Stark the next time I see him.

Sure.

So, THEM revives the Red Skull, who learns you're also still alive.

I never saw that coming, let me tell you. (*a small, knowing smile*) And I'm guessing he was still holding a grudge from our last fight because he sent operatives to attack me.

I read the report released by the Avengers. That was quite something. The operatives were able to hide their appearance from others using hypnosis, so to anyone near you it must have looked as though you were fighting something that wasn't there.

It looked like I'd lost my mind, which of course was the intent. The Skull wanted to turn the public against me, and I started to think the attacks were all in my head and there had to be something wrong with me. Once I figured out what was happening, that led me to the Skull and his island fortress.

Even though THEM found and revived him, he felt no loyalty to his benefactors.

They were a means to an end for him. They'd made this thing he called a "Cosmic Cube," which kind of acted like a genie's lamp, doing the bidding of whoever wields it. Don't ask me to explain how it works, but my understanding is that A.I.M. scientists didn't so much create it from scratch as they found a way to tap into some form of strange power source. (*pauses*) Stark once described it as "extra-dimensional energy" that essentially lets its user warp reality itself to fit their desires.

I've tried to understand it from reading various S.H.I.E.L.D. documents, but I'm no scientist.

The Cosmic Cube, created by A.I.M.

It's way above my pay grade, but it's the sort of thing Stark and Reed Richards could talk about for days. I leave the deep thinking to smart people like that. I'm just a soldier.

You're selling yourself short. You were able to outmaneuver the Red Skull.

I played to his ego. His vanity. I convinced him once he got done reshaping the world to his whim, what better way to top it off than keep me around as a trophy. His ultimate victory.

And he went for it.

I'd like to think I got the drop on him, but he was probably just too wrapped up in the moment. He even put on this ridiculous suit of knight's armor as he prepared to declare himself king of the world. Once he realized what I was doing, he destroyed his island in an attempt to kill me, but when I knocked the Cube from his hand into the ocean he went after it.

Armor and all.

So far as I knew at the time, he and the Cube went straight to the bottom and were buried under tons of rock from the destroyed island.

You'd beaten him again.

Sure, but I had no idea he'd be back. You'd think I'd learned my lesson after the first time, but life is nothing but surprises.

DAILY ⌒ BUGLE®

NEW YORK'S FINEST DAILY NEWSPAPER

CAPTAIN AMERICA RETIRES

Star-Spangled Avenger Reveals True Identity, Hangs Up Shield

NEW YORK—People across the country and perhaps around the world were stunned earlier today when Captain America announced his retirement.

One of our greatest World War II heroes, he was found remarkably frozen in ice, suspended from aging for decades until his discovery by the Avengers. He joined their ranks and helped them carry out a number of missions to protect our country, so his surprise announcement has unleashed a cascade of reactions.

"He's in his prime," said one citizen interviewed on the streets of New York. "No one could even match him!"

Added another, "I still can hardly believe it. What made him do it?"

That is the burning question now asked of Steven Rogers, the man who has worn Captain America's mask since WWII. Whatever his reasons are, he seems to be keeping them to himself, at least for now. This is a developing story!

Then there are the surprises you've sprung on the public, yourself.

It was because of Sharon. There might have been a time when she told you it was her fault, but it wasn't. This was all me.

You mentioned earlier that she turned down your marriage proposal.

She'd made a pledge to serve S.H.I.E.L.D. Swore an oath to defend the nation, just as I once did.

Duty before self. It's a concept with which you have rather significant experience.

But underneath the costume there's still a heart in my chest, and it felt broken. I need to stress here that this was *my* reaction at that time. Sharon did nothing wrong, and I honestly believe our relationship has only gotten stronger over time. She just wasn't ready to divide herself that way, and in hindsight neither was I.

Yet it did affect your judgment in the moment.

I'm still human, and sometimes humans make dumb mistakes when our emotions run high. Over time, we showed each other we did not need to be married to be committed to each other.

So, now the world knows Captain America is really Steve Rogers, a man from another time. There was quite the mix of reactions.

Tell me about it. Everything from some people feeling betrayed to many offering words of support and encouragement. And of course there seemed to be no shortage of people vying to replace me. (*laughs, shaking his head*) I can't fault them for their passion.

Some of the men who would be Captain America

In today's attention-seeking world, it makes perfect sense that some would try that.

It never occurred to me. (*shrugs*) Another sign I was out of step with the times, I guess. They were well meaning, but once people started getting hurt by actually trying to *be* me, I knew I couldn't let that stand. Fury knew it too, and for a time he even convinced me it might be easier to forget about being Steve Rogers than Captain America.

How would that even work, given the number of people knowing the two are one and the same?

With Fury's help, we faked Captain America's death for a bit to trick Hydra so we could lure them out of hiding, and we also set up "Steve Rogers" as a fake identity. That thankfully didn't last long either. I mean, hair dye and makeup? Why on Earth did I think I'd ever want to live like that?

Not that it truly helped. It didn't stop the Red Skull from finding you.

Once again, he survived after I was sure he'd been killed during our last battle. I've lost count of how many times I've been wrong about things like that.

He also found the Cosmic Cube you thought was lost too.

And revenge was on his mind, let me tell you. At first he was content to just torture me with the thing. He beat me, tormented me, even transported me to another world in some other reality. He wanted to break me, mentally and emotionally.

But you're rather stubborn, in your own way.

I guess that's one way to put it. Eventually, he started to get frustrated that I was managing to hold on, but then he realized a faster way to get at me was to go through the people I most cared about.

Like Sharon Carter.

Exactly. He used the cube to swap his body and mine, so he could pretend to be me while I was trapped behind his face. He brought Sharon to us, and of course she thought the Skull was me. At the same time, he's transporting me to different locations where he can commit crimes and let "the Red Skull" take the blame. He even turned Rick Jones against me for a time, because Rick didn't know it wasn't me telling him he could never be a good partner to me. That may have hurt the most, because it took such a long time to set things right with Rick.

And all during this, you had your own hands full.

Ultimately, the Skull transported me to Exile Island in the Caribbean, where many of his allies and minions had fled to avoid arrest, prosecution, or worse.

WILSON, SAMUEL THOMAS ("SAM")
KNOWN ALIASES/ALTER EGOS:
Falcon, Captain America

An interesting choice. I read what you told Director Fury, in that it seemed the Skull hoped the other Exiles would kill you, thinking you were him.

It probably would've worked too. After all, I wasn't in my own body. I didn't have super-strength or speed, or even my shield. I still don't know if I might've been able to fight my way out of there, if not for Sam.

Sam, and his falcon, Redwing.

Oh, yes. We can't forget Redwing.

Is it really true he answered a job ad from someone in the Caribbean looking to learn falconry?

(*laughs*) Lucky for me, right? Turns out it was one of the Skull's people who placed the ad. After he took the job and arrived on the island, it didn't take long for Sam to figure out the truth about them and how they were treating the local population. He'd been trying to motivate them to revolt, like a one-man resistance. Having seen during the war how effective such defiance can be if it's channeled the right way, I decided to help him.

It was you who convinced Sam he needed to be more than a man, but also a symbol.

A symbol of revolution, and hope.

And you suggested he adopt a masked identity, as well as his new moniker, "the Falcon."

Well, I *do* have some experience with masks, costumes, and inspiring names. Thankfully, the locals were already in a place where they just needed that extra push—someone to show them the way—to convince them they could take on their oppressors and win. Sam and I provided that push. Once they joined the fight, the Exiles didn't stand a chance, and the locals sent them running.

And the Red Skull was aware of all this?

Not at first. He was so preoccupied with trying to ruin my name and reputation, he didn't realize that his extensive use of the Cube might attract unwanted attention.

In this case, A.I.M.

How about that? They'd not only been looking for the Cube, but also working on a way to retrieve it as well as restrict who could use it, and even destroy it, which is apparently what they did. We didn't know any of this at the time. To us, the Cube just seemed to melt while the Skull was using it to fight us, and then the Skull himself appeared to disintegrate.

But let me guess: That wasn't the last you'd see of him.

Now you're starting to catch on.

And this was the beginning of your long-term partnership with Sam Wilson.

Indeed it was.

Scenes of revolution on Exile Island.
Photo Credit: Alvita Jeune

III.
REASSESSMENT

Captain Rogers' adjustment to his remarkable
circumstances was no easy feat. He'll be the
first to admit it continues to this day, in some
ways very much akin to the ongoing care one
might receive for what ails them, physically,
psychologically, or emotionally. Unsurprisingly,
Captain Rogers has attempted to reconcile himself
with our world. On the battlefield during World War
II, he was confident in the reasons why he and his
fellow soldiers fought. The stakes seemed clear cut
in black and white, and the nation's commitment to
victory was steadfast. Now, he sees that many of us
perceive areas of gray.

As Captain Rogers stated earlier, his status
as a "man out of time" was never something he
assumed for himself. I've started to recognize
the ways how we--the people of this time--have
just labeled him as that. From our perspective, we
easily see the gulf of time across which his life
was paused. But as a character in a halted video
might experience, this gap is imperceptible to him.
I wondered whether his inner conflict lies as much
with that disparity of viewpoint as it does his
situation itself. Against the background of earthly
conflicts, this dichotomy of how we see him and how
he sees himself becomes tricky for us to bridge.
But Captain Rogers' life is not as tethered to this
world as our lives are, a circumstance that, once I
recognized it, helped clarify for me his devotion
to the abstract and timeless American Dream beyond
the concrete manifestations by which you and I may
define it today.

INTERVIEWER: *Steve, I'd like to get your take on the alien activities on Earth that found you unexpectedly back with the Avengers as you tried to prevent an interstellar war.*

STEVE ROGERS: Sure. You know our efforts were more to prevent the conflict between the Kree and the Skrulls from destroying our planet as essentially collateral damage. We were not coming at either of these races like soldiers went at the Axis.

Yes.

Still, I needed to get up to speed on just who we were dealing with and why each wanted to scrub the other out of existence. The issues between the Kree and the Skrulls went back a million years. I'm not exaggerating—one million years. How can we even relate to their fear of and anger toward each other?

What happened?

The warlike Kree cohabitated on their homeworld with a peaceful race that called themselves the Cotati. Because of their vastly different cultures, they just left each other alone.

Forgive me for pointing out the lesson we can learn from that.

Agreed. One day, the Skrulls arrived with superior technology they were willing to share—in exchange for total loyalty to them because they're Skrulls—but with a catch: They would share with only one race. They chose seventeen beings of each race, transported them to an environment totally alien to them, and gave them a year to accomplish whatever they were able. The Skrulls kept their word and returned in one year. The Cotati had cultivated a lovely garden using native seeds and water while the Kree had constructed an entire city. Well, the Skrulls went with the gardeners.

And the Kree went to war.

Exactly. The Kree wiped out every one of the Skrulls *and* the Cotati. They commandeered the Skrull ship, mastered their technology anyway, and eons of fighting began.

I can appreciate the level of concern you all had for our world becoming a theater of war for these two races.

I'll admit to having a personal stake in this as well. I wanted to face the Skrull responsible for using my image and my reputation to place the Earth in direct jeopardy by suggesting I wanted to disband the Avengers. It was a deceitful tactic and very much in line with how we now know the Skrulls to behave. Their plan could have cost us the Earth.

How did all of this begin to become clear to you?

Rick Jones found himself unhappy with the direction of the Avengers. I was aware how much he wanted full membership status and a costumed identity, in particular being named the new Bucky in partnership with me. As this never came to pass, he moved out of Avengers Mansion and we lost touch. In that time, the Kree soldier Mar-Vell psychically reached out to Rick, which allowed Rick to free Mar-Vell from imprisonment in the Negative Zone.

So from that time Rick fought alongside Captain Marvel?

Their partnership was a bit more complicated. I don't entirely understand how it worked but Rick was able to swap his physical place on Earth with Mar-Vell's in the Negative Zone and did so willingly for quite some time. But early on, they did work to free each other from this bond, and in doing so nearly freed the villain known as Annihilus from the region and onto Earth. That did not happen, thanks to the Avengers. What did happen, though, was Mar-Vell stole the Avengers' Quinjet in his attempt to return to the Kree galaxy, while Rick remained with us.

MAR-VELL
KNOWN ALIASES/ALTER EGOS:
Captain Marvel

I guess we can't blame him for wanting to go home.

Well, again, more context we did not have at the time. Mar-Vell's presence on Earth triggered a Kree would-be despot named Ronan the Accuser to attempt to overthrow Kree leadership and kill Mar-Vell. This conflict led the Avengers to uncover a Kree plot to devolve and destroy the Earth.

Now we're coming into the part of the story with which I'm familiar.

The establishment of the Alien Activities Commission, which came after the Avengers for alleged criminal activities. Among those activities was their attempts to assist Rick and Mar-Vell, which the Commission wanted to label as harboring a fugitive and obstructing justice. When seen with clear eyes, the Commission was a tool for bigots who needed a trip to Liberty Island to read a reminder of what this country means to people around the world . . . and soon, perhaps, around the universe. (*recites from memory*) "A mighty woman with a torch, whose flame is the imprisoned lightning and her name Mother of Exiles."

"The New Colossus" by Emma Lazarus.

You know it. I like that, friend. America is admired for welcoming all, even a soldier from the Kree galaxy. The Commission sought to corrupt that flame.

Transcript of MTN World TV News coverage of Alien Activities Commission hearing.

REPORTER: Coming to you live from Washington following stunning testimony before members of the newly formed Alien Activities Commission. This hearing has brought to light plans by an alien race known as the Kree to revert humans to Neanderthals and subjugate the planet. I know this must sound unbelievable, but witnesses assure us it's all true.

WITNESS (off camera): It sure is true!

REPORTER: Wait! Excuse me, sir, come back! You were among the men who testified. You witnessed it all?

WITNESS: Yes, ma'am. I worked for the government as a technician at an Alaskan research station. I survived the effects of the Kree weapon, myself.

REPORTER: You claim you were devolved into a prehistoric human.

WITNESS: It was horrible, I tell you, horrible! Those Kree monsters turned some kind of ray on us, turned us into savage cavemen. They intended to do the same to all humanity.

REPORTER: Ultimately, the Kree plan was foiled by the Avengers. You witnessed this, too?

WITNESS: Yes, the Avengers rescued us, all right. I'll give them that. I heard enough, though, to know that that Captain Marvel is a Kree, whatever that is. He's one of them.

REPORTER: Thank you, sir. Also testifying were Reed Richards and Ben Grimm of the Fantastic Four. While they were called as expert witnesses on the Kree, being the first humans to encounter the aliens on Earth, they also weighed in on the Avengers' roles in the incident. Dr. Richards testified that while he knows little about the Kree and has never met Captain Marvel, he said he would accept the judgment of the Avengers that this hero from the far-off, scientifically advanced galaxy of the Kree poses no threat to us on Earth. Signing off from Washington.

(transcript ends)

And upon their return from this hearing, the Avengers discovered their headquarters ransacked by angry protesters—and you waiting for them.

Who they *believed* were me, Iron Man, and Thor. They were Skrull imposters, all of them. The one who looked like me proclaimed the Avengers' actions to be irresponsible and declared the Avengers disbanded for all time. So, the roster of Quicksilver, Scarlet Witch, the Vision, and Goliath went their own ways.

When did you learn of all this?

I was in the dark about it all until a chance gathering at Avengers Mansion with Thor and Iron Man. The Vision burst in and collapsed, and we thought he was dead. As it turned out, the android was suffering from internal damage, and we were lucky to have Hank Pym on hand to repair it internally as Ant-Man. Once restored, Vision told us of our, well, "appearance" in the mansion. Iron Man shared with us a handwritten letter from Edwin Jarvis, who had given his resignation from the mansion after witnessing the same thing.

For Jarvis to resign was rather extraordinary, given his longtime association with Tony Stark and his parents. He'd looked after you and the other Avengers in a similar capacity, after Stark donated his mansion for use as your headquarters.

I don't know that I've ever seen Jarvis that rattled, but he had good reason. According to Vision, he along with Quicksilver and Scarlet Witch had been attacked by creatures who appeared in the form of grazing cattle and suddenly transformed themselves into duplicates of the Fantastic Four.

Sounds like they encountered the prime suspects you were seeking.

Doesn't it? We tracked down and engaged the Skrulls, who fought back using the combined powers of our allies with enough effort to defeat us and make their escape with at least Quicksilver and Scarlet Witch aboard. We knew our next step.

Pursuit.

But our departure was delayed by an attack on us ordered by H. Warren Craddock of the Alien Activities Commission in the form of Mandroids.

Item No. 0137—Mandroid Armor Mark 1

HEIGHT: 7'5", WEIGHT (WITHOUT OPERATOR): 300 POUNDS

This armored suit was developed by Anthony Stark and Stark Industries for use by the intelligence agency S.H.I.E.L.D. Composed of a highly durable foamed-steel alloy, a Mandroid combat suit is capable of amplifying the wearer's natural abilities into superhuman ranges, with running speeds measured up to 45 mph and strength tests measuring up to twenty times more than normal capabilities. Life-support systems can protect the wearer from environments ranging from 70,000 feet above to 800 feet below sea level and are capable of circulating and replenishing air for up to two months. Weaponry includes high-neutronic-frequency stun cannons, a 250-watt laser torch, and an electro-gravitic tractor/repeller field generator able to push or pull up to 950 pounds.

Although Mandroid armor is designed to be worn for maximum capabilities, an unmanned Mark 1 suit can be remotely controlled through a laser-guided transmission beam.

From what I understand, those are formidable opponents.

I sure found them to be. Thankfully, Iron Man had the sense of knowing exactly what to do against them and managed to short out the armored suits without harming the operators inside. But before we could resume the pursuit, we received an in-person distress call from Triton of the group of moon-dwellers we know as the Inhumans. We assisted Triton in locating Black Bolt, leader of the Inhumans, and helping to quell a revolt against his leadership by Maximus the Mad.

What we discovered was that Maximus had given his allegiance to the Kree, and just as we were responding to this news, Rick Jones was taken by Kree forces and kidnapped into space.

That had to have been troubling.

It affirmed my resolve. I swore an oath in that moment against Kree and Skrulls alike. The Avengers were coming for our friends, and their day of reckoning was at hand. I led a team of Avengers that included Iron Man, Thor, Vision, and Clint Barton in the guise of Goliath. We traveled in the *Bogey-Baby*, a spacecraft of unknown origin powered by the hammer of Thor itself. Things went pretty smoothly

BLACKAGAR BOLTAGON
KNOWN ALIASES/ALTER EGOS: Black Bolt, ruler of the Inhumans

TRITON
KNOWN ALIASES/ALTER EGOS: Prisoner 423-IX

The Bogey-Baby

until we encountered a full-blown fleet of Skrull ships heading directly to Earth.

I've come to understand that you were critically outnumbered.

Outnumbered, outgunned, out of about everything you could name, most likely. But one thing the *Bogey-Baby* did have aboard her was some sort of defensive image projection device that made her appear as one of a vast group of approaching vessels. Somehow, the strategy worked as the Skrulls sent just one ship to intercept us. While Iron Man was able to withstand the near-vacuum of space to start our attack, the rest of us didn't have those advantages. That's where the *Bogey-Baby*'s Starling fighter ships came in handy. We each jumped into a cockpit and sped out after Iron Man.

That ship was tricked out.

I expected no less of anything given to us by Nick Fury, and that ship definitely gave us the initial upper hand against the armada. We were able to board the Skrull ship as Goliath patrolled the area and kept watch. We confronted the Skrull commandant to demand our fellow Avengers be released to us. As he answered, we were interrupted by a video transmission from the Skrull Emperor, who showed us an image of Mar-Vell constructing a device he called an Omni-Wave Projector.

And what was that supposed to accomplish?

I found the Emperor's description impossible to believe, but it apparently was capable of instantaneous intergalactic communication as well as being reconfigured into what we were told was the ultimate death ray. Before this weapon could be wielded, we witnessed Mar-Vell turn on his captors and free Quicksilver and Scarlet Witch. Then the Emperor ordered the execution of Plan Delta, which we took as our cue to engage the Skrulls hand-to-hand. That's what got an underling to confess the details of this imperial plan. The Skrull ship had launched a small craft with a nuclear warhead capable of destroying a planet. And it was headed toward Earth.

What was your plan to stop that from happening?

Goliath, of course. I ordered him to stop at nothing, including the loss of his own life, to prevent that craft from reaching Earth. I'm guessing I don't have to tell you that Goliath was successful in accomplishing his mission.

I'll hold that truth to be self-evident.

I like what you did there. But we have reached a point in this story where I cannot call the details my own. On one hand, Goliath was on his own, one soldier tasked with saving the world. On the other hand, our own fates were determined by what we later discovered were the actions of our own Rick Jones amplified through the cosmic power of Mar-Vell.

How so?

We found our Skrull adversaries had been frozen in place, perhaps in time, by a flash of light with no apparent source. With no other clear course of action, we set course for the Skrull galaxy itself. Before we could get there on our own, the lot of us were swept from the ship into a Kree stronghold, flung there by forces that also brought Mar-Vell, Quicksilver, and Scarlet Witch. Once there, I faced a sight that has haunted me over and over since my revival in this time. I stood before a seemingly dead Rick Jones.

I can understand how you must have felt. How did that come to pass?

As I said, these details are not my own. I am authorized to give you a copy of this report by Rick Jones himself.

POST-ACTION REPORT -
AVENGERS INTERNAL USE ONLY

Contact and conversations with Kree leaders
during time of Kree and Skrull activities on
Earth as reported by Richard "Rick" Jones
(transcript of oral report)

After I was kidnapped and transported to Hala, the
Kree homeworld—which was crazy, by the way—I was taken
before Ronan the Accuser. He recognized me from being
part of the Avengers' attack on the Kree citadel built
near the Arctic Circle, and ol' Chrome-Dome was not
happy about that—even though he's the one who took off
to his homeworld in the middle of the fight—but, yeah.

I was called out by this massive green blob of a
floating head with all these waving tentacles for hair
who said it was the Supreme Intelligence, the rightful
ruler of the Kree. It appeared to me on a massive TV
screen and said it was the sum of the mightiest minds
of the Kree and not really a living being. It must
have existed inside the computer system. Anyway, this
Supreme Intelligence said it had been overthrown from
leadership, weakened, and locked away. Because some
sort of energy shield protected the top brass of the
Kree and the Skrulls, this green head thingy projected
its mental waves to Earth and caused that politician
H. Warren Craddock to create all these problems for
the Avengers. It even said it had caused all of the
actions that brought me before him then and there.
Well, I had no other explanation for all the weird
stuff that's happened to me, so I just went with it.

I probably should have been more aware of what it
was doing because it said that I, Rick Jones, would
decide the fate of "worlds without end," whatever that
meant, and then I felt myself dragged into a portal of
energy that dumped me into the Negative Zone right in
front of Annihilus. Great, right?

But something else wasn't right. My mind was
alive with images coming from across the universe. I
could see Mar-Vell working on something I somehow knew
was an Omni-Wave Projector. I could see Quicksilver
and Scarlet Witch fighting for their lives against
attacking Skrulls. I saw Iron Man and Cap and Thor and
Vision fighting Skrulls as well, but I knew that image
was coming to me from even farther away. I saw Ronan

flying toward Earth. I saw Craddock screaming about
the Avengers. I saw Hawkeye—no, wait, Clint was Goliath
at that point—facing even more Skrulls. And there in my
mind was the Supreme Intelligence somehow responsible
for all of it.

As I came to my senses, Annihilus grabbed me by
the throat and started to choke the life out of me for
helping to banish him to the Negative Zone. I couldn't
breathe. I started to panic. And then I don't know what
the heck happened, but I fought back by shooting this
energy beam out of my forehead right into Annihilus'
ugly face. My brain beam blasted that thing into
the darkness. Then the beam stopped and I was just
floating alone in the nothingness.

The green head returned and told me we had one
hope. It said if I concentrated hard enough, I could
unlock visions of heroes stored deep within my mind
who could save us from the Kree. So I focused. I
pulled the most detailed memories I could from my
mind of Cap and of Namor, and then I imagined each
of the heroes I could remember from those old comic
mags I used to read back at the orphanage. Somehow
my imagination became _real_. Every one of those heroes
just materialized out of my brain and they came out
swinging at the Kree soldiers. The big green head
commanded me to send my creations into action. All
I could feel was a giant pain like a white-hot poker
stabbed through my brain from one temple to the other.
But I did it. I mentally commanded these comic heroes
of World War II to save us and they did. The android
Human Torch threw fireballs and the Patriot kicked
Kree fighters in the jaws. A wild version of the
Vision cracked Kree heads together and the Blazing
Skull swung soldiers around by their ankles. The Angel
and the Fin fought until my mind no longer had the
strength to control the heroes and they all faded back
into my imagination, I guess.

But that didn't stop the pounding and aching in
my head. I thought the pain would drive me mad, but
the Supreme Intelligence kept pushing me toward what
it called my "fateful test." I had to do it. I had no
choice. I reached out, pointing at nothing, and this
bright bolt of light or fire or something shot from my
fingertips. I had no idea at all what I was causing
as it was happening, or how, but the big brain seemed
to expect that. It said my comprehension had yet to
overtake my power. I regained my senses long enough

to realize that the beam had frozen Ronan and every Kree soldier in their tracks—and I mean frozen like a statue. Turns out that was not just the Kree where we were, but the Skrulls had frozen up, too, and that was in a whole other galaxy. I never would have believed it had I not been told by the Avengers who saw it themselves.

The Supreme Intelligence then forced me to watch how my power had reached all the way to H. Warren Craddock, the same guy who ran the Avengers completely off Earth. I could see him clearly in the middle of New York, and I could even read his mind. The bolt zapped Craddock but nobody else. And something started happening to him right before my eyes. He started changing into a Skrull! The hypnotized crowd saw it too. The Skrull got pulled into the crowd, which by then was a mob—a frightened, kill-crazy mob! A few seconds of shouting and hitting and it was all over. Once the Skrull guy's spell was finished, the crowd just drifted away.

The Skrull was dead—and in a way, I killed him.

The Supreme Intelligence said I could not be blamed for what happened. It was the end of a chain of events that began when Ronan weakened the Supreme Intelligence so it could no longer influence the leaders of the Kree and the Skrulls. Once they forced Mar-Vell to build and use the Omni-Wave Projector, that gave the big green head what it needed to unleash powers inside me and inside all humans. In some distant future, it said, every human would be able to do what I did. He made it sound like no big deal. It was all so heavy, man, that I just blacked out.

Next thing I knew, I was up and around—and I had no idea why. The big green head said it was once again able to keep the Kree and the Skrulls at an uneasy peace, and it sent us all back to Earth. That's when I learned I'm alive only because Mar-Vell chose to be linked to me once more.

(transcript ends)

Richard "Rick" Jones
before Ronan the Accuser

Mar-Vell made the sacrifice to connect his life energies with Rick to ensure Rick's survival.

Yes, he did. It was a choice that cost Mar-Vell a measure of his personal freedom. I have thanked Mar-Vell for that sacrifice many times. This all was orchestrated by the mind of the Kree Supreme Intelligence. Without that being's assistance, Rick and any number of us might have been lost. That truth makes the subsequent events of this conflict even more regrettable.

That's a shame to hear. What happened next, Steve?

We again found ourselves subjected to a power of unimaginable level that returned us all to Earth unharmed. With H. Warren Craddock discovered to have been a Skrull imposter, all charges against the Avengers by the Alien Activities Commission had been dismissed. But our work was not yet done. I had ordered Goliath to stop the Plan Delta nuclear warhead, which he clearly did, but we soon discovered Goliath was nowhere to be found. We knew only that wherever he was, he likely was powerless, as the growth serum developed by Henry Pym had stopped working for him.

How did you start such a search?

H. Warren Craddock, now known to have been a Skrull imposter

I'll be honest with you. I was looking at this through a wartime frame of mind. I said openly that we could not rule out the possibility that Goliath had sacrificed himself for the success of the mission. After all, those were my orders. To save Earth, he could have destroyed the Skrull craft with himself aboard. For reasons of their own, Thor and Iron Man separated from the group to conduct their searches individually; Thor from Asgard and Iron Man from Tony Stark's new townhouse. My plan was to check with Nick Fury as S.H.I.E.L.D. already had begun the search, but before I did, I had a gut feeling to catch up with a TV newscast. We had been off Earth long enough that certainly something could have happened anywhere on the planet to draw Goliath's attention.

Were you able to get any clues?

What we saw was chilling. The screen filled with images of protests verging on riots in the streets. Americans were chanting and screaming in favor of going to war against anyone and everyone. And not just conventional war but escalating our attacks to nuclear missiles. They called themselves the Warhawks, and something about them felt . . . inauthentic. These weren't the sentiments I believed would send Americans into the streets. I took Rick, Quicksilver, and Scarlet Witch with me in the Quinjet to investigate in person. Sure enough, thanks to Thor's timely arrival and intervention, we learned the riot was not at all genuine but the work of Ares, the Olympian god of war. Thor was not the only surprise arrival to the Warhawks' riot.

As I recall the incident, this was the return of Goliath.

Well, the return of Clint Barton, you're right. But he appeared in a new heroic uniform and announced himself as Hawkeye. And with Hawkeye was Hercules, whom he encountered on his lengthy journey back to the Avengers. Another story better told by him than by me.

POST-ACTION REPORT ---
AVENGERS INTERNAL USE ONLY

Events surrounding Skrull Plan Delta and return to
Earth following time of Kree and Skrull activities
on Earth as reported by Clinton Barton while active
under codenames Goliath and Hawkeye
(transcript of oral report)

I was piloting the one-man fighter craft Starling
One launched from the Earth vessel Bogey-Baby and
maintaining surveillance of activity surrounding a lone
Skrull warship as my fellow Avengers Captain America,
Iron Man, Thor, and Vision engaged its occupants. While
I began the operation as Goliath, by my choice I was
no longer under the influence of the growth serum
developed by Dr. Henry Pym and at the time possessed
no superhuman size or abilities.

I received a communication from Captain America
with orders to pursue a vessel I observed departing
the Skrull ethercraft Beta-31 warship referenced in
other reports. Cap ordered me to "stop" the vessel
"at any cost including your own life." I acknowledged
his order and pursued the vessel, catching it as it
neared entry into hyperspace. I forced entry onto the
bridge of the Skrull vessel and faced several members
of its crew.

I fled the bridge and hid within the ship's
infrastructure while pursued by armed Skrulls. In
the moment, I was desperate for anything that might
work against the Skrulls. I attempted to will myself
into reactivating any remaining growth serum in my
system, but that resulted only in blowing my cover. As
the Skrulls fired on me, they struck the surrounding
bulkheads and loosened pieces of conduit and other
materials that made up the ship. I quickly fashioned a
bow from pieces within reach and let a few makeshift
arrows fly to create a diversion. Cap always said I
could turn a piece of string and two sticks into a bow
and arrow. In that moment, I believed his words and I
believed in myself as an archer—as Hawkeye. I believed
that, once again, I was a hero.

Apparently, my diversionary shots wreaked some
kind of havoc aboard the ship as the Skrulls lost
interest in pursuing me in order to tend to whatever
damage I had caused. I took advantage of the situation

by reboarding the <u>Starling_One</u> and getting the hell outta there. Not long after my escape, the Skrull ship went off like the Fourth of July. I considered my directive from Cap accomplished. Before I could set a course for Earth, the <u>Starling_One</u> had become trapped by the gravity of a nearby planet and I was forced to make a crash landing.

As it turned out, to my great relief, the planet that pulled me in was Earth and I was met at the crash site by members of a traveling carnival who spoke little English. Their leader, a man named Rudolfo, told me I had landed in Yugoslavia. I told him I was an archer with the Avengers, and while that meant nothing to him, he did offer me a bow and quiver filled with arrows that I used to show off a little to his group. I impressed him enough to earn a lift to Belgrade.

We encountered a severe storm along the way, and a flash flood swept the horse-drawn wagon I was in into a ravine. As the wagon was balanced just so against a tree, I knew I had no hope of getting out of it alive without some help. Rudolfo brought a man he introduced as Hercules, and it quickly became clear by the man's impossible strength that I was in the presence of the god Hercules, well known to us in the Avengers. Hercules, as it turns out, had linked up with the carnival himself while suffering a bout of amnesia he had contracted in battle. Who knows how long he might have continued his travels with them had I not found him.

Once we reached Belgrade, I contacted Kevin O'Brien of Stark Industries while trying to reach Tony Stark, and Kevin arranged for me and Hercules to be flown back to the United States. Upon our return, we were immediately attacked by soldiers of Ares, and I ended up invading Olympus with the rest of the Avengers. My report on that activity already has been filed.

(transcript ends)

BARTON, CLINTON
KNOWN ALIASES/ALTER EGOS:
Goliath

Experiencing the hateful unrest of the Warhawks as pawns of Ares was one thing. Not long afterward, I chanced across more hatred—this time aimed directly at me. It was a television ad unlike any I had seen before.

TV AD STORYBOARD: WHO IS CAPTAIN AMERICA?

VOICEOVER: Good day, my fellow Americans. This is a man many of you know: Captain America.

VO: For years, Captain America has been a one-man vigilante committee, attacking anyone he deemed a criminal. Some were clearly such—

VO: But others were private citizens, men the recognized legal agencies had never molested.

VO: In fact, recognized legal agencies are hardly ever involved in Captain America's headlong pursuit of his individual concept of law and order. He is unwelcome, for example, at S.H.I.E.L.D.

VO: Who is Captain America? He wraps himself in our nation's flag, yet no one in government is responsible or will take responsibility for his actions.

HARDERMAN: Perhaps the reason for this lies in chemicals, which, many rumors allege, created his unnatural abilities in a secret laboratory!

HARDERMAN: Yet he continues to roam the streets, striking at will at those who displease him! He claims he does it all for America!

VO: Your America?

THIS PUBLIC REMINDER PAID FOR BY THE—
COMMITTEE TO REGAIN AMERICA'S PRINCIPLES

That must have been hard to hear.

I won't lie. I was mad enough to chew iron and spit rivets. None of that commercial was true. The words were negative distortions of my actions, and the photos were taken completely out of context. This was created to turn the public against me. I had been devoting my life to my only goal: making America a better place to live for everyone however I could. I tracked the commercial to the founder of the Committee to Regain America's Principles, a man named Quentin Harderman, who said he would change his tune on TV if I took part in a charity boxing exhibition.

And you agreed?

I would have agreed to anything to get him off my back. What I did not know was that I had played into a plot to frame me for murder hatched by members of a group that called itself the Secret Empire. Their goal was nothing short of dominating an unsuspecting America through propaganda and lies. With the help of Sam as well as Professor Charles Xavier and two of his X-Men, I unraveled the plot, which stretched all the way to the highest elected office of our nation.

Highest . . . are you saying . . . ?

Let's just say that the revelation of the Secret Empire's leader, his quest for unchecked power, and how he took his own life rather than submit to authorities was enough to shake my trust in the basic framework of America. I questioned the virtues of our leaders. I felt crushed by my realization that while I was fighting for a better nation, its very leaders were working to dismantle our freedoms from within.

What a world to come home to.

I joined the Avengers and traveled to different galaxies with the goal of protecting our nation and our planet from those with no regard for our basic liberties. I fought to protect us from alien threats only to discover our own citizens turning against each other and conspiring to strip basic liberties away from us all. I had no regrets about taking up that fight. What I regretted in a way was that I did it as Captain America. My homecoming got me asking whether people today deserved a Captain America. I wondered whether they ought to experience their world without one. My conclusion was that it was time for Captain America to die.

You . . . you couldn't have meant that literally, Steve.

No, I wasn't going to harm myself. In the moment, I wasn't even sure whether I had the guts or even the right to just retire the persona of Captain America, let alone end the existence of a living symbol of our country. But personally? I was a man no longer interested in being a living legend. I had seen America rocked with scandal, manipulated by demagogues with sweet, empty words. I had seen on our soil things I had watched in the newsreels of my youth about wartime Europe, which had driven me to assume the duties of a soldier. And over the years, where had all my efforts to help my fellow man get me? Americans gripped by the lies of the Secret Empire turning on me. What I did—who I was—had just lost its meaning for people. When no one can trust their leaders, how can they trust their heroes? How can I blame them for not wanting to?

America no longer was the single entity I thought it was when I took the name Captain America. Nothing was that simple anymore. In the land of the free, each of us is able to do what we want to do, think what we want to think. That's as it should be, but it makes for a great many different versions of what America is. And knowing that the eyes of this nation were upon me, that people the world over looked to the examples set by Captain America, which America was I supposed to symbolize?

I can't begin to answer that. I'm sure you couldn't either.

I settled on one central point. The government created me in 1941 to act as their agent in protecting our country. Over the years, I always tried to serve my country well. I wasn't perfect but I did my best. And then I faced a government that was serving itself. So I asked myself whether Captain America must die, and if I had the courage to carry out my verdict. The answer to both questions was yes. But try as I might, after putting my uniform away, I could not sit by with the powers I had and not use them for good. I needed to fight—but for no one's ideals but my own. It was the birth of the Nomad.

ROGERS, STEVE
KNOWN ALIASES/ALTER EGOS: Nomad

I trust in your sincerity, Steve, don't get me wrong. But you prepared yourself to fight on our behalf as Nomad only to take back your Captain America uniform a short time later. What changed your mind?

A terrible, bloody challenge from the Red Skull. There are Americans every bit as bad as the Red Skull, who abuse America's ideals . . . and I didn't see them. I thought I knew the good guys from the bad guys.

Things are more complex today.

Maybe you shouldn't say that as a point of pride.

I'm resigned to it, Steve, not proud of it.

INTERVIEWER'S NOTE: Captain Rogers had an edge in his voice I was not accustomed to hearing. I wondered whether he extended that into assuming I believed those simpler times fostered simpler or more naive people. I wanted to correct the course of our talk.

I refuse to resign myself to events and their consequences. Had I been paying more attention to how the American reality differs from the American Dream, had I not tricked myself into thinking that what I believe is decades out of date, I never would have left the job I started. The man Nomad is . . . well, that man makes Captain America better.

You took back the Captain America mantle because those feelings and values that had always guided you once again were validated.

I know it sounds corny, but it gets in your blood. I know in a lot of ways I'm a relic—a throwback to a generation most people have never known. Have I mentioned how surreal it is to walk battlefields on which I fought, and they've been "historical" sites for decades? And their significance seems to lessen in importance with each new generation and every passing day. But I know that's not entirely true. There are still young people discovering this history and doing whatever they can to keep it visible and relevant.

Such efforts offer hope that the very harsh and even painful lessons we learned all those years ago might not be completely forgotten.

All those years ago for you, friend. Not for me.

Of course. There are those—myself included—who appreciate how you represent a unique treasure far beyond your physical abilities and the great services you've performed for us. You represent a direct line to that history. Through you, we can experience that world and that time for what they were as they happened, and I think it starts with the person who so loved their country that they were willing to do anything to serve it during its time of need.

INTERVIEWER'S NOTE: *I watched Captain Rogers consider my words. What I intended as praise and affirmation made him shift in his seat. He did not meet my gaze; he muttered his response into his chest.*

I'm just a soldier. That's all I ever was, just like so many others, many of whom gave far more than I ever did.

Steve, you may regard yourself that way. I assure you that many of your fellow Americans did not. I want to propose something because I believe this is the right time to do it. I want to leave you with this.

You're giving me a box of homework?

This is some insight into the time you missed. These are items I pulled from the National Archives. They have quite a collection of documents and reports, newspapers, photographs, personal journals or at least pages from them. The letters written to you—Captain America, I mean—are among the most interesting. There also is one item I've brought that I believe you'll find of particular interest.

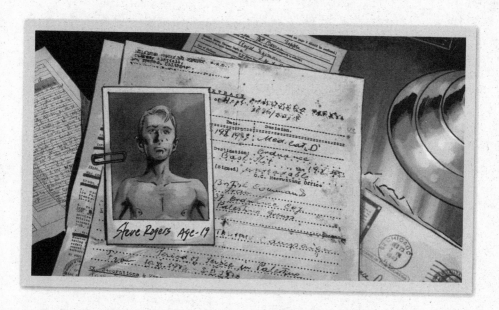

S.H.I.E.L.D.

MEMORANDUM

"Joseph Reinstein" was an alias for Abraham Erskine, a German scientist whose death was faked in 1940 following his defection to the United States. Working in secret, he continued his research into human genetic enhancement. Even with private writings such as this, Erskine rigorously maintained his cover identity until his assassination in 1941, shortly after administering his experimental Super-Soldier protocol to Steven Rogers. He was killed before he could fully record the details of his research so that it might be replicated, leaving Rogers as the sole successful recipient of Erskine's original efforts.

TRANSLATION

It's late and I know I should be trying to rest, as tomorrow promises to be a monumental day, but I cannot sleep. The anticipation is too powerful to ignore, and I find myself pacing my room, anxious to proceed.

Tomorrow, after years of work along with months of preparation just to get us to this point, we will finally be ready to test the formula on our subject. All the examinations we have made with our candidate give me high hopes for success. If this works, it will give the American military a tremendous advantage over our would-be adversaries. An army of "Super-Soldiers," stronger as well as faster and more agile than the enemies they might face in battle.

But strength of body is only part of the equation. Indeed, locating a prime physical specimen has never been a component I've viewed as crucial to the success of this program. We interviewed and tested hundreds of potential candidates, many of whom came to us from backgrounds where their physical strength was an asset. Young men raised on farms, employed in factories or construction, and even soldiers who've already benefited from a military conditioning program designed to help them survive the rigors of war.

However, if tomorrow we are successful, those who undergo the life-changing process we've developed will be the vanguard of a new breed of soldier, possessing superior physical and mental acuities far exceeding those of our potential enemies. Yet how do we ensure the army we propose to create will not one day grow beyond our control, and utilize their newfound abilities not for the good of the country they've sworn to protect, but instead some heretofore unobtainable yet ignoble ambition?

To avoid such undesirable scenarios, we must ensure those we seek to imbue with these gifts must first and foremost be of worthy character—brave, but also selfless. Powerful, yet gentle; resolute on the battlefield but also mindful that even in war, there are rules to which civilized men are beholden. I believe there are such men who can rise to this challenge. We must simply expend the effort necessary to find them.

I believe Steven Rogers to be such a man, hopefully just the first of many.

Abraham Erskine, alias Joseph Reinstein

INTERVIEWER'S NOTE: This excerpt from Professor Reinstein/Erskine is something Captain Rogers had never seen before we met. I was able to watch his reaction as he read it for the first time, then sat in silence for several moments before we resumed our conversation.

Wow. That's ... that's quite something. (*clears throat*) I mean, I knew he always thought highly of me, and I often wondered if I was truly deserving of the praise he offered. At the time there was a part of me that wondered if he was just saying things to keep me relaxed about the experiments.

While I'm sure he did do that, I think it's safe to say there was far more to it. For a man who only knew you as a teenager the Army had classified as unfit for service, he was rather insightful. He had you pegged from the beginning, looking past the scrawny kid to see the person within.

I'd like to think I was just the first person he found, and he simply didn't get the chance to discover others who could do the same job.

We'll unfortunately never know how successful he might have been. What we do know is that attempts to replicate what he accomplished with you have all fallen short to varying degrees, and that's without discussing the moral implications of how some went about it.

Let's discuss it then.

You were upset to learn the government had forcibly experimented on other soldiers in an attempt to replicate Professor Erskine's work.

Absolutely. (*taps his chest*) I volunteered. I understood the risks, and the
professor warned me the experiment
might even be fatal. I was given the
choice. Isaiah and all those other
men? What was done to them—those
chosen for the program and most
especially those who weren't? And
to tell their families they'd died in
battle? (*pauses, blowing out his
breath*) It's simply evil.

*In hindsight, the false notifications
may have been easier for them to
process than what really happened
to them, at least for those families
who never learned the horrible truth.
Only seven of the original three
hundred test subjects survived*

BRADLEY, ISAIAH
KNOWN ALIASES/ALTER EGOS:
Captain America

the procedure. Ultimately, Isaiah was the only one to live through the test program and the war.

And they thanked him with a court-martial and prison, and for what? Some stupid trumped-up charge. He deserved medals for his heroism, proper care after his health began to fail him, restitution to his family for the pain they were forced to endure. All of them deserved so much better. We, as a nation, failed them. The only think I can do is fight to make sure nothing like that ever happens again.

INTERVIEWER'S NOTE: *Though his voice remained level throughout the last part of this exchange, I noted how he was clenching his fists so tightly, the blood left his fingers. I decided to end our session for the day and leave him with the box. Until we resumed a few days later, I had no idea whether he even had opened it.*

Captain America and Bucky, August 1944

CAPTAIN AMERICA CAPTURES SPY RING!

ut—
? p.3

THE TRUE

DAILY 🎺 BUGLE ☆☆☆☆

NEW YORK'S FINEST DAILY NEWSPAPER

NAZI VICTIMS RESCUED BY CAPTAIN AMERICA

Saboteurs Fail with Captain America on the Scene

CAPTAIN AMERICA

PREVENTS DAM EXPLOSION

Thanks for seeing me again, Steve. You've been on my mind for sure.

I spent the last couple of nights going over some of the letters and other materials you left with me. It was certainly a trip down Memory Lane, but not always what I expected.

Because many of them are things you never saw?

Right, but many of the letters and other documents acted as their own prompts in other ways. A date, a particular turn of phrase or a reference to something from back then, almost always evoked some kind of memory.

How did that make you feel?

What would you have me say? I can tell when someone is asking a question for the chance to hear a story, and that includes you. You know by now that I want to share with people this experience of mine. I have insights that might help others lead better lives. But I also am getting better at knowing when you are asking for *you*. So when you push me to express my feelings about a topic, because you strike me as genuine, I answer for you.

My mother gave me good windows into people and this is one of her best. She said that when people ask how you're feeling, take the moment to tell them honestly. If next time they ask again, it's because they truly want your answer. And if they start answering you honestly when you ask, they're a friend you should keep.

(pauses) Someday, we're going to talk about our moms. You want to know how that box made me feel? Happy? Homesick? Sad? Resigned? All of the above, I suppose, and other feelings I can't easily describe. I mean, since Stark and the others found me, almost anything has acted as a memory trigger. An old song—or even a newer one if its lyrics contained certain words. A smell, an old movie on TV. Visiting a museum can definitely do it. I went to the World War II museum in New Orleans. It was like going home again.

Going home to your life before Dr. Erskine and the Super-Soldier Serum?

My life before the serum wasn't much to speak of. Manhattan didn't offer much to my parents before they died, and didn't offer anything to me beyond libraries and movie theaters. But then, when I wanted a doorway to escape into fantasy, I faced a harsh reality instead. Scenes in the newsreels of the war in Europe formed my resolve that I keep to this day, that freedom is worth fighting for. I just wasn't equipped to fight.

Until you were.

I believed with every fiber of my being that I should take my fight to the Nazis. Dr. Erskine made that possible.

It was a process you were told could kill you.

I was willing to give my life on the battlefield but I was denied. If the Super-Soldier Serum procedure took my life instead, I was willing to face that consequence.

And the procedure itself?

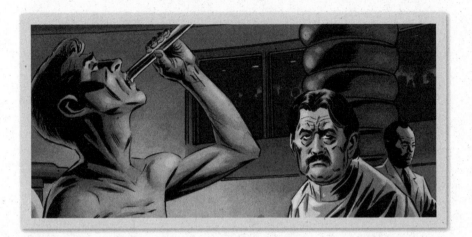

A three-step process that, to hear me describe it, may sound anticlimactic. I got an injection. I drank a concoction. I let myself be exposed to a form of radiation. The properties of each component and their reactivity to each other and to my body is something I never got the chance to fully understand. I just know that it worked.

How did you feel?

Physically, I felt pain and dizziness. I thought I might black out but I fought against it. And then, somehow my body just . . . got larger. I became stronger. In a matter of minutes, I became a new man.

Beyond physically, Steve, how did you feel?

I mean . . . I felt *new*. I felt actualized, as if Dr. Erskine helped me manifest in my physical form the potential I carried in my heart. I had hoped it would work but I never imagined I would be . . . this. It was a miracle.

I'd say it still is, especially given the fact that Dr. Erskine was murdered as soon as you transformed and was prevented from creating more soldiers like you.

I still fight for those who might have been.

Even with Dr. Erskine's passing and his Super-Soldier Program allegedly on hold—though we now know better—it didn't take long for the Army to put you to work. Those newspaper clippings tell part of the story. Here's the other part.

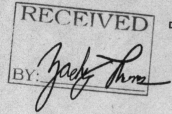

DEPARTMENT OF THE ARMY

5 December 1942

FROM: PERSONNEL
TO: PRIVATE ROGERS, STEVEN G.
SUBJ: PERMANENT CHANGE OF STATION

Effective 20 December 1942, you are ordered to report
no later than 31 December 1942 to Camp Lehigh,
Virginia, for duty with the 2nd Infantry Battalion,
309th Infantry Regiment, 78th Infantry Division.
Proceed from your current location in sufficient time
to report by the date specified. Unit of assignment
is responsible for rations, quarters, supply, health
and welfare, and maintenance. Failure to observe
these orders is a violation of Articles 86 and 92
of the Uniform Code of Military Justice, subject to
trial by court-martial and punishment included but
not limited to confinement, forfeiture of pay, and
dishonorable discharge.

FOR GENERAL PHILLIPS

R. Perlman
LTC PERS
Commanding

REGRADED UNCLASSIFIED BY
AUTHORITY OF DOD DIR. 2200. 1 R
BY _____

Unidentified photographs
recovered from Steve Rogers's
personal possessions at the
time of his purported death

**BARNES,
JAMES BUCHANAN**
KNOWN ALIASES/ALTER EGOS:
Bucky, Winter Soldier,
Captain America, Revolution

(*smiles*) Yeah, that whole "cover identity" bit. General Phillips and others were worried the Nazis would send spies or assassins to finish what they started with the professor. Or they'd want to capture me to take back to Germany for study. That was always a concern, so the Army in its infinite wisdom decided to try hiding me in plain sight.

Hiding you as a lowly private—one of several million across America at the time—does seem to have been a master stroke.

There I was, just another dogface training for war and marching around the parade grounds. Doesn't mean I didn't stick out. (*laughs*) Did you know they had to tailor my uniforms to fit me? My size wasn't available from supply. My helmet and my boots were the only things that fit off the shelf.

Even before being sent to Europe, you were chasing down Nazi spies, saboteurs, and assassins. You prevented bombings on military bases, factories, dams, and bridges.

And I still managed to get home in time for bond drives and photos with movie starlets. (*shakes head*) Definitely not the life I imagined all those times I tried to enlist.

It was while you were at Camp Lehigh that you met Mr. Barnes and trained him to be your partner.

Excerpt from the personal journal of
James. B. Barnes, discovered April 1945

What a day!

All this time, Captain America has been hiding right under our noses. And who would've thought it was none other than my best friend, Steve Rogers?

Him being here is just a cover story to keep Cap's location secret. If the Nazis ever found out where he was, they'd stop at nothing to get to him. All those times I wrote about what a klutz he is and how he's always getting in trouble with Sergeant Duffy? It's all an act! And those times where he's late to duty or says he forgot to do some work detail like peeling potatoes or spit-shining boots? It's because he was off doing Captain America things. Talk about your good acting. Steve gives Bogart a run for his money. Nobody, not even me, ever suspected he was faking that all along. He did what they told him to do, hiding the truth from everyone including me.

He didn't mean to give up his secret. That was all my fault. Earlier tonight, I walked into his tent

while he was putting on the Cap costume! He didn't know I was there until it was too late. The first thing he did was make me swear I'd keep his secret, but then he asked me to be his partner! He warned me the training would be intense, but I think I'm ready for it. I've already been exercising and running the same obstacle courses the real soldiers use to train. They take me to the ranges and let me fire rifles and pistols, and I've got some of the highest scores. I've taken hand-to-hand combat classes, but Steve promises me I'm going to be getting a lot more of that training.

The funniest thing about all of this? I'm liable to get in the same kind of trouble Steve does whenever

Sergeant Duffy thinks he's been goldbricking but he's really out being Captain America. Whenever I'm peeling potatoes, I'll be able to smile, knowing we're carrying out important missions, even if the public never learns who we really are.

I wonder if I'll get my own costume?

I learned Bucky kept a journal only after I came out of the ice. (*holds up the copied pages*) Reading this again, I can feel how excited he was that night, and to be honest I was relieved that I could talk to someone about this big secret I'd been keeping. Finally, I had someone with whom I could just be myself. You have no idea how much that meant to me back then. I think keeping all of that to myself was the hardest part, especially when I'd get letters from kids.

DEAR CAPTAIN AMERICA,

MY NAME IS BILLY AND I WANTED to SEND YOU A LETTER to WISH YOU A MERRY CHRISTMAS. I AM VERY GREATFUL YOU ARE SPENDING CHRISTMAS AWAY FROM YOUR FAMILY AND FITING to KEEP US SAFE.
I HOPE YOU CAN COME HOME SOON.

THANK YOU!

YOUR FRIEND
BILLY

Capt

c/o

A letter delivered to
Captain America C/O
the War Department,
December 1944

A letter delivered to
Captain America C/O the War
Department, July 1944

Dear Captain America,

We are learning about you in our class and I wanted to send you a card for your birthday but my teacher told us nobody knows when your birthday is so we decided that maybe July 4th should be your birthday. I hope you are doing well over in the war. When you come home can you come to visit us. Our school is in Kansas but my teacher says you can go anywhere you want so please come see us so I can draw a picture of you for my daddy.

Happy Birthday from your new Friend

Elizabeth

PS my Brother wants to know if you can use your Shield as a sled when it snows

I tried to read every letter I received and even tried to write back to the kids who sent one, but after a while it became too much. The Army supposedly had a team of clerks handling my mail at one point, but I never got the chance to meet any of them. They'd still send me some of the special ones, but (*holds up the letters he's just read*) I never saw these.

There are many more like those in the National Archives. What did you do with the ones you actually received?

(*smiles*) I kept them in my footlocker. In the military and especially if you're deployed, storage space for personal items is a luxury. Most of the time, you get whatever can fit in your duffel bag or backpack along with your uniforms and other Army gear. Whatever else goes in there has to be chosen with care, and I've seen guys cry when they realize they have to sacrifice a favorite book or even an envelope of photos or letters from home because there's just no room. If you're lucky enough to get a footlocker, you only really have access to it when you're not in the field. What's special enough to take overseas with you but also something you're willing to leave in a box you might never see again?

I've never thought about a military deployment in that way, but it's so obvious how something like that can be so important to a soldier's morale. I understand your footlocker and its contents were preserved after you were listed as missing in action.

Yeah. I was never declared dead, so the Army stuck the footlocker in a warehouse, where it was then forgotten for decades until after I joined the Avengers. When Baron Zemo and the Masters of Evil took over the mansion, Zemo destroyed it. (*pauses*) He made a point to go through the footlocker and tear up every photo and letter, and break everything else it contained. Every connection I had to my past life, gone.

That must have been painful.

His tearing up my only picture of my mother was the cruelest part. Still, I remember being angry with myself at the time. Zemo and others had killed Blackout and beaten Jarvis, Hercules, and Black Knight to within an inch of

Sarah Rogers, circa 1928

their lives, and there I was crying over some old photos and letters. It was Monica Rambeau who helped me realize it was okay to be upset, given everything else fate had taken from me.

My understanding is Zemo actually undid the harm he caused you.

(*a small laugh*) I definitely didn't see that coming. After he became the leader of the Thunderbolts, Zemo actually traveled back in time and retrieved the footlocker from a point before he destroyed it and brought it back to me. Based on everything I've heard Reed Richards and Tony Stark say about how bad it is to disrupt timelines and everything else, I keep waiting to see what effect my footlocker has on future history.

Perhaps a forgotten C-Ration in there that could alter our timeline?

Given the power that I know a can of ham for breakfast has over a gastro-intestinal system, anything's possible.

Steve Rogers and James Barnes, circa 1945

IV.
RECOMPENSE

Memories hold power over us all. When our minds transport us back to times of great joy or great sorrow, when we feel ourselves moved to laughter or tears equal to the intensity of what we experienced in the moment itself, we are reminded of what we can be reduced to under that power.

Steve Rogers is a man unlike us in many ways but exactly like us in most. He continually confronts specters from his past even as he aids his fellow Avengers in safeguarding our collective future. Comparing memories of his early life with his experiences today has led him to crises of confidence and conscience.

What Captain Rogers trusts more than the intangible properties of his mind are the tangible capabilities of his body. But even in light of the uncounted hours of training he has performed, his superior physical form does not make him infallible. When we next met, I was ready to explore how he might respond should his body not bend to his will and passion for the Dream.

INTERVIEWER: *I'd like to return to our discussion of the Secret Empire, specifically the activities of the Elite and the Royalist Forces of America.*

STEVE ROGERS: My first encounter with the Secret Empire started with an attack on the American psyche through propaganda and lies. The next time we crossed paths, they'd developed technology that didn't rely on the gullibility of the American public but rather a person's susceptibility to a sonic frequency generated by a device operated by a simulated brain.

This is the device you came to know as a Madbomb.

That's right. It's a weapon capable of inducing mass chaos by transmitting waves that encourage people to lash out at each other and destroy whatever is around them. The first device was unleashed on the public in New York, and it also happened to affect me and Sam Wilson. We fell under the influence of the transmission and started to fight each other for no reason we could recall. As I fought through my own madness, we moved into the city streets, where I discovered the device and shattered it with the edge of my shield. Then we were contacted by an agent of S.H.I.E.L.D. and brought to a government facility, where we were briefed on the capabilities of the Madbombs already set off in public. One bomb the size of a toy whistle had been enough to incite the residents of a small town to reduce it to rubble. Another, more sizable Madbomb had influenced 200,000 city dwellers to wipe out a large section of their business and residential areas. Now, an allied spy had discovered and photographed a Madbomb that was significantly larger than we ever imagined. S.H.I.E.L.D believed this device was capable of inciting the population of the entire United States to riot at once and destroy our country from within. Our mission was to eliminate the bomb.

That must have felt like a daunting task.

But one we were up to, especially after we received doses of energy at a frequency intended to immunize our minds against the frequencies of the Madbomb. Our travels took us to the Badlands of South Dakota, where we got a glimpse of an Elitist vision of America led by the face and voice of a composite computer image. We battled for our lives underground against Elite soldiers while the U.S. Army commanded by General Argyle Fist worked to breach the compound from the surface. Once we discovered the mammoth Madbomb wasn't on site, we were off to the East Coast in search of Professor Mason Harding, an electronics genius who our government was convinced had a hand in creating this unimaginable weapon. Turns out our intel was correct, but what we didn't know was that Harding himself had turned against the Elite and their vision for a New America. He confessed to us that his ultimate Madbomb, the size of a Titan missile, was protected by a sonic security system.

That was helpful.

Professor Harding even gave us devices to place in our ears to counteract the sonics. The only trouble was that to gain immunity from the sonics, Sam and I had to commit to stuffing Madbomb technology into our ears. The device was hidden on the grounds of an estate owned by William Taurey, the individual responsible for this insane plan to destroy America and take control of whatever remained. I led a group of soldiers in seizing the grounds and we were making quick work of things. I followed Taurey, who was dressed in the finest clothing of the Colonial era, right up to his white powdered wig, into the estate's manor hall. He stood before a crowd of Colonial-costumed Elitists and announced that they would celebrate here while America tore itself apart under the influence of the massive Madbomb.

I'm sure that didn't sit well with you.

The irony is that I held off revealing myself just long enough to learn that Taurey and his lieutenants were just as eager to face me as I was to face them.

I'm not sure I follow.

I was just as confused in the moment. I overheard a conversation that they were carrying a two-hundred-year-old grudge against me because of the actions of my family. According to an old family diary I had read, Captain Steve Rogers of the Continental Army happened to intercept a William Taurey, a turncoat informant who intended to inform the British of General Washington's movements. That Steve Rogers challenged that William Taurey to a duel and killed him before his message could be delivered.

The Elite knew about this and wanted you dead because of it?

The drive for vengeance can run deep and long, friend. But I will tell you that my dedication for justice makes me just as passionate. I walked onstage and right up to Taurey. I announced that federal forces had occupied the manor and they all were under arrest. But when it came to Taurey, I took him at his word. I asked for a pair of pistols, gave one to him, and told him he had gotten his wish. There I stood ready to represent Captain Steve Rogers of the Continental Army in a duel to the death. We faced each other, pistol barrels jabbed into each other's chests, and I told him to take his best shot. It takes guts, not words, to duel. I told him that his beef with me wasn't some sense of lost family honor. He was driven only by hate.

And?

Hate isn't sustainable. It isn't replenishable. It's never enough. Taurey wasn't strong enough to follow through with pulling that trigger. I was sure he wouldn't be. His quest for power crumbled on that stage as he was taken into custody.

But what happened with the Madbomb?

That's a story for Sam to tell.

LYø.

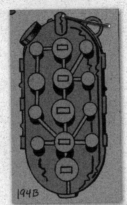

Item Nos. 194A, 194B, 194C—Madbombs

The transmitted mind-waves of "Peanut" caused the citizens of a small town to wipe their village off the map. "Dumpling" was capable of destroying a heavily populated city. The "Big Daddy" was primed to be detonated at the first hour of the nation's Bicentennial.

POST-ACTION REPORT -
AVENGERS INTERNAL USE ONLY

Debriefing on activities as part of "Operation
Madbomb" submitted by Samuel Wilson
(transcript of oral report)

I arrived in Philadelphia operating as the Falcon ahead
of a United States Army squadron briefed on our plan to
search Taurey Towers for a device known as a "Madbomb"
or any evidence as to where the device might be. As
soldiers and law enforcement worked to block traffic
and citizens from the area of the building, I flew
toward our objective.

My goal was to reach the Madbomb before it could
be activated by members of a group we knew as the
Elite, which was working to sow chaos throughout the
country, and amid that chaos seize control of the
federal government. Once activated, the Madbomb was
capable of transmitting waves of mind-controlling
energy at a range we estimated at 3,000 miles, more
than enough to cover the continental United States.
This artificially generated madness would sweep the
nation faster than any plague and could have proven as
deadly or deadlier.

I remember arriving at the top of Taurey Towers
struck with the resolve not to let any Americans fall
enslaved to the grip of the Madbomb. I knew the device
I sought was estimated to match the size of a Titan
missile and that Elitists referred to the device as
"Big Daddy." I encountered a pair of Elite foot soldiers
manning a sonic battery. I was able to incapacitate
them before they could use the battery or inform anyone
else of my arrival.

Once inside the tower, I alerted members of the
operation strike force, who arrived at the top of the
tower via helicopter. Our arrival was discovered by
Elite guards, who fired upon us after we made our way
deeper into the building. We returned fire to suppress
the guards and continued our assault.

I discovered the room holding the Madbomb as well
as a group of operators in the process of activating it.
As I heard one man say the device needed ten seconds
to reach full charge, I engaged the operators and
knocked them unconscious. Based on Professor Harding's
briefing on the Madbomb's operation, I knew to locate
the acceleration switch of the sonic feeder and pull it
into the "Maximum Sonics" setting. I held the switch

in place as I felt myself being bombarded with sonic mind-waves. Despite my mental preparations as well as the technological counteragent provided by Professor Harding, I could feel the waves ripping into my mind. The waves were strong enough to vibrate and crack surrounding equipment. I imagined what they were doing to my flesh and blood.

I fell away from the sonic feeder as it, too, was shaken into pieces by the waves. The air filled with flying debris as I clutched my head in my hands. The facade of the top floors crumbled away and revealed the Madbomb to the outside world. But overburdened by the sonic bombardment, the Madbomb, too, lost structural integrity and exploded. I survived the explosion thanks to the quick actions of members of the squadron, who pulled me from the room in time. As soon as I heard a soldier contact Captain America via walkie-talkie, I asked to speak to him first. I recall my words to him being, "Hello, Cap. It's A-OK here. How stands the nation?" I was greatly relieved to hear his reply.

"There's no doubt now, Falcon. The nation stands!"

(transcript ends)

Despite the decades separating your past from your present, your past has an uncanny knack for catching up with you.

You noticed that, did you?

The Red Skull, for example. He remains a persistent adversary.

(*smiles humorlessly*) That's one way to put it. The universe—or is it the Multiverse, or even the Omniverse?—seems intent on making sure we never stray too far from each other.

You both were born of World War II, so it seems strangely poetic that you remain so connected. He certainly seemed to think that much, especially when the ravages of time decided to have their way with him.

The effects of the gas that put him into suspended animation during the war and kept him from aging began to wear off, causing him to age much more rapidly than normal. Like you said, it was as if time was coming to collect an outstanding debt. All of a sudden, he was an old man, staring death in the face. Of course he decided if he was going to be cheated out of this second life he'd been given, the same should be true for me.

The Skull used one of his people to brainwash Jack Monroe.

Right. Jack was operating under the Nomad mantle I'd used for a time. Under the Skull's control, he slipped a drug into my food that counteracted the effects of the Super-Soldier Serum in my blood. As a result, I began aging rapidly just like the Skull had.

MONROE, JACK
KNOWN ALIASES/ALTER EGOS:
Nomad

COX, DAVID
KNOWN ALIASES/ALTER EGOS:
The Slayer

This wasn't his only scheme to hurt you.

No, he also went after two friends of mine.

The Skull brainwashed Dave, turned him into the Slayer, and sent him after me. Dave's a wounded vet and an avowed pacifist following the experiences that cost him his right arm and so much more, so what the Skull did to him was particularly cruel. I hated having to fight him, but I had no choice. I'm just glad he eventually recovered, both physically and emotionally, from that ordeal.

He also captured your friend Arnold Roth.

"Captured" is putting it too lightly. The Skull, Zemo, and their underlings *tormented* him. That he had to suffer that way just so the Skull could get to me still infuriates me. Everything I ever feared about revealing my real identity to the world—how someone might use the people I care about to hurt me—came true with Arnie. I know he forgave me for it, but I'll never truly forgive myself.

So, you went after the Skull.

By then, I was feeling the effects of the poison given to me, growing older with every passing hour, and after I dealt with Zemo and the rest of the Skull's people we finally stood face-to-face. He'd decided we needed to confront each other one last time before dying together.

ROTH, ARNOLD
KNOWN ALIASES/ALTER EGOS:
None

You learned more about the man behind the mask on that day than you'd ever known.

His mother died giving birth to him, and his father hated him for that. He might have died at his father's hand that very day, but for the doctor who delivered him. The doctor saved him, and the Skull ended up hating him for that, thanks to the life that he ended up living.

Raised in an orphanage. Living on the streets of prewar Germany. A chance meeting with Adolf Hitler, who sees the pain and evil dwelling in his heart and creates a monster for all time.

He wanted me to know his whole sordid, secret story before the end, because he believed it was our joint destiny to die together. He injected us

Captain America cradles the body of Johann Shmidt, A.K.A. the Red Skull (Image taken from surveillance camera footage later retrieved by S.H.I.E.L.D.)

both with a poison to kill us within hours, but he succumbed to its effects before I did.

Since we're sitting here talking, you obviously fared better.

It's nice to have friends. Black Crow saved me from the poison that killed the Skull. Once I was back at the Avengers Mansion, Hank Pym figured out a way to reverse the poison and aging effects on my body, using equipment found at the Skull's headquarters. That was enough restore me to my old self. Or is that, "young self?"

You lived to serve another day.

(*shrugs*) The life of a soldier. It doesn't pay well, but the perks are worth it.

Speaking of pay . . .

THE DAILY GLOBE

DAILY EDITION

75¢

CAPTAIN AMERICA RECEIVES BACK PAY FROM US ARMY

Star-Spangled Avenger Nets Nearly $1M From Uncle Sam

MANHATTAN—It may have taken decades, but the United States Army has made good on its commitment to one special soldier.

Captain America enlisted in the Army in 1941, months before the Japanese attack on Pearl Harbor. Following his disappearance during the closing months of the war in Europe, the Army recorded him as missing in action. As years passed and his official status remained unchanged, his soldier's pay continued to accrue, including standard pay raises given to the military and for promotions he received in accordance with increasing time in service. Though the exact amount and methods of calculation were not disclosed, the end result is a tidy sum for the Sentinel of Liberty.

My only regret is that it didn't start me as a captain and go from there. (*laughs*)

I'd heard rumors that they officially promoted you to captain, but I found no official record of that.

They wouldn't have done that, at least not publicly. "Private Rogers" was my cover identity. As I wasn't the same kid who'd enlisted at that point, Private Rogers I stayed.

Coming into a lot of money can be life changing, but it doesn't surprise me that you'd do something altruistic with it.

I thought the hotline was a good idea, at least in the beginning. With computers overseeing the operation, I figured it wouldn't take very many actual people to monitor things, but I hadn't counted on the sheer volume of calls.

That's where the Stars and Stripes came in.

The whole project would've been dead in the water without them. These computer hobbyists volunteered to help triage the incoming messages, figuring out which ones were the most urgent and coordinating responses based on point of origin. All of that information was routed to me.

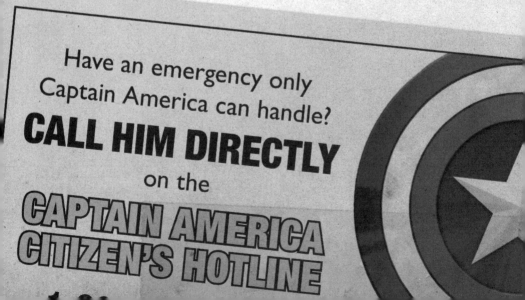

Have an emergency only Captain America can handle?
CALL HIM DIRECTLY on the
CAPTAIN AMERICA CITIZEN'S HOTLINE

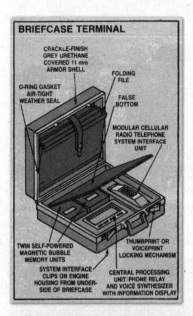

BRIEFCASE TERMINAL

CRACKLE-FINISH
GREY URETHANE
COVERED 11 mm
ARMOR SHELL

O-RING GASKET
AIR-TIGHT
WEATHER SEAL

FOLDING
FILE

FALSE
BOTTOM

MODULAR CELLULAR
RADIO TELEPHONE
SYSTEM INTERFACE
UNIT

TWIN SELF-POWERED
MAGNETIC BUBBLE
MEMORY UNITS

THUMBPRINT OR
VOICEPRINT
LOCKING MECHANISM

SYSTEM INTERFACE
CLIPS ON ENGINE
HOUSING FROM UNDER-
SIDE OF BRIEFCASE

CENTRAL PROCESSING
UNIT/PHONE RELAY
AND VOICE SYNTHESIZER
WITH INFORMATION DISPLAY

Headquarters for the Captain America Hotline, Brooklyn Heights, NY

Portable Computer Terminal Used by Captain America to Receive Hotline Updates

By taking all of that on, you put a lot of responsibility on yourself.

I've served the American people my entire life, and I know what it's like to feel as though you're not being heard. I wanted a direct connection to them, rather than having their concerns routed through government bureaucracy. Maybe it was naive of me, but it felt like the right thing to do and I don't regret it.

Sam Wilson revived the idea not all that long ago.

His version takes full advantage of modern technology, social media, and the way people communicate now. Computer technology's also come a long way since I had the original idea. Maybe it'll stick around this time.

While there's no arguing you used your Army pay for a noble purpose, it's not surprising to learn there were strings attached.

(*laughs*) Since the Army never saw fit to discharge or retire me, the Commission on Superhuman Activities decided I must still be on active duty, and thus still answerable to them as a government employee. After everything that had happened since Stark and the others pulled me from the ice, the idea of just being a rank-and-file soldier didn't work for me anymore. Besides, I'd already been through this with the government before and I wasn't about to put up with it again.

This is reminding me of when we talked about your time in action as Nomad. You were becoming disillusioned again.

That's a fair conclusion. But back then I *chose* to resign my role as Captain America. This time, I basically was fired from the job. Since the moment I put on the uniform and took up the shield, I had been given autonomy in my actions. However, those in office at the time believed that I was under contract to do their bidding. They said they would find someone else to do the job if I wasn't up to it anymore. It was a lot for me to consider, and I felt like I needed to process the situation with someone. I reached out to some friends and confidants.

Do you remember what you were grappling with in the moment?

I struggled with the idea that the America I represented felt in conflict with an America other people desired for themselves. I never felt that I represented the political platforms of America but more her intangible properties as outlined by her Founders . . . qualities of liberty, justice, human dignity, our pursuit of happiness. How would I protect those when the people who wanted to tell me what to do might hold different definitions or even different opinions of what those qualities represent or how they are manifested in the country at the time? I do what I do driven by ideals. Maybe the beliefs I held were out of step more than I realized at the time. Maybe I should have been functioning as an enforcer of policies rather than a damn idealist. I considered what would be my worst-case scenario by going along with this mandate. Could they ask me to do something that felt un-American to do? Would they? Would I be sent overseas to fight in a war? Would I be allowed to stay an Avenger? How would I feel seeing someone else in Captain America's uniform? In *my* uniform?

Those were important questions to ask yourself.

And the next morning, I answered them for the Commission.

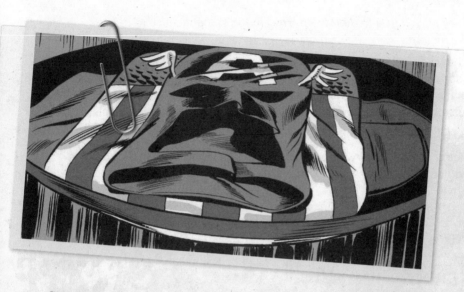

Statement made to the Commission on Superhuman Activities by Steven Rogers in regard to his continuing activities as Captain America

Gentlemen, I have given the matter we discussed yesterday a great deal of thought, and I regret to say that in all good conscience I cannot accept your terms of employment.

Captain America was created to be a mere soldier, but I have made him far more than that. To return to being a mere soldier would be a betrayal of all I've striven for, for the better part of my career. To serve the country your way, I would have to give up my personal freedom and place myself in a position where I might have to compromise my ideals to obey your orders.

I cannot represent the American government. The president does that. I must represent the American people. I must represent the American Dream, the freedom to strive to become all that you dream of being. Being Captain America has been *my* American Dream.

To become what you want me to be, I would have to compromise that dream, abandon what I have come to stand for. My commitment to the ideals of this country is greater than my commitment to an enlistment contract, which should have expired decades ago. I'm sorry, but that's the way it must be.

Gentlemen, I believe these are yours.

(Reporter's note: *At that point, Rogers placed the Captain America shield and uniform on a table and left the meeting room.)*

They stayed true to their word. They found someone else to put on the uniform.

They did. I thought I was prepared. But I'll be honest, I felt alienated, lost ... saddened. I had spent years of my life living up to the role as a symbol of all that was good in America. It was unthinkable to walk away from that. But I just couldn't bring myself to start serving America someone else's way.

So what did you do then?

Being a hero is in my blood. I knew I had to be the best hero I could be without being Captain America.

THE GOSSIP GUTTER

Hello, Gutter Guys and Dolls! Today we start with scoop on the supes. In the gutter today is the Captain. Captain who? Well, it sure isn't Captain America—at least not anymore!

When Steve Rogers told members of the Commission on Superhuman Activities where they could store his shield (if ya know whatta mean!), what he also left behind is his crime-busting persona he's had since the days of World War II. These days, he answers to simply the Captain, thank you very much.

And get a load of these new duds in a snap by a faithful Gossip Gutter reader (and you know who you are, sweetie!).

Looks like he's trying to be the super answer to "What's black and white and red all over?"

Try as I might, your faithful gutter snipe has tried her best to get the straight scoop from Steve Rogers himself but to no avail. So how about the next best thing, my pretties? Here's a quote from Tony Stark, industrialist and man about town (who is no stranger to this gutter), who allegedly created the shiny new shield that the Captain now carries.

"As I've told other reporters, we at Stark Enterprises want to provide our heroes the equipment they need to keep us safe and sound," Mr. Stark said, "and any publicity we get as a result never hurts."

When it comes to getting that name of yours in the press, Mr. Tony, know that you're always welcome here with me in the gutter!

You must feel good to know that Tony Stark can come through for you when you need him to.

For as long as it lasted, anyway.

Things were good until they weren't?

So, you've met Tony?

I'm very aware of his mercurial temperament.

You have a very diplomatic way of phrasing things.

If you like, I can just call him an a—

And we don't have to let Tony Stark derail our conversation when he's not even here, do we?

Of course not.

But it's worth noting that my first, most visible activity as the Captain was a conflict with Iron Man during a time that Tony was actively reclaiming any body armor and other technology with any connection to what he had developed. When he told me he was going to storm the Vault—

You mean the maximum-security prison? That Vault*?*

That Vault. Tony wanted to reclaim the armored suits of

the Guardsmen working at the prison. I believed that was counter to our national security. I thought I had convinced him to wave off the idea.

But you didn't.

But I didn't. And when I arrived at the Vault to make myself clear, Tony hit me with an electrical charge great enough to distract me while he made a getaway. Given that technically I wasn't authorized to act in the interest of the government, I took off too.

What else did you accomplish in your time as the Captain?

Remember that the Avengers had disbanded around this time—temporarily, thank goodness—so my thought was to assemble a less-formal grouping of heroes just in case the need for fighters arose. I recruited Sam and a few others.

We rounded up a few escapees from the Vault, essentially cleaning up Tony's mess. We took on the Serpent Society and prevented them from turning the residents of Washington, DC, into reptilian monsters through a mutagenic chemical in the water supply. But when I learned that the Red Skull or someone calling himself that had resumed his criminal activities, the Captain's time was about to reach an end.

LYONS, PRISCILLA
KNOWN ALIASES/ALTER EGOS:
Vagabond

MONROE, JACK
KNOWN ALIASES/ALTER EGOS:
Nomad, Bucky, Scourge

Which brings us back to your old nemesis, the Red Skull.

Despite my thinking he was dead, you mean? Yes. He'd somehow managed to infiltrate the Commission as well as other groups. His agents were behind the push to get me to give up the Captain America persona —as well as deciding who would assume it next.

TOP SECRET—EYES ONLY

COMMISSION ON SUPERHUMAN ACTIVITIES

FROM: ROCKWELL, D.
TO: Distribution List CSA-001, ULTRA-Level Clearance
SUBJECT: Captain America

With Steve Rogers surrendering his role and uniform, we're left with a decision. Do we simply acknowledge Captain America has "retired" and craft a plausible scenario for such a turn of events, or do we find a replacement?

There are obvious challenges to the latter idea, but I believe announcing Captain America no longer serves this country would do greater damage to public confidence not just in him but also other superhumans the American people believe stand ready to protect this country from all threats, terrestrial and otherwise. With that in mind, is there really a choice?

The biggest obstacle is, of course, finding a suitable candidate who possesses physical abilities on par with Rogers', but I think there's more to it than that. Captain America must be a symbol--the embodiment of everything for which this country stands. There are, in my estimation, very few individuals who meet those specific requirements. Indeed, there may be only one. Please review the attached dossier and forward your questions, comments, and concerns to me by end of business tomorrow.

Mr. Walker was an interesting choice. While you both have somewhat similar backgrounds such as prior military service and comparable beliefs, such as devotion to duty and love of country, you're not exactly interchangeable.

Like, John's an Army vet. His experiences were of course much different than mine, and while I'd like to think it still gives us common ground and a foundation for mutual respect, we've certainly had our differences. I know he joined the Army because he wanted to be like his brother, who he greatly admired.

But that wasn't enough, and he underwent a process to augment his body so that his strength and speed far surpassed a normal human's.

WALKER, JONATHAN ("JOHN")
KNOWN ALIASES/ALTER EGOS:
Super-Patriot, Captain America, U.S. Agent

It wasn't the same as the Super-Soldier formula I was given, but still more than enough to make him superhuman. I understand the process responsible for his augmentation carried incredible risk, but John was one of the lucky ones. After a brief stint as a professional wrestler, he adopted the persona of "Super-Patriot."

He branded himself a super hero, but—

But he certainly didn't act like one. He was a vigilante, and he enabled others to follow him. They pretended to support me, but it was a sham. They were extremists. I'd had an earlier run-in with him, so I knew what he was capable of. The Skull's manipulations of Commission members is the *only* way he ever would have been considered as Captain America.

Though Mr. Walker assumed the role with noble intentions, the decision cost him dearly.

(*sighs*) Yes. The very people he enabled to work with him as Super-Patriot felt he'd betrayed them by taking on my—Captain America's—mission. They killed his parents, which sent him on a revenge quest against those responsible.

This forced the Commission to suspend him.

Sure, but that only lasted until another threat revealed itself.

MORGENTHAU, KARL
KNOWN ALIASES/ALTER E
Flag-Smasher

HOSKINS, LEMAR
KNOWN ALIASES/ALTER EGOS:
Battlestar, Bucky

DUNPHY, DENNIS W.
KNOWN ALIASES/ALTER EGOS:
Demolition Man, D-Man,
the Serf, Scourge

Mr. Morgenthau was holding hostages at a research station in the Arctic.

The very sort of thing you'd send someone like Captain America or another Avenger to investigate, right? So the Commission sent Walker along with Lemar Hoskins.

Battlestar.

Right. He even worked with Walker under the "Bucky" identity at one point. Hoskins hung back just in case Walker ran into trouble, which ended up being a smart move. With the weapons tech he'd fashioned to round out his Flag-Smasher persona, Morgenthau bested and captured

Ice Station Able, located near the North Pole

Walker. He was furious that they'd sent Walker instead of me, and he ordered Hoskins to report back to the Commission and bring me into the situation, or else he'd kill Walker and his other hostages. It was all a ruse on Morgenthau's part, designed to get close enough to convince me he'd turned against ULTIMATUM.

The Underground Liberated Totally Integrated Mobile Army to Unite Mankind. The anarchist group.

Right. He left them after learning the whole thing was being financed by the Red Skull.

The same Red Skull you thought had died right in front of you.

Literally in my arms.

And then he got better.

That's one way to put it. He'd been manipulating everything behind the scenes for months. Douglas Rockwell was a double agent who'd infiltrated the Commission to help the Skull put his plans into motion, and he paid for his duplicity with his life.

The so-called Red Dust used by the Skull.

Yes. With help from Hoskins along with Dennis Dunphy— sorry, Demolition Man—we were able to rescue Walker, and Morgenthau led us to the doomsday weapon ULTIMATUM was constructing to deliver an electromagnetic pulse powerful enough to disable the world, so we could destroy it. (*pauses*) I thought we'd lost Dennis on that mission, but I'm glad he eventually proved us all wrong.

But the Skull wasn't finished.

Not by a long shot. I followed Walker to where the Skull had lured him, an office building he was using in Washington, where I learned to my horror that not only had the Skull survived our last encounter, but he—or someone—somehow got their hands on my DNA and cloned me, which enabled him to inhabit that cloned body.

And yet, you managed to defeat him despite being, for all intents and purposes, equals.

We never even fought. He fell victim to the same Red Dust that killed Rockwell and others. The overdose turned his face into a permanent caricature of the Red Skull. He got away from me that day, but I think you know it wasn't the last time we'd meet. After that came the cleanup. The Commission forced Walker to step down as Captain America and asked me to serve once again in that capacity. While I was reluctant at first, it was Walker himself who convinced me to do it.

I think I speak for many people when I say you made the right decision.

I'd like to think so.

Even with Mr. Walker's physical modifications and his sense of duty—despite whatever differences you two had, so far as personal beliefs or convictions—you are admittedly a hard act to follow, and an even harder person to replace. There have been numerous efforts to duplicate the gifts you were given by Professor Erskine's Super-Soldier formula, but nearly all of them have fallen short.

And even the serum I was given wasn't perfect. Under the right conditions, it was susceptible to outside contamination, and me along with it.

THE DAILY GLOBE

75¢

DAILY EDITION

Captain America Busts Up Drug Lab

STAR-SPANGLED AVENGER ESCALATES HIS WAR ON DRUGS

NEW YORK—Concerned about the escalating trafficking of "Ice," the powerful and addictive methamphetamine for sale on streets throughout the city, Captain America has chosen to attack the problem head-on. After first taking on street-level dealers, he redirected what many describe as a personal crusade against these dangerous and illegal narcotics straight at the source, figuratively speaking. In this case, it meant tracking Ice from many of those dealers to their place of manufacture and distribution.

According to witnesses who spotted the Sentinel of Liberty entering a nondescript warehouse in the city's industrial shipping corridor, the building was consumed by a powerful explosion shortly after his arrival. Police are investigating but have not yet determined whether the blast was caused by Captain America or perhaps an unfortunate mishap inside the drug lab itself. At last report, he was unharmed in the explosion and has since returned to Avengers Mansion in Manhattan.

This is a developing story.

It started with Fabian Stankiewicz.

Yes. My research has indicated he'd long been troubled by substance abuse.

He'd been in trouble with the law and even the Avengers, but he made efforts to turn his life around, to the point where he's even helped me on a few missions.

You've tried to help him on several occasions too.

Drug addiction wreaks terrible havoc on the human body and mind. I was able to see past that to the man I knew Fabian wanted to be, so I did what I could to aid him. I helped him land a job as a member of the Avengers' support crew. His technical genius and other gifts were invaluable to the team.

Despite all of this success, he still lapsed.

STANKIEWICZ, FABIAN

KNOWN ALIASES/ALTER EGOS:
Mechonaut

(*sighs*) Yes. Addiction's a disease, and it's not one you cure so much as work continuously to keep at bay. I blame myself for not seeing the signs early on, but I missed them. Then all of a sudden, it seemed, he was addicted to Ice.

Is this why you chose to take on the drug problem?

(*laughs, but it's forced*) You know that "the drug problem" is much bigger than any one man can fight, but I did go after what I considered the immediate threat to people I cared about, so I started small. I confronted street dealers, forced them out of business, and with the appropriate "persuasion" convinced them to tell me where their product was being made. That led me to the lab, but I was spotted by a kid who called himself "Napalm," because he apparently had a gift for explosives.

Police reports indicated the entire building was wired with explosives that all but consumed its interior and contents, including this "Napalm" person.

So I heard. I thought I'd managed to escape the explosion with little more than some minor burns around the edges, but there was definitely more to it than that. I still managed to inhale enough of the fumes from the Ice saturating that lab that it had a pronounced effect on me. I started getting irritable and paranoid with friends and colleagues. I flew into uncontrollable rages and took my anger out on everyone from street punks to innocent bystanders.

Daredevil tried to confront you about your increasingly erratic condition.

And I beat him nearly to a pulp. Black Widow was the one who finally knocked me on my can and got me back to the Avengers Mansion, where Hank Pym figured out what was wrong with me.

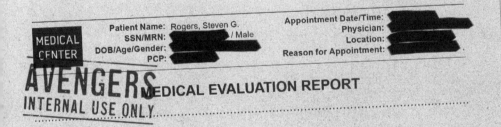

	Patient Name:	Rogers, Steven G.	Appointment Date/Time:
MEDICAL CENTER	SSN/MRN:	▮▮▮▮ / Male	Physician:
	DOB/Age/Gender:	▮▮▮▮	Location:
	PCP:		Reason for Appointment:

AVENGERS MEDICAL EVALUATION REPORT

INTERNAL USE ONLY

Diagnosis of Steve Rogers, as reported by Dr. Henry Pym
(transcript of oral report)

With superhuman powers come superhuman problems, especially when we're talking about anything related to caring for the body and mind of someone possessed with such gifts and their associated foibles.

After a complete battery of tests, I've verified the presence of methamphetamine in Steve's blood. Under ordinary circumstances, such toxins should metabolize out of the bloodstream after some time, which can of course vary between individuals. Given what I knew about Steve's heightened metabolism and superior physical conditioning, I would've expected this already to have happened. Instead, it seems the chemicals used to manufacture this particular methamphetamine variant, "Ice" as it's known on the streets, have instead bonded with molecules of the Super-Soldier Serum present in Steve's blood. I believe it is this unique combination of factors that has brought about the acute effect on his emotional balance.

Given the severity of his condition and the fact I can detect no signs of the Ice weakening or otherwise being processed out of his system, I believe the only course of action is to submit Steve to a complete blood transfusion.

(transcript ends)

The obvious side effect of this treatment, aside from curing you of the issues brought about by the Ice, is that the transfusion—

Removed all traces of the Super-Soldier Serum from my blood. At first, I was worried I couldn't *be* Captain America without the serum and its effects on my body, but I quickly put that doubt to rest . . . or so I thought. Still, I decided I didn't need what I thought was a drug in my body. I could do it all on my own, training and working to maintain my physique and fitness the old-fashioned way.

But that ended up being short-lived.

(*nods*) A later physical conducted by Dr. Kincaid, the physician who oversaw the health needs for all the Avengers, showed that enough of the serum molecules remained in my system that it was able to replicate itself back to its previous levels. As I told the doc at the time, "Once a Super-Soldier, always a Super-Soldier." Still, it was nice to see that I could do the job without the serum, at least in a crunch.

Do you suppose that outlook prepared you—at least a bit—when it was determined the serum in your blood was beginning to deteriorate?

KINCAID, KEITH
KNOWN ALIASES/ALTER EGOS: N/A

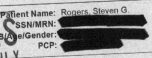

Patient Name: Rogers, Steven G.
SSN/MRN:
DOB/Age/Gender:
PCP:

Appointment Date/Time:
Physician:
Location:
Reason for Appointment:

MEDICAL EVALUATION REPORT

From: Kincaid, K.
To: Avengers, Distribution List 63-M-384
Subj: Deteriorating Condition of Rogers, Steven G.

My latest examination of Mr. Rogers confirms our earlier hypothesis that the serum carried in his bloodstream is weakening. Further, the process appears to be accelerating at an alarming rate. Left unchecked, it may well prove fatal.

Our latest series of blood tests builds on the conclusions reached by Dr. Henry Pym, in that the formula given to Mr. Rogers in 1941 acted like a virus, affecting his genetic makeup at the molecular level. Dr. Pym and I concur that this is almost certainly why he was able to regain his superhuman abilities following the complete blood transfusion he received. However, our latest findings indicate the serum's enhancing effects are susceptible to degradation over time in the face of prolonged physical activity. In Mr. Rogers' case, such activity far exceeds that of a normal person, with the resulting adrenaline increases acting to continuously reduce the effects of his genetic augmentation. I predict he has perhaps twelve months at his present rate of physical activity before he risks total and permanent muscular paralysis.

I believe that this deterioration can be slowed and perhaps even arrested if Mr. Rogers agrees to restrict his activities to "normal" human levels. Minding such limits could even allow him to maintain his mobility and fitness for the remainder of his life. But I suspect that's not an option Captain America would choose.

That was an eye-opener, to be sure. In hindsight, I was pretty stupid about the whole thing.

You mean your resistance to Dr. Kincaid's advice?

For starters. Instead of listening to him, I continued doing what I'd been doing. Facing off against adversaries and other troublemakers—the usual. All that did was further aggravate my condition. My strength was failing me more frequently. It reached the point that I asked Fabian Stankiewicz to build a special armored tactical vest with equipment and weapons to help me compensate for my . . . um . . . shortcomings.

A temporary measure, of course.

If you mean my entire body seizing up while fighting the Serpent Society before I had a heart attack and almost died in the desert, you'd be correct. Luckily, Hank Pym came to my rescue again, but while he saved my life, there was nothing he could do for my body. I was in a coma. I couldn't wake up, I certainly didn't know I had been taken to a state-of-the-art medical facility deep within Stark Enterprises headquarters. All I kept seeing were these flashbacks. Missions with Bucky, facing off against enemies like the

Red Skull. I have to tell you . . . there was a point when I was ready to just let go.

You mean die.

That's exactly what I mean, but . . . I couldn't. I just couldn't give up like that. There was still too much to do. Too much to fight for. It was Tony Stark who rescued me. He used one of his fancy machines to reach me while I was unconscious and pull me out of my coma. I woke up to find I was paralyzed from the neck down. The prognosis was I'd never walk or really do anything ever again.

Except, fate keeps underestimating Henry Pym and Tony Stark.

(*smiles*) Right.

Captain America Exoskeleton, designed by Tony Stark

The exoskeleton Mr. Stark and Dr. Pym devised allowed you to move with your former strength and speed.

Sensors implanted throughout my body helped control my movements, and Stark even made sure I couldn't go overboard and inflict more harm than I wanted. It was all a stopgap measure, of course. I'd pushed myself beyond the ability of Hank or anyone else to help me. Sooner or later, my heart would give out and that would be it. I was on borrowed time, so I decided to make the most of what little time I might have left. (*pauses*) It was during all of this that I learned my old friend Arnie Roth had contracted bone cancer. It left him with less than a year to live, and he wanted to spend that time helping me.

That's a devoted friend.

Someone I never imagined I'd meet again until he chanced across me one night in Brooklyn Heights. Arnie was the best pal a kid from the Lower East Side could have had. He kept bullies away from me. He had me over for dinner when my mother was struggling to make ends meet. He ended up going to war as a sailor. I had a chance to lend Arnie a hand when he had gotten in deep with a loan shark. He spent his final months running my hotline, doing whatever he could to lend a hand. I'm just glad I had the chance to thank him for being such a good friend to me. We don't always get chances like that.

INTERVIEWER'S NOTE: I opted to pause our conversation here, as I could tell the memories we'd evoked were affecting him. When we resumed, he seemed eager to move past these particular recollections.

THE DAILY GLOBE

$1

CAPTAIN AMERICA
M.I.A., BELIEVED DEAD

I finally got to the point where I knew I had one day left. A single day, to wrap up all my affairs. Say my goodbyes, prepare for . . . what, exactly? How do you prepare for the end of your existence?

It's a question humankind has pondered since the dawn of time.

Well, it wasn't as though I had anything significant to add to the discussion. I just know at that point I was tired. Physically, mentally, even spiritually. I'd spent my entire adult life serving this country and even the entire world, and I felt as though there was still so much to do . . . that I hadn't done enough.

PRIORITY

TRANSCRIPT—NEWS REPORT

BLACK_WIDOW: It is my sad duty as an Avenger to report that Captain America has succumbed to a debilitating illness.

NEWS_ANCHOR: Black Widow spoke these words one month ago. With a trembling voice, she reported that Captain America was missing, presumed dead. Now, as of today, the search for his body has been paused, so that our nation may pay tribute to his spirit. Here in Arlington National Cemetery, tens of thousands have come to pay their respects to the star-spangled legend who, at the president's insistence, has been honored with a state funeral, largely ceremonial since the revered champion has yet to be found. Five-star general Ulysses R. Chapman hushed the crowd with his solemn statement.

GENERAL_CHAPMAN: I know no words that can express the grief and loss we as a people feel at this moment. For generations, Captain America has been our protector, our defender, our friend. I can honestly say that as I look to a future without him, I am a little bit afraid for each and every one of us. He was the best and the brightest, the symbol of a nation, the greatest hero this country has ever known.

(transcript ends)

And yet as the saying goes, "Old soldiers never die."

They just get transported to an advanced lab and resurrected.

Sharon Carter.

Yes. She took me out of Avengers Mansion just before I actually died, and kept me in hibernation long enough to oversee my treatment, which included a blood transfusion from none other than the Red Skull. His cloning me meant he carried the Super-Soldier Serum in his blood, so I guess you could say he was returning the favor, after a fashion.

Naturally, there was a catch.

There's always a catch with the Skull.

And it seems that, like him, there are other enemies from your past who simply refuse to leave this life.

HATE-MONGER
KNOWN ALIASES/ALTER EGOS:
Adolf Hitler

It's astonishing to think that—

(*holds up hand*) Don't even say his name.

—that particular Hate-Monger could survive all this time, transferring his consciousness into body after body with technology developed during World War II.

There's still a lot that went on during the war that people don't know about. Hopefully most of it will stay buried, perhaps forever lost to time. But given humanity's habit of messing with things it doesn't understand or should just leave well enough alone? I'm not holding my breath.

The Skull agreed to give you some of his blood—originally cloned from you—so that you could be restored to your former self and help him fight the Kubekult, who at the time possessed a Cosmic Cube containing Hi—I mean, "Hate-Monger's"—consciousness.

And of course the Skull wanted the Cube for himself.

But you were able to destroy it, along with the Skull. Apparently, at any rate.

Remember what we said before about the Skull?

It seems true of Hate-Monger, as well. He disappeared when you destroyed the Cube.

Yeah, but we know how these things go by now, don't we?

V.
RECONSTRUCTION

Given everything he has faced, Steve Rogers has uncounted reasons to ask himself what many who have served our nation have asked. Was this path the right choice for my life? Have my sacrifices been worth it?

I've talked with Captain Rogers about times he had questioned his convictions, even his perceived worthiness to be the living representation of the ideals upon which our nation was founded.

But what of the times when the country to which he's pledged himself has doubted him? More than once, his loyalty has been called into question. He's even been punished by those who believed he'd betrayed the oath he swore and the ideals he'd promised to support and defend. I was ready to ask how such accusations weigh on him, a man to whom such vows are more than mere words but instead an intrinsic part of who he is.

INTERVIEWER: *Being accused of treason isn't to be taken lightly by anyone, under any circumstances. But to be brought in handcuffs before the president of the United States so he could level such a charge at you?*

STEVE ROGERS: I've had better days, if that's what you're asking.

Of course. What I meant was—

I've been wounded. I've even been killed. I've lost comrades in arms. Almost everyone I ever knew or loved from my life before the ice was taken from me. And despite all of that I still stood up, saluted, and did whatever job was asked of me. But after all of that, to be there in the Oval Office, before the man representing literally everything to which I'd given my entire adult life, as he called me a traitor? That might well have been the single worst day of my entire life, and that's saying something. It was like a knife through my heart.

I honestly can't even imagine what you must have wanted to say.

Even then, the hardest part was seeing the disappointment in General Chapman's eyes. It's one thing to be accused by a civilian—even your commander-in-chief—but for someone who's worn the uniform and sworn their life to serving their country? That sort of wound cuts a lot deeper.

THE WHITE HOUSE
WASHINGTON, D.C.

EXECUTIVE ORDER

By virtue of the authority vested in me as President of the United States, by the Constitution and the statutes of the United States, it is hereby ordered as follows:

1. I hereby declare that Steven Grant Rogers is no longer a citizen of the United States, and no longer enjoys the rights and privileges thereunto pertaining.

2. Upon arrangement and agreement with the government of the United Kingdom, Steven Grant Rogers is to be transported from the United States to the United Kingdom via the most express means.

3. As of this date, Steven Grant Rogers is by law forbidden from entering the United States or any of its recognized territories and protectorates, any US embassy, or any military facility controlled or otherwise employed by the United States armed services.

4. These actions will remain in effect until expressly rescinded by a future executive order, either by my hand or that of a successor.

All things considered, you took the president's decision with surprising grace, if the reports I've read are to be believed.

To be fair, the evidence against me was pretty overwhelming.

Security camera recordings of your intrusion upon a high-security military site already under siege by supremacist soldiers.

Yes.

Apparently as an ally with the Red Skull. THE Red Skull.

I can't deny that.

Along with evidence of a second offense that I'm told remains under Top Secret classification.

I have a good idea to what you're referring.

I'd call that a tough hill to climb, Steve.

I can't honestly take issue with his reaction. He had the interests of an entire country to consider, and in that moment I looked like a threat to national security. I can't say I'd have done anything differently had our positions been reversed.

I guess I shouldn't be surprised you'd look at things that way.

Don't get me wrong. I was still angry, just not at him. I wanted payback from those responsible.

Machinesmith, and the Red Skull.

Given my remarkable "resurrection" with the Skull's assistance, it made sense to think I might have traded national secrets for my life. What I didn't know was that while I was in a coma and awaiting the Skull's blood transfusion, Machinesmith scanned my mind and essentially made a digital recording of it. Everything, memories, knowledge—and, yes— secrets—including one I shared with no one else except the president: information about the Argus cannon.

Argus cannon? The puzzle piece I could not find.

I'm assuming so.

And Machinesmith used that knowledge to construct his own version of this new, secret weapon.

SAXON, SAMUEL
KNOWN ALIASES/ALTER EGOS:
Machinesmith

He used *me*. I wanted to clear my name, but the more immediate threat was Machinesmith threatening to use what he'd taken from me against the United States in a bid to drag them into a war with Moldavia. I couldn't stand by and let that happen, no matter the personal cost.

The Argus cannon, as created by Machinesmith

You at least had one ally: Sharon Carter.

Thank the heavens for Sharon. Through good times and bad, she's always been there for me. (*pauses, with a wistful smile*) She's just like her aunt, that way. With her help, we headed to Moldavia. Machinesmith was reported as being there, along with his version of the Argus cannon. Given his intellect, building something like that even from the information gleaned from my memories was child's play for him. Moldavia also made sense for his base of operations if he was looking to incite a war between that country and the U.S.

He also knew you'd come after him.

Like I said, he's no dummy. He was on to us pretty quickly, sending a team of advanced, cybernetically enhanced soldiers after us. They should've planned better, as that didn't work out so well for them.

Speaking of planning, my sources note you and Sharon stole a fighter jet from an American military base, and used it and yourselves as bait to attract fire from the Argus cannon.

Unconventional, I admit, but it worked. We bailed out just before the cannon shot us down, but from that we were able to pinpoint the weapon's location.

I'm sure Agent Carter loved that bit of improvisation.

(*laughs*) No, she really didn't. Still, we made it to Machinesmith's base and destroyed the cannon. Unfortunately, I underestimated him. He's perfected the process of transferring his consciousness into a cybernetic body, the same procedure that originally saved his life. What I didn't know was that he also could transfer into almost any kind of electrical system.

Like a computer or computer network.

Specifically, the computer systems that control the S.H.I.E.L.D. Helicarrier.

S.H.I.E.L.D. Helicarrier

With the access codes he pulled from my mind, he was able to hack the carrier's main computer and set it on a collision course with Mt. Hood in Oregon. The worst part was, he was ready to kill thousands of people to distract us from his real mission: assassinating the president and getting his hands on the nuclear launch codes he holds. Machinesmith transferred himself into another of his cyborgs that he'd sent to Camp David, posing as one of the Moldavian delegates the president was meeting with in the hopes of averting war.

Such power at his disposal, and this is what he chose to do with it.

He used the secrets I carried in my head to attack the country I'd sworn my life to defend. I knew I had to stop him, or die trying. And I guess that meant calling in favors from unlikely parties.

Of all the people to ask for help in getting back to America, you went to Doctor Doom.

Desperate times, desperate measures, and so on. I simply told him that any war involving Moldavia would almost certainly affect the entire region, including Latveria, so it behooved him to help me prevent that.

Agent 13's report describes Doom as "ambivalent" despite his decision to help you.

He knew the real score, but I suppose he was putting on a good front. (*shrugs*) I don't know and I didn't care. It got me back to the States in time to stop Machinesmith, who by this time had used his cyborgs to defeat the president's Secret Service detail and steal, with his mind-reading powers, the secure codes for the nuclear football, which he now also possessed.

VON DOOM, VICTOR WERNER

KNOWN ALIASES/ALTER EGOS:
Doctor Doom

He had at his fingertips the ability to launch our entire nuclear arsenal. You arrived in time to disable his remaining cyborgs, but it seems Machinesmith had one more play.

He transferred his consciousness into the nuclear football. (*pauses*) That sounds more insane every time I think about it.

Not quite as insane as you destroying the football, leaving the aforementioned arsenal inaccessible for a time.

(*sighs*) Imagine if we could do that with the world's other nuclear powers.

A welcome idea, to be sure. I suppose we should state the obvious: Machinesmith was gone, but you knew he'd return at some point.

It's definitely a sort of recurring theme with my various adversaries.

More importantly, the president knew from his own experiences with Machinesmith that you hadn't betrayed the United States. He reinstated you, formally, as Captain America.

Even handed my shield back to me personally. (*smiles*) But, not before he tried it on for size. He thanked me, but that wasn't nearly as important as having his trust in me restored. The idea that anyone might consider—even for a moment—that I could betray the country I've served my entire life is just too horrible to consider.

Following the return of your American citizenship, I'm thinking that you somehow turned up in Japan. Is that true?

Oh. Well, first, yes, but I also understand your confusion. You've not accounted for our conflict with the Onslaught entity.

The sentient psionic creature you fought in Central Park.

That's the one. His goal was to transform the human race into a collective consciousness. If that's not a violation of life, liberty, and the pursuit of happiness, I don't know what is. And it took all of us—Avengers, X-Men, anyone we could find—to take this thing down. Doctor Doom coached Vision and Rogue into merging forms while Namor, Giant-Man, and Wolverine hammered at the force barrier between us and it. Jean Gray used her psychic abilities to bring down the mental barriers Bruce Banner uses to keep the Hulk in check, and that gave us the upper hand. Hulk cracked Onslaught's psychic armor and released a blast of energy unlike any I had witnessed. Even as the entity released from that armor declared itself as a form beyond the physical, we still came at it. I yelled out "Avengers assemble!" and prepared myself to enter this void, fight the battle, and not return.

And yet, here we are.

Here we are.

Can you explain what happened?

There are people way smarter than this soldier for you to ask about that. All I need to know is that somehow Franklin Richards was—

Just to clarify, you're referring to the son of Sue and Reed Richards of the Fantastic Four.

I am. Franklin was able to save us all by moving us from one reality to another of his own making. And then, he moved us all back here. So, there you go, an idea for your next book, free of charge.

Well, thank you. Our world certainly missed you for those months. Do you have any recollection of what happened to you in this universe of a child's making?

I've not talked about this before.

And you don't have to now, Steve.

True.

INTERVIEWER'S NOTE: *Steve paused here and I was struck by his expression. It was one of reverie, perhaps of loss but not of grief. He was searching his mind not for words but seemingly more for memories—ones that weren't there anymore. I wanted to help how I could, so I directed him from content to process.*

How are you feeling, Steve?

(*smiling wryly*) I see what you did there.

Blame my mom.

Heh. (*pauses*) The simple truth is that I just don't remember vividly what I experienced in that . . . existence of mine. It has left my mind, perhaps by design. Here's what remains. I sense that I lived a life of battle, of dedication, of service to a cause. It was a different life but not a kind of life unknown to me. Does that help at all?

It does. Thank you. If I may, I appreciate that you trust me with this story, Steve.

I do. (*pauses*) When I returned, I did my best to commit the details to a private journal. It's not something I revisit, so I don't know what I wrote down in that moment when the memories were fresh. I will loan it to you. You gave me the box, I'll give you the journal. You can read what's there and decide for yourself what's worth including. Deal?

Deal.

INTERVIEWER'S NOTE: I did read that journal. It consisted of only a few handwritten pages and Steve's record was more like note-taking, without a chronological order. To present his memories as written would prove too confusing and would, I believe, violate a level of privacy he is owed from this experience.

In this other world, Steve lived in Philadelphia and worked in a factory. He had married Peggy Carter, and they were parents to a son, Rick, who was of elementary-school age. And that version of Steve had dreams about his life as Captain America. He met a man named Abe Wilson, who recognized him as Captain America and returned to him Cap's shield, which somehow Abe had kept hidden. And then Steve discovered through the Nick Fury of this imagined reality that his family was nothing more than Life-Model Decoys programmed to distract him from his calling as a hero.

At that point, he could have returned to a peaceful, blissful existence with them, never knowing what he once meant to his nation and the world. But from what he was able to recall at the time of his writing, Steve gave up his family to resume his duty.

There were other details of missions and victories and the people who came into his life as Captain America—all of them part of this alternate reality. The main focus of his journal was recollections of time spent with a family created by Franklin Richards and in turn created by that imagined reality's Nick Fury in order to keep that world free from Captain America.

Steve Rogers proved that even in that artificial construct of reality, Captain America yearns to fight for ideals on behalf of those who can't. That's all any of us needs to know of this very personal experience.

What else are you wanting to discuss?

I was referring to notes from an earlier discussion we had regarding the Kree–Skrull War, and you had made reference to the Kree Supreme Intelligence saving Rick Jones and others. Your words were, "That truth makes the subsequent events of this conflict even more regrettable." I wondered whether you were referring to another somewhat extended absence from Earth with the Avengers.

I was, yes. Rick Jones had been contacted in a dream by the Kree Supreme Intelligence. This led us to information that during a conflict between the Kree and the Shi'ar, Earth had been established as some hyperspace midpoint in their military travels. This fight was not Earth's, but that juncture was affecting the stability of our sun. This was a matter for the Avengers, so I called a meeting, only to learn that a group of Avengers members had threatened to destroy a Shi'ar ship and took some of its crew as prisoners. My goal was to resolve the threat to Earth without getting caught in the muck of an intergalactic war.

What was your next move?

My best play was to convince the two sides to stop fighting before events truly got out of hand. When Vision explained that space vessels of each army were using our sun as an energy source to activate an inert wormhole for travel, which could lead to our sun going nova, I became confident this diplomatic mission was the only solution. I proposed dividing our ranks into three teams: one to stay on Earth, one to meet the Kree, and one to meet the Shi'ar.

What was your destination?

The Kree Empire, along with U.S. Agent, Iron Man, Crystal, Hercules, the Black Knight, and Sersi. That changed, however, when Hank Pym gave Clint Barton enough of his growth serum to allow Clint to resume duty as Goliath, just as he did the last time we went into Kree space. We used the wormhole to arrive in Kree space and made entry into a space station we encountered almost immediately. We were attacked by Shi'ar commandos while Iron Man accessed the station's computer network. When he discovered Kree reinforcements had nearly arrived, he did what he thought was prudent and left on his own to engage them.

How did that turn out?

He conceded our surrender to the Kree Empire.

Well, that's one way to get their attention.

It did secure our passage to the Kree homeworld of Hala, I had to acknowledge that. But my attempts to engage Kree leadership during our transport were fruitless, so my strategy once we landed had turned to escaping their custody. Sersi used her powers to disguise us all as Kree accusers, which acted as a free pass for us to move about. Iron Man, of course, made a play to strike out on his own, but Goliath went along just in case. We attempted to get to the Capitol Citadel of the Kree Empire but were attacked and again captured. When we were brought to face the Supreme Intelligence, he sentenced us to execution. Somehow Goliath had managed an attempt to break us all free and nearly succeeded. I was left behind.

That isn't something Avengers do.

I can't blame them. I had been led away by Kree accusers to face the Supreme Intelligence on my own just before the plan was hatched. Turns out that the Supreme Intelligence had intended to absorb my consciousness into his immortal group intellect until he got a taste of who I really am. He said my desires for freedom and independence made me unsuitable for his needs.

He wanted a fighter who craved power over others. What he got was a hero who fought against such tyrants in the name of liberty and personal rights. That's a good thing.

And here's a bad thing. I remained completely unaware of the Supreme Intelligence's plan to detonate a Shi'ar nega-bomb that completely and utterly destroyed the Kree Empire. Uncounted billions . . . *billions* were killed in an instant. And all because the Supreme Intelligence believed this was the only way of evolving the Kree toward perfection as a race. The very idea of my facing yet another horrific genocidal plot in the name of creating a superior race turned my stomach. When the Avengers returned, it was up to me to relay the Supreme Intelligence's plot to those who risked their lives to stop it from happening. I even had to explain the plot to Kree survivors Captain Att-Lass and Doctor Minn-Erva, who barely had time to conceive of this destruction let alone grieve the fallen. Att-Lass chose to end his own life, as he believed his ignorance of the plan made him culpable in it. Minn-Erva's attempt to stop him ended her life as well.

How does one even respond to that?

Given that Att-Lass' final words were a plea to the Avengers to destroy the Supreme Intelligence for his crime, that left us two responses. We could carry out Att-Lass' wish or go home. The Black Knight was all for carrying out the death decree.

And you?

I absolutely disagreed. I stood before my fellow Avengers sickened by the loss of so many lives. But I couldn't kill in cold blood. The Supreme Intelligence is a sentient being. To kill him was unthinkable . . . *is* unthinkable to me. My preference was to let the Kree survivors decide their leader's fate. With the war over, the threat to Earth had dissipated. My gut wanted it to pay as much as anyone standing there. But the Avengers don't serve as judge, jury, and executioner.

So, you returned to Earth.

Not right away, no.

POST-ACTION REPORT - __
AVENGERS INTERNAL USE ONLY

Events surrounding the Kree-Shi'ar final conflict and
the death of the Kree Supreme Intelligence on Hala as
reported by Tony Stark while active under codename
Iron Man
(transcript of oral report)

You can file my report alongside the one I'm sure
Captain Rogers will be making in regard to the
Avengers' actions on Hala, the Kree homeworld.
Following our return from our unsuccessful mission to
prevent the detonation of a Shi'ar nega-bomb, Rogers
informed us that the bomb was key to a plan by the Kree
Supreme Intelligence to mutate the Kree and help them
clear an evolutionary dead end to become the greatest
race in the universe. This was confirmed by Minn-Erva, a
Kree scientist who revealed she was aware of the plan.
She said that the sacrifice of billions upon billions
of Kree would be rewarded by the offspring of nega-bomb
survivors being a race of beings we would fear.
        For being complicit in this plan, Captain Att-Lass
decided to take his own life, as he served the Supreme
Intelligence without question. Before he died, he
begged us to make the Supreme Intelligence pay for its
crime against the Kree.
        After some discussion among us with Captain Rogers
dissenting, I made the decision as the only founding
member of the Avengers present to destroy the Supreme
Intelligence. I believed it to be a machine rather than
a being, a soulless piece of hardware, that we would
prevent from taking a similar action ever again.
        Joining me in this mission were Eric Masterson
under the codename Thor, Dane Whitman under the
codename Black Knight, Simon Williams under the
codename Wonder Man, Hercules, Vision, and Sersi
the Eternal.
        As we approached the being, it told us that it
had monitored our debate. It said we were acting with
moral certitude without really knowing whether it was
alive or merely a construct. It then conjured from our
minds the images of beings from our past to serve as
its defenders against us. Those proved to be easily
dispatched, which led me to believe that maybe the
Supreme Intelligence had been damaged in the nega-bomb
explosion.

We reached the heart of the being's support system, which Vision said was an amalgamation of cybernetic material and organic tissue. That information prompted Thor to drop out of our final assault. The Black Knight leapt onto the spherical case containing the amalgamation and drove his photon sword into it. The Supreme Intelligence ceased to exist with a cry of agony I may never forget.

I reported our success to Captain Rogers and prepared for our return to Earth. I stand by these actions.

(transcript ends)

The cybernetic material and organic tissue at the heart of the Supreme Intelligence

Just as Iron Man and the others returned, a Shi'ar ship arrived and Lilandra came forth to take possession of Hela and the territory of the Kree Empire in the name of the Shi'ar Imperium. She assured us that the wormhole stargate near our sun would never be used again, which is all I wanted to hear.

You had no words for her?

Well, I did. I wished her luck as she had that day become one of the most powerful beings in the universe. I told her she had the power to cherish life rather than destroy it. And I agreed with her that from that day forward, things wouldn't be the same.

Certainly not the same between you and Tony Stark.

Something that could have gone without saying.

Of course. I apologize. But it was this rift that prompted you to step down as the head of the Avengers, correct?

I called for disciplinary action against the members who took part in the action. The majority of the Avengers voted against that. They saw the action as appropriate conduct during wartime. I convened a seminar on super-human ethics for the membership, but only three of them showed up, none of them the ones I felt should be there in the first place. That really set me to thinking.

Care to share about what?

About whether I was the right person to be running the Avengers or even representing American values as a hero. I felt my professional style had fallen out of fashion with Americans. Maybe people like the Punisher or Cable or Wolverine were the answer to the types of threats facing our nation. But if the values for which I'd striven during my entire career as Captain America were untenable, who would I be without them?

Those are big questions to answer by yourself, Steve.

As it turned out, I didn't have to. Clint found me and took me out. Not on patrol, mind you, but out as a friend, which I truly felt I needed. I didn't have civilian friends in my life. Every time I had tried to put together a regular life for myself, one without the shield, before long it would fall apart. I came to believe that being a good Captain America meant being a lousy Steve Rogers.

Let me understand. Being a good Captain America requires the sacrifice of a good Steve Rogers?

I'm saying that being a good Captain America is easier for me than being a good Steve Rogers. Being a good Steve Rogers takes time and effort for me, and it's better for all of us that I not skimp on what it takes to be a good Captain America.

Is it really better for you, Steve?

KEY PLAYERS, AVENGERS—KREE-SHI'AR CONFLICT

CAPTAIN AMERICA

U.S. AGENT

IRON MAN

MOCKINGBIRD

CRYSTAL

HERCULES

SCARLET WITCH

THE BLACK KNIGHT

THOR

SERSI

CAPTAIN MARVEL

THE VISION

SPIDER-WOMAN

WONDER MAN

SHE-HULK

HAWKEYE

No. Easier, not better. The Avengers and my headquarters crew were the only people in my life then, and without my being able to inspire them, I felt I should distance myself from them rather than fail them.

But Clint was there.

And you might never guess who else came up pretty big for me that night.

Bigger than Goliath at your table?

That's pretty good but no. It was Tony, and he opened up to me. He started by apologizing for not trying to explain his actions at the Vault. He spoke of his actions in Kree space and how he was more dependent on his armor to stay alive than I ever imagined. He mentioned how I'd been abandoned on Hala, but I understood that. He needed to try and stop the nega-bomb and I would have done the same.

And when it came to the Supreme Intelligence?

He didn't budge on that and neither did I. Where Tony did drop his armor, so to speak, was when he imagined I might not have survived the nega-bomb blast on Hala. In that moment, Tony said, he realized there was no one among those who do what we do that he would miss more than me. He said that he and a lot of the other Avengers really do see me as inspiring and have respect for me. He called me an idealist in a world that is far from ideal. He said he couldn't keep the ugliness of what we do from getting to him and hardening him, and that he valued how I could.

That's quite a confession.

And I made a few of my own. I told him I sometimes am too quick to judge and too slow to forgive. I said I didn't like how our ideological differences had bent our friendship out of shape. I offered him my hand in friendship once again. But I did leave my post after all, and Black Widow very capably succeeded me to lead the Avengers.

THE DAILY GLOBE

75¢

LY EDITION

SUPER HERO BUSTS REPORTER FROM GITMO

GUANTANAMO BAY NAVAL BASE, Cuba— The super hero and Avenger known as the Falcon apparently aided the escape of a *Daily Bugle* reporter being held at the Guantanamo Bay detention camp within the U.S. naval base in Cuba.

Security camera recordings released by military sources show the Falcon swooping into the base with the help of his vibranium glider wings under cover of night and emerging with the imprisoned reporter. Falcon left the base while carrying the reporter and evading gunfire from sentry towers. Neither appeared to be injured by the gunfire.

Bugle city editor Joseph Robertson identified the prisoner as Leila Taylor, a community activist and occasional columnist for this newspaper. Taylor was being held as an enemy combatant on unspecified

charges after being taken into custody by the United States Coast Guard, Robertson said.

Military forces have begun a search for the Falcon and Taylor, who they suspect have not left the island, given current weather conditions. Hurricane Mitch is expected to make landfall near the naval base in the coming hours.

At some point after that, you resumed your partnership with the Falcon. I know he's someone you've long regarded as a close friend.

Without question, yes.

The two of you paired up in your hunt for the operative referred to as the Anti-Cap, did you not?

I was never big on that reference but yes. When I started my search for him, I was looking for Sam as well. He was stuck in Cuba after trying to rescue a friend from government custody in Gitmo. All I knew about this other operative was that he was at least as strong, fast, and resilient as me. He also was wearing a uniform similar to mine and he carried a shield. He was described to me as "you without the conscience."

Kind of plays right into the nickname.

But still. I don't think any label applied to this man. I knew he was dangerous and that I needed to find Sam and his friend before he did. Turns out that he was an experiment run by the U.S. Navy, a test subject for a super-steroid intended to improve upon the serum that made me who I am. But this super-sailor, to borrow the term, was uncontrollable. His tactics were savage. His views on why he existed were the complete opposite of mine.

And they were?

He said while I was a product of America's hope, he was the sum of America's fear.

I'd venture that in the long run, hope is greater than fear.

Which may be why we were able to bring him down. As for Sam's friend, she was on the trail of something she thought was illicit drugs that turned out to be the very stuff used to create this super-sailor. We got her out safely.

Did you ever learn who this super-sailor was? How he ended up in this situation?

No. We took him to friends in Wakanda to prevent his handlers from killing him. My hope was that I could help him . . . somehow. In a way, I thought saving this young man might help me atone for not being able to save Bucky all those years ago in what was seeming more and more like a past life. And that thought made it all the more worse when I believed my efforts to save him ended up killing him.

I didn't realize that he died.

That's just it. I only *believed* he had died. Because he was a sailor, we gave him a burial at sea. What I didn't know was that his death was faked with Sam's help so Sam could untangle himself from problems with the government and with the Rivas cartel, all stemming from his actions in Cuba.

Things got very complicated. Even I had moments of doubting Sam amid everything. And in the end, when I found myself facing the super-sailor for what would be the final time, all I had to do was outlast the drugs that were working their way out of his system.

How did you manage it? From the sound of things, he was stronger than you.

I kept in mind that his ways—murder, terror, fascism—never were my ways. In my years of service, my biggest regret is all of the people who see the symbol but miss the point. Our greatness, our strength, comes from our principles, not our weapons. The super-sailor never realized that there is a fine line between patriotism and fanaticism. Ultimately, he chose to die for the country he believed he served over being retaken by the people he actually served.

The people you both knew would kill him as a failed experiment.

Regrettably, yes.

If I understand the timing of these events, this would have been happening about the same time that Scarlet Witch suffered her mental collapse.

That's correct.

Did you have any indications of her distress ahead of the incident at Avengers Mansion?

Not that I recognized at the time. Wanda assisted me and Sam in some capacity during our dealings with the super-sailor. I did experience several incidents of what I now believe were delusions Wanda planted in my mind. It's clear by Tony's actions at the United Nations that I wasn't the only person affected by this ahead of her psychic influences.

So you were present for his address to the General Assembly?

I left just before that happened to deal with a different matter, which held my attention until I received the Avengers' Code White signal.

And that is?

Damage control efforts after the attack on the Avengers Mansion

That requires any and all heroes to report immediately to Avengers Mansion. When I arrived, the mansion had suffered extensive damage from a powerful explosion on the front grounds. Jarvis told me Scott Lang had died in the explosion just as I noticed a Quinjet arriving at high speed. I recognized Vision at its controls about the same time I realized it wasn't coming in for a landing but had targeted the mansion on a collision course. The crash took out even more of the mansion, but Vision emerged with a message for us.

What did he have to say?

We don't have a recording of this. What I recall is that he said the Avengers were about to be punished, but not by him as he no longer controlled his own form. He said our time was over. And from his unhinged mouth came five metallic spheres maybe a bit bigger than softballs, each of which opened up to become an Ultron robot. They engaged us and we struck back. I figured out we could incapacitate these Ultrons by severing the head from its body. But their assault sent She-Hulk into a rage she was unable to control, and when I stepped in to calm her, she attacked me. She might have taken me out completely had I not been able to place my shield between my head and the armored S.H.I.E.L.D. vehicle she brought down on me. That earned me a visit to the hospital to get my shoulder put back into place.

As for the rest of the Avengers?

Captain Britain and Wasp were listed in critical condition, She-Hulk was in S.H.I.E.L.D. custody, Vision was being shipped to Stark Enterprises in two separate crates, and Scott . . . we assumed had been disintegrated in the initial blast. When we were summoned back to the mansion, we were greeted by dozens of heroes, all of whom had answered the call to help. Nick Fury demanded they disperse for fear they would contaminate a live crime scene. I told everyone we should listen to Colonel Fury, but it was just then we received the news that the U.N. had voted to disavow the Avengers.

That couldn't have come at a worse time.

Given that a Kree fighting force had chosen that moment to hover its warship over what was left of the mansion, I couldn't agree more. I stopped a Kree soldier and demanded to know what was happening. He said they had come to witness the end of the Avengers as foretold by the latest incarnation of the Supreme Intelligence. As the fighting wore on, Hawkeye suffered a blast to his quiver that he must have known would be catastrophic. He grabbed hold of a Kree soldier, used his jetpack to get them airborne, and steered them into the intake of one of the warcraft's engines. The resulting explosion was enough to drop the whole ship onto the streets of New York.

NEWS   10:02 *LIVE*

KREE INVADERS ATTACK NEW YORK

ON DAY TWO OF A CONTINUED ASSAULT ON AVENGERS MANSION, KREE FORCES ARRIVE VIA WARSHIP TO TAKE THE FIGHT TO HEROES ASSEMBLED AMID THE RUINS OF THEIR HEADQUARTERS.

I remember the coverage of that.

We finally got a grasp on what was happening when Doctor Strange arrived in his astral form to offer an explanation. He asked us whether there was anyone we knew who was capable of wielding this level of mystic power, of orchestrating this level of chaos. In an instant, I knew the answer.

Wanda Maximoff.

Wanda. Somehow, sometime in the past, she used her hex powers to conjure two sons into existence. When Agatha Harkness discovered the situation, apparently she used her own powers to erase them. That was enough to send Wanda into a psychosis. Doctor Strange explained that as her mastery of magic had not come about through a spiritual under-standing, she'd never gained a sense of magic's consequences. This reality she had built around her had taken a toll. She struggled constantly to maintain her reality in light of every single change, great or small, that she made to it. And finally, she lost all control over it.

She was in serious need of help, it seems, and without it, things would get even worse for you.

For all of us, possibly for all of us on the entire planet. We asked Doctor Strange to point the way to her, which he did. And I went into her realm to talk to her. I told her what she was experiencing wasn't real. I told her I was there to help. She responded by conjuring the Red Skull and a group of Nazi soldiers, who fired upon me. Then Doctor Strange took over, and the two of them threw magic at each other the likes of which I'd never witnessed. He conjured a giant eye—to show her the truth, he said—and she dropped like a wounded bird from the sky and into my arms. She was alive, breathing, but she was gone.

At that point, what did you do? What could you do?

Nothing at all, but fortunately that wasn't up to us. Magneto arrived silently from the sky, took her from me, and flew away. And then . . . we all just left. No one said it aloud but we knew it was all but the end of what we had called the Avengers.

NEWS   11:01 *LIVE*

AVENGERS DISASSEMBLE

NEW YORKERS GATHER TO SHOW THEIR SUPPORT FOR SUPER GROUP CALLING IT QUITS. RUINED MANSION TO BECOME LANDMARK MEMORIAL FOR THE FALLEN.

But the truth is that six months later, you were back at it.

I never would have predicted that then. It was a matter of circumstance, and then of a meeting of minds.

Care to elaborate?

The incident started when something or someone diverted enough electrical energy from Manhattan to overload the security system on the Raft, which is the high-tech, ultra-security outpost of Ryker's Island Maximum Security Penitentiary.

REC   CAM 1

The place where super-criminals are incarcerated.

Yes. An East Coast version of the Vault, in its way. I was on my way to a security conference in Washington, DC, in a S.H.I.E.L.D. helicopter before we headed to the scene. On our way in for a landing, we were struck by a bolt of energy and downed on the facility's helipad. It turns out that Spider-Man had thumbed—well, webbed—a ride aboard the helicopter until he got pitched from the 'copter into the drink. Spider-Man swam up to the helipad just in time for us to see Electro silhouetted in the air against a huge shaft of energy. Spider-Man took off to engage him and quickly was overwhelmed by dozens of Raft inmates now on the loose. I jumped in to free him from their attack and found us joined by Daredevil, Luke Cage, and Spider-Woman.

That had to help some.

So did the arrival of Iron Man, who caught me just as I had been flung into the air by Ironclad. By morning, 42 inmates were known to have escaped

the facility and 45 remained. As Tony noted, we officially did that half-assed. But what struck me was how this insanely dangerous, out-of-control situation that no single one of us could have handled alone ended up in the hands of heroes assembled more or less by fate. People who willingly tossed aside how much they personally had on the line. Who instinctively did what they do best, giving no pause to the gravity of the fight in front of them. And just when it seems like it's anyone's guess which way the fight would go, the team comes together and it's done.

That story rings a bell.

Doesn't it? Just like the original Avengers, this group came together on its own. There were 42 criminals who needed to be recaptured and we already had a team together to do it. Thinking back, I should have known in my gut that we needed a team in place for just this sort of emergency. Maybe, when we closed the mansion and ended the Avengers, we threw the natural balance out of whack. I told Tony if the old Avengers didn't want to assemble, maybe these new ones would. We don't need tech or a salary, no U.N. or government involvement, just us helping people who need help with the big problems.

And a cool clubhouse.

Well, we needed a place to convene.

You sure can't beat the top floor of Stark Tower.

Top three floors, actually. And Jarvis was back.

Forgive me, but how did you convince Tony Stark to do the Avengers all over again?

Didn't have to convince him. He said he trusted my instincts.

So, when you began your investigation of the Kronas Corporation, why didn't you involve your new team of Avengers?

No need. That was an operation of Colonel Fury's through S.H.I.E.L.D., and my participation was mission critical. The Red Skull appeared to have been killed and they wanted me to investigate. Fury said the bigger issue was that when he was killed, the Red Skull once again had possessed the Cosmic Cube, but it wasn't present at the scene of the killing. Our hunt took us to Paris, a place I'd not been for a long time.

By your tone, I'm guessing a very long time.

Not since August of 1944, when I worked with the French Resistance during their uprising there. Back then, I brought some friends along.

Unidentified photographs
recovered from Steve Rogers's
personal possessions at the
time of his purported death

THE HUMAN TORCH
KNOWN ALIASES/ALTER EGOS:
Jim Hammond

RAYMOND, THOMAS
KNOWN ALIASES/ALTER EGOS:
Toro

NAMOR
KNOWN ALIASES/ALTER EGOS:
Sub-Mariner

Members of the Invaders?

That's what Churchill called us first and it sort of stuck.

Take me back to that time, Steve. This would have been about a year before you woke up here.

Sure was. Paris was new to us. We were already in France as part of Operation Dragoon, so we worked our way up from the south and met leaders from the Maquis to help plan an attack. I'd seen a lot before I got to France, including plenty of combat . . . but the savagery the Nazis inflicted on those people . . . I never had seen anything like it. That's why it really galls me when I hear my own people dismissing the French as cowards. We're talking about a people who never gave up fighting the Nazi occupation. Their country may have surrendered but they didn't. I saw men and women—civilians—take on Panzer divisions, knowing that their own loved ones would be slaughtered in retribution. So, we were proud to help them take back Paris.

I'm sure that was very gratifying.

The victory parade came right through the Champs-Élysées. My friends and I watched from the sidelines as it was the people of France's day, not ours. I've never forgotten what they paid to get that day, which is probably why Paris always has been one of my favorite cities.

After following the Cube's trail to Paris, I was called to Arlington National Cemetery to investigate a pair of grave desecrations.

I can appreciate you would want to help, but why not—

Why not find someone else? These were graves of former Captain Americas.

I had a lot of respect for William Nasland, respect he earned, and Jeff Mace was a good friend of Bucky's. He may not have been overseas in the trenches but he saved a lot of American lives, including mine once. When Bucky and I were both M.I.A. and presumed dead, the war was still on and President Roosevelt didn't want our G.I.s losing faith. William Nasland

NASLAND, WILLIAM
KNOWN ALIASES/ALTER EGOS:
Spirit of '76, Captain America

died saving John F. Kennedy during his first campaign for the U.S. Senate. He died wearing my uniform. That's how Jeff Nash became the next Captain America. He finished the job Nasland started that day, and because of them, Kennedy lived long enough to become president, long enough to change this country for the better.

I'm sorry, but those men aren't widely known for their work as Captain America.

Their names had been highly classified, yes. But this despicable act was a shot at me. I wanted to know who took that shot. Not long after, I was ambushed by Crossbones, a known associate of the Red Skull, but he mentioned it was a Russian who had set him up to attack me. That was enough for Fury to connect us to Aleksander Lukin, a major Cold War player who went on his own when

MACE, JEFF
KNOWN ALIASES/ALTER EGOS:
Patriot, Captain America

the Soviet Union collapsed. He had established an oil supplier called the Kronas Corporation, which shared a name with a small Russian village not far from Stalingrad.

I'm assuming you have a reason to remember that village.

In November of 1942, Bucky and I were on the Russian front and ran into Nazi forces as the cold wind cut through us and the snow fell. Among the enemy were Russians, some prisoners, some deserters, fighting along-side the Nazis against their own people. That was part of what made the Russian front uglier than what we were used to. Stalin's forces were about to launch an operation to trap the entire Nazi invasion force inside the snow and ice of Russia with no supply lines and no way home all winter.

Sounds ambitious.

And on top of that, word had leaked that the Germans had some sort of super-weapon nearby that they were waiting to spring on us. That was enough to get the Invaders involved, and the Russian officer in charge of our anti-super-weapon mission was Colonel Vasily Karpov. I didn't like Karpov or his tactics, but he managed to get information we needed. The weapon was in Kronas, heavily guarded. We arrived an hour before dawn with Bucky taking point to clear our way.

Did that make you nervous, putting him up front?

Let me tell you the real secret of what Bucky was. The official story said he was a symbol to counter the rise of the Hitler Youth. There was some truth to that, but like all things in war, there was a darker truth underneath.

What truth was that?

Bucky did the things I couldn't. I was the icon. I wore the flag. While I gave speeches to the troops in the trenches, he was doing what he had been trained to do. He was highly trained. He wouldn't have been out there with us if he wasn't. And Bucky radioed the all-clear.

Care to elaborate for me? Bucky had been highly trained? In what?

INTERVIEWER'S NOTE: *I felt unsettled at this point. Captain Rogers had not looked at me the whole time he recounted his war story. He stared forward, his head slightly bowed. His gaze, nearly unblinking, bored into the floor. I felt he was seeing straight into his past. I could not fathom how this encounter was replaying in his mind. In flashes of memory? In long stretches of light and noise? As my words hung between us, Captain Rogers looked up. Yet it appeared to me that his vision of the war remained uninterrupted. He was seeing through me, perhaps watching whatever acts young Bucky committed in wartime. I wondered whether my questions had unlocked more than I was ready for.*

Steve?

We should have been able to waltz right in, but it all went to hell. Nazis started crawling out of the woodwork like they were expecting us. Then we see Master Man, Hitler's personal Super-Soldier. We had been expecting him or something like him, of course. The Torch, Toro, and Namor took to the sky. We faced threats like this all the time but I can only imagine what this kind of combat looked like to the Russians. Men on fire doing battle above them.

And as they were, you sought the super-weapon.

Finding the secret weapon wasn't a problem. We just looked for where the Nazi guards were heaviest in number. I took out a machine-gun nest with a

Master Man,
Hitler's personal
Super-Soldier

grenade, and as Bucky and I made our way to the shed it protected, a beam
of electric-green fire thicker than water from a firehose nearly disintegrated
us where we stood. Seeing how it melted a path through everything in front
of it, I quickly grasped the nature of our mission. The beam leapt again,
tearing through houses and people indiscriminately, and through the flames
I saw the Red Skull at its controls.

What was your next move?

When he saw us, he cut and ran. What I couldn't have known at the time
was that he was setting the device to self-destruct. The devastation was
just a cover for his escape. The Skull knew what we would do.

You tried to save Kronas.

Namor and the Torches broke off their battle with Master Man, and he
disappeared with the Red Skull. By that time, the fires had spread too
quickly. We couldn't stop Kronas from burning to the ground. Karpov
arrived and was much more interested in the Skull's abandoned weapon
than helping us assist the villagers. When it exploded, his men burned
along with the weapon.

How . . . how could he?

He told me I was unable to understand. Karpov said we and the Germans
had our Super-Soldiers and secret weapons while the Russians had nothing
but their winter. Within an hour, we were in the air and on the trail of the
Skull. The last I saw of Vasily Karpov, he was wandering through what was
left of Kronas, surveying the damage I'm sure he blamed on me.

You never heard what became of Karpov after you left him?

Oh, I heard.

PROJECT WINTER SOLDIER: CONFIDENTIAL FILE
RECOVERED BY CAPT. STEVEN ROGERS

TOP SECRET

Translated by

Doctor's notes—
5 May 1945

Comrade Karpov's package arrived this morning., though whether
we will be able to get anything useful from it is yet unknown.
The physician aboard Comrade Karpov's submarine has speculated
that the subject's immersion in freezing water may have preserved
him, as it prevented his wounds—consisting of several severe
lacerations on the left side of his body and the loss of his
left arm at the shoulder—from bleeding out. Since they had not
the facilities to test this theory onboard, he was kept in cold
storage until he could be transported to Moscow.

They have told me he was on a plane which exploded, but
I doubt this. He must have leapt before the blast. From the
appearance of his wounds, he was in close <u>proximity</u> to a small
explosion, but perhaps 20 feet away, already falling to the
water below.

Tomorrow we will begin the process of allowing the subject's
body to regain its heat, in the hope that his blood will still be
viable for testing. We are using an approach for this that one of
our spies smuggled out of Hitler's most secret laboratories.

I have not personally witnessed it, but have read of cases
where a body that is flash-frozen has been completely revived. The
case of the mother and child in Stalingrad frozen in a snowbank
along the road for two hours, for example. I have little hope
that will be the case here, but Comrade Karpov and his superiors
are more interested in the analysis of his vital fluids than in his
revivification. Apparently Comrade Karpov once saw the subject in
action, and believes it probable that he, like his partner Captain
America, has the much-rumored Super-Soldier Formula flowing
through—or rather, frozen inside—his veins.

Doctor's notes—
7 May 1945

Yesterday exceeded all expectation. Subject's body temperature was
increased over the course of several hours, and his wounds were
dealt with, to prevent bleeding. When his temp. was close enough

DECLASSIFIED AND RELEAS
BY S.H.I.E.L.D.

to normal, it was as we thought . . . his tissue and blood were still viable. But, as I predicted, he was in fact <u>deceased</u>. Either the explosion, the fall, or his time in the water had killed him.

One of my colleagues had an idea that had <u>not</u> occurred to me. Since he had been frozen so soon after his demise, he suggested trying to revive him as if he were only recently deceased. We administered electricity, Cardio-Pulmonary Resuscitation, and adrenaline directly into the heart. And though I can still hardly believe it, the subject was brought back from death.

It is not exactly the miracle that I have previously read of, though perhaps because of the time the subject was submerged in the icy waters, or perhaps because of the explosion that put him there. But whatever the reason, though we now have a <u>live</u> subject, there appears to be <u>considerable</u> brain damage. The subject has <u>no memory</u> of his previous life.

What he does have, as he tragically demonstrated on two of our aides—remarkable with only one arm—are <u>reflex memories</u>. He knows the things he did before; how to fight, particularly, how to speak four languages, including, thankfully, Russian, and many other things. But he has no idea how or why he knows these things. He is nearly a blank slate, but an incredibly dangerous one. Thus, he is being sedated while further testing is completed.

Doctor's notes—
21 May 1945

Two weeks of work, to no success. A battery of blood tests was run on the subject, but it appears he is nothing more than human. There is not a trace of any additive or "super" formula in his system. After much discussion between our superiors and Comrade Karpov, it was decided that the subject is to be put back into stasis, for what purpose, I do not know.

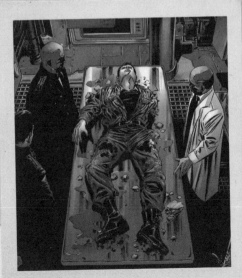

Major General Vasily Karpov
HEAD OF SPECIAL SECTION
Department X

TOP KGB CLEARANCE ONLY

Project: Winter Soldier
June 1954

Volkov's man at MI-6, Parsifal, has proved his worth. The schematics for Advanced Robotic Appendages and Attachment he provided two months past were revolutionary. Our science team finished a working prototype and attached it to the American without incident. With the new appendage in place, clearance was given for Department X to begin work on the Winter Soldier Project.

It has long been my plan to turn this American symbol back against our enemies. He was no aid to developing our own Super-Soldiers, but he will still be a valuable tool, in the right hands.

It was our own experiments in Mental Implantation during Sensory Deprivation that provided the breakthrough. And because of the American's memory loss, it was quite simple. We were able to reprogram the American's mind. We gave him a purpose and we made him loyal to no one but us. Once that was accomplished, we had simply to train him and prepare him for a field evaluation.

Hopes are high that he will be a successful operative. I believe, because he walks and talks just like them, because he exudes "America" with his every breath, that the enemy will never see him coming.

TOP SECRET

PROJECT WINTER SOLDIER: CONFIDE
RECOVERED BY CAPT. STEVEN R

Translated by

Report—
Codename: Winter Soldier—
Field test, 5 November 1954

All objectives achieved. Codename Winter Soldier encounters no difficulty on mission.

As predicted, Americans and allies mistake him for one of their own. Allow him unimpeded entrance into West Berlin.

Winter Soldier spends evening in Berlin nightclub along many U.S. and U.K. servicemen, unsuspected. Jeep overturns at 02:45 killing three soldiers en route to base from nightclub. Crash not investigated. Assumed drunken roadway incident. On mission completion, Codename: Winter Soldier crosses border, returns to handlers without incident.

Future assignments under evaluation.

[report ends]

WINTER SOLDIER—MISSION REPORT.

Cairo, 11 January 1955

> Objective: United Nations Diplomatic Team.
> All targets eliminated without incident. Fire reported as accident.
> [report ends]

WINTER SOLDIER—MISSION REPORT.

West Berlin, 14 May 1955

> Objective: NATO General James Keller.
> Target eliminated with prejudice.
> [report ends]

WINTER SOLDIER—MISSION REPORT.

Madripoor, 1 January 1956

> Objective: British Ambassador Dalton Graines.
> Target eliminated, along with acceptable collateral damage.
> Madripoor authorities have no leads.
> [report ends]

WINTER SOLDIER—MISSION REPORT.

Algeria, 1 April 1956

> Objective: French Defense Minister Jacques Dupuy.
> Target eliminated with prejudice. Algerian Nationalist Movement
> implicated.
> [report ends]

WINTER SOLDIER—MISSION REPORT.

Paris, 12 May 1956

> Objective: Algerian Peace Conference Envoy.
> All targets eliminated.
> [report ends]

WINTER SOLDIER—MISSION REPORT.

Mexico City, 17 February 1957

> Objective: United States Colonel Jefferson Hart.
> Target eliminated with prejudice.
> [report ends]

AVENGERS
INTERNAL USE ONLY

PROJECT WINTER SOLDIER: CONFIDENTIAL FILES
RECOVERED BY CAPT. STEVEN ROGERS

Translated by

Scientific analysis.
7 June 1957

A comprehensive mental evaluation of Codename: Winter Soldier was conducted over the course of the past week. Diagnoses are varied, but most in Dept. X Science Team believe that his mental state is becoming unstable. In the three years since he was awakened from stasis, it appears his mind is seeking to fill in the holes from his memory, or possibly rebelling against the implanted programming he received originally. The subject has recently begun to exhibit more than usual curiosity, even to the point of questioning orders from superiors, and once in the past month, he attacked a fellow operative, nearly killing him. On interrogation, he could not explain his actions.

One theory is that just as he has reflex-memories, which allow him to be such an effective operative, he may also have a deeply buried sense of who he was, or at least of what kind of person he was. As such, this deeply buried idea may be causing him mental stress and triggering turmoil in his thoughts. Another theory, which is more disturbing, is that he may actually be remembering his previous life, though in small pieces only. It is therefore our recommendation that Codename: Winter Soldier be kept in stasis between missions, and that he undergo Mental Implantation at every awakening. We believe this will correct his instability issues, so he can continue to be of use to Department X.

[Report ends]

WINTER SOLDIER: CONFIDENTIAL FILES
RECOVERED BY CAPT. STEVEN ROGERS

Incident Report,
12 March 1973
re: Codename: Winter Soldier

I regret to report that after more than fifteen years of selective use around the world, all to great success, last month's Winter Soldier mission into the United States did not go as planned. The target, Senator Harry Baxtor, was eliminated, and the death was made to appear accidental. But after that, something went wrong. Codename: Winter Soldier failed to appear at his extraction point.

His handlers waited, and listened in to police transmissions, but he did not arrive, and the local authorities reported nothing that implied he'd been apprehended. Following protocol, our agents in the U.S. began a wide search for Winter Soldier. All extremes were taken to recover this valuable asset, including several sleeper-agents breaking cover. Through that considerable effort, we were able to track some of his movements. Security camera footage showed him in civilian garb at the Dallas train station, boarding a train to Chicago. In Chicago, he was seen boarding a bus for New York City.

His movements in New York are unknown to us, but for two weeks he was completely off the grid. It was only through sheer luck that he was found by one of our agents, sleeping in a flophouse on the Lower East Side. It took several of our agents, in the garb of New York policemen, to take him into custody. Yet even after subsequent mental conditioning, Codename: Winter Soldier has no answers for his conduct, or any memory of his time out of our control.

While troubling, the incident appears to be an aberration, requiring nothing more than closer watch. It is further recommended that in future he be excluded from missions on American soil.

From the personal journal of
Major General Vasily Karpov

September 1983

Against advice, I have taken Codename: Winter Soldier to the Middle East as my personal bodyguard. I am getting old and I know there are only a few years left for me, so I wish to spend them watching this twisted creature defend my life. I almost feel sorry for him, as he tenses up whenever anyone approaches, ready to dive in front of a bullet for me.

It will never make up for what he and his people did to me in the war, how they shamed me in front of my own men, but even after all these years, it still makes me smile to see Captain America's partner serving Mother Russia. Let us see what kind of damage he can do to his country's efforts in the Middle East. These next few years should be amusing. I am glad that Yuri transferred me. To hell with him.

TOP SECRET

**PROJECT WINTER SOLDIER: CONFIDENTIAL FILES
RECOVERED BY CAPT. STEVEN ROGERS**

Project Winter Soldier—
Final Orders.
4 August 1988

In accordance with Major General Karpov's final orders before his death, Project Winter Soldier has been decommissioned.

Codename: Winter Soldier has been placed back into stasis after his years in the Middle East alongside the Major General.

No incidents were reported by the Major General during this time, but it is recommended that if Codename: Winter Soldier is revived from stasis in future, thorough mental reimplantation be done to assure control of the operative.

Codename: Winter Soldier will be stored at an undisclosed location, along with much of Department X's abandoned experiments.

[end files]

That must have been a lot to take in at once.

I knew that Lukin had placed this file in my home for me to find as part of his psychological war with me. I called Fury to have him read the file. He took it to verify its authenticity while saying its details matched everything S.H.I.E.L.D. already had on the Winter Soldier. This file also was all I needed to know that Lukin possessed the Skull's Cosmic Cube. There was no other way he could have obtained those documents. And I understood something else.

What was that, Steve?

Bucky once said to me that if I didn't have him, there wouldn't be a single person in the world who really understood me. The first thought that struck me after I finished that file was that I might be one of the only people in the world who then understood him and what he had become. I knew there was some part of him, of who he is, still trapped inside. Somewhere inside that thing they turned him into was whatever was left of Bucky Barnes' humanity. He was my partner. He was my friend. I owed it to him to find that part. And there was something else.

I'm listening.

I knew that if Bucky understood he wasn't in control of his actions, he would hate that more than anything. I know what he would want. He'd want me to do whatever it took to stop him. I just had to find him another way out of this.

How did you find that other way?

Like the song says, with a little help from my friends.

An oldie but a goodie.

Maybe to you.

Who did you seek out?

Sam found me first, thanks to a tip from Colonel Fury. And then Tony. We knew Lukin would move the Cube to the highest bidder. Tony was able to track the Cube's energy signature to West Virginia and an underground Kronas research facility with a nuclear-safe vault. The biggest problem with that wasn't one I expected. Tony's business entanglements with Lukin prevented him from assisting us in our search for the Cube. If Iron Man was seen on the scene, he likely would have lost his business. So Sam and I went on our own. When we arrived, we found out the Winter Soldier was the one with the Cube.

Everything was coming together.

Sam engaged troops at the facility. Sharon had arrived with a S.H.I.E.L.D. strike team. I went after Bucky. I chased him to a system of tunnels below the facility.

You caught him there?

He caught me first, and he tried to kill me. I wondered whether any part of him remembered what he used to be. We punched and grappled and fought. He told me he would be the man to kill me. So, I just stopped fighting. I knelt on the ground and told him that if he truly didn't know me, he should shoot me.

He shot you, didn't he?

No. Well, he shot *at* me. And as he did, I threw my shield to come at him from the back. When he was hit, he let loose of his satchel and out tumbled the Cube.

A Cosmic Cube. One of the greatest powers of the universe, capable of shaping energy and matter to the will of its user.

Bounced right to my feet. I picked it up. I held it before me as I looked at Bucky, and I ordered him to remember who he was.

Oh, my . . . Steve, when you find another way out for someone—

That wasn't part of my plan, I promise you. But it worked. Bucky knew it worked. He knew it up to the point that he grabbed it from me and crushed it in his robotic hand. He cursed its existence as he did so, and when the energy he released from the Cube dissipated, he was gone. Sharon and Sam said Bucky was dead. They were sure he couldn't live with what was done to him. I disagreed. I said Bucky is a survivor and that he was out there, somewhere.

And you were right. You would see him again.

But not for a long time.

VI.
REQUIEM

SUPERHUMAN REGISTRATION ACT

~~FUGITIVE~~

REAL NAME: STEVEN ROGERS
CODE NAME: CAPTAIN AMERICA
SEX: M
EYES: BLUE
HEIGHT: 6'2"
WEIGHT: 240 LBS.

POWERS: PEAK HUMAN PHYSIQUE, HIGHEST
POSSIBLE HUMAN-LEVEL STRENGTH/SPEED/AGILITY/
ETC., MASTER STRATEGIST AND COMBATANT

EQUIPMENT: INDESTRUCTIBLE SHIELD, CHAIN-MAIL
UNIFORM

ENHANCED HUMAN

S.H.I.E.L.D DIRECTORATE

SHRA ID 0 04 815 16 23 42

I'll admit that going into this session with
Captain Rogers, I brought with me specific insights
into events that have come to be known collectively
as the first "Superhuman Civil War." My thoughts
on this were shaped by my conversations with
Tony Stark.

I believed those insights might better inform or
guide me in our own discussion of those events. I
should not have assumed as much. As has often been
the case during these interviews, the man who each
day embodies and fights for the ideals promised
to the people of this country in its founding
documents is a far more complicated individual than
his identity and costume might suggest.

It's well known that Mr. Stark and Captain
Rogers were on opposing sides of that conflict.
We all know who sacrificed the most as events
unfolded. I went in eager to explore the other side
of this most important story.

INTERVIEWER: *We've already discussed your experiences being accused of treason and even being deported from the country because it was felt you'd somehow betrayed your oath. Did you experience similar feelings when the Superhuman Registration Act was first discussed?*

STEVE ROGERS: I think the record's pretty clear at this point that I had misgivings about that whole thing from the very beginning.

SUPER HERO INSIDER

SHI

NEWS   GOSSIP   CELEBS   PHOTOS   VIDEOS

NEWS

SUPERHUMAN REGISTRATION IS ON THE HORIZON

U.S. House introduces bipartisan measure to subject heroes to government oversight, including registering their true identities

WASHINGTON—Action could come quickly in the U.S. House of Representatives on what already is being called the Superhuman Registration Act.

House Resolution 421 would update the United States Code to require such individuals, including those of extraterrestrial or paranormal origin, to catalog themselves as "living weapons of mass destruction."

The new bill's hyper-focused attention on such terminology is sending ripples through Washington as well as United Nations headquarters in New York City.

In this extraordinary bipartisan plan, a mechanism will be devised for managing individuals possessing "superhuman" abilities—those acquired either through a natural consequence of their birth or as the result of artificial or technological enhancements.

If made law, the act would require any American citizen as well as noncitizens living in the United States or its territories and identified as a "superhuman" to register their actual identities with a special governmental body tasked with overseeing the initiative.

Such individuals would further be compelled to undertake specialized training to act as deputized agents working on behalf of the government. While there is no requirement to serve in this capacity, even those superhumans wishing to abstain from such work would be required to register.

The Baxter Building, where the registration talks took place

You were fervently against the entire idea, at least at the time. The notion of accountability to higher authority would seem to be an easy thing for you to accept.

We've established that I have no druthers with being held accountable, but for my *actions*. What bothered me was the idea that, as a default position, we were being viewed as potential enemies unless we agreed to a level of control and oversight. After everything—*everything*—we'd done to protect the country and the entire world from threats that, if we're being honest, to this day make me shake my head in disbelief, this was something I had a hard time accepting.

But you also harbored other concerns.

The new law would require us to register both our costumed identities as well as our real names, at least for those of us who make that distinction. I'd already had experience with the wrong people knowing who I was and using that information to hurt people I cared about as a way to attack me. It's one thing for me to knowingly put myself at risk, but I couldn't do the job knowing my actions might spark vengeance against people I love.

Even though that information was not intended for public release.

And in the history of the United States government, no secrets have ever leaked, right?

Fair point. Still, coming from someone who's spent his entire adult life as a soldier and is accustomed to following orders, your reaction surprised a great many people. The American military has always operated under civilian authority and oversight. How did you distinguish that from the superhuman situation?

The American military exists to protect American interests. We can argue the merits of those interests all day long, but one key distinction for those who serve is that every person who does so joins the ranks voluntarily. I know that wasn't always the case, and smarter people than me can give you compelling reasons for and against compulsory military service. That doesn't interest me except in this context: With few exceptions, superhumans don't ask to be what they become.

You did. At least, in a sense. You understood the risks you took when you agreed to be a test subject for Professor Erskine, and you accepted the assignment you were given when his experiment made you what you are.

That's one of the reasons I agonized over how I felt about registration. Back then, during the war and when the draft was on, I tried to join and was rejected because I was unfit. At the time, I saw the professor's project as a way to do something I wouldn't otherwise be able to do: serve my country when it needed every able-bodied American it could find. I may have questioned that decision from time to time since then, but I've never regretted it, and as a soldier I swore to obey the orders I was given.

So, how was registration and agreeing to oversight—in your case, a continued agreement, all things considered—different, at least in your eyes?

The Superhuman Registration Act was an American law requiring me and my colleagues to answer to the American government. Even though I'm an American citizen and my abilities were given to me through the American defense apparatus, that's obviously not the case for every superhuman. More importantly, my fellow superhumans and I see ourselves as serving all of humanity, rather than a single nation, but what if other countries began enacting their own equivalents to the law? What if one country's law came into conflict with another's?

You were concerned about being answerable to a single governmental authority, even when it's your own.

If one government could control all of the superhumans and label them as being instruments of one nation's security, then they also get to decide which entities or actors are threats to that security.

The United Nations was also consulted during the law's development, and it voiced support of being part of the larger oversight process, perhaps to alleviate concerns such as yours.

If the proposal from the beginning had been a multinational effort, we might have been onto something, but that it ended up being a law enacted only in the U.S. just made me more skeptical.

Were you surprised when Tony Stark came out in vocal support of the new law?

(*sighs*) Yes, at least at first. When Reed Richards testified to Congress the first time they tried to do this, Stark was in his corner, and for what I believed to be the right reasons, and they were able to sway at least some opinions.

Then Stamford happened.

★ EXTRA ★

DAILY 🎺 BUGLE®

NEW YORK'S FINEST DAILY NEWSPAPER

Stamford Disaster Pushes Congress to Act on Superhuman Registration

CONNECTICUT CONSEQUENCES

WASHINGTON, DC—Even as state and federal resources are dispatched to Stamford, officials in the nation's capital are meeting to discuss the fallout of the devastating battle that ravaged the stricken Connecticut city.

In a series of closed-door sessions, members of the Homeland Security and Armed Services committees in both chambers of Congress as well as the House Oversight and Accountability Committee met with representatives from the Commission on Superhuman Activities to discuss a renewed effort to pass legislation designed to govern the activities of the world's super-powered individuals.

SUPERHUMAN REGISTRATION ACT

It's the right thing to do, and it's the law.

Over six hundred people killed, including sixty children. The New Warriors had absolutely no business confronting Nitro and others, in Stamford or anywhere else. As Tony said, they should have called us to help them. On that, at least, we agreed. This was a terrible, wholly preventable tragedy, and for what? TV ratings.

In principle, you understood and acknowledged the need for accountability, and even training those with superior powers in how to use them properly and responsibly. I see it as an outgrowth in how you took Bucky and Rick Jones under your wing. You were okay with them being your partners, but they had to do it the right way.

I understood the need to hold the New Warriors to account, along with Nitro and his colleagues. I understood the need to hold ourselves to a standard of conduct that was above reproach, so we would naturally engender the trust of the American people and everyone else around the world.

But—

I drew the line at how they planned to enforce the new law. The penalty for not registering included imprisonment in a special facility designed to house superhumans. Taken out of the country and held beyond the reach of any constitutional rights or protections. (*leans forward*) For the crime of existing, and for not surrendering their right to privacy.

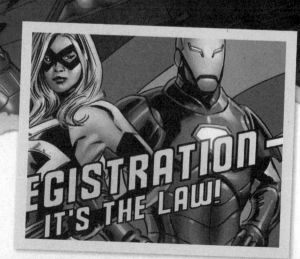

IE DAILY GLOBE

$1.00

DITION

WON'T REGISTER'

Captain America, Others Who Refuse Superhuman Registration Face Imprisonment

EGISTRATION —
IT'S THE LAW!

Punishment for noncompliance seems odd, considering the individuals involved. As Mr. Stark discussed during one of our interviews, how do you make Thor register? Or Captain Marvel?

How do you imprison Bruce Banner for the crime of being an accident victim? Or any of the X-Men for being born the way they are? How does a society founded on individual liberty get to this place? Is it because people actually *fear* the differences they claim to celebrate? Do people fear the different ones among us not so much for what they've done, but for what they might do *because* they're different? How many pages of history have been written to show us just how that sort of thing is a bad idea?

WANTED
BY S.H.I.E.L.D.

TRAITOR

STEVEN ROGERS
A.K.A. "CAPTAIN AMERICA"

The above-named individual is charged with Non-compliance against the Superhuman Registration Act. As such, they are now considered a fugitive from the United States Government. Harboring such persons is prohibited. Federal law provides severe criminal penalties for aiding and abetting superhumans violating this Act, with a maximum penalty of up to ten years in prison.

What began as a solitary act of defiance evolved in rather short order to you becoming the figurehead for what many dub the resistance movement.

I knew I'd likely inspire others to follow my example. I didn't realize how quickly that would catch on.

You formed your own team, the "Secret Avengers," to resist the Registration Act.

I figured it would be better to have some organization, rather than individuals going off on their own. At first, it was a means to help those superhumans who wanted out of the country to avoid registration, that sort of thing. However, we still took to the streets, trying to prove we were still the same heroes people looked to not just for help but also as symbols of what was good rather than evil.

During my interviews with Mr. Stark, we discussed how even as you actively resisted registration, you and others like the Secret Avengers were continuing to act as you always had: confronting those who wished to do harm. Mr. Stark made the point that you were doing so because you were still heroes. "Good people who'd chosen for their own reasons to use their extraordinary abilities for a cause greater than themselves."

Tony Stark said that?

He may have promised me not to reveal such platitudes for fear of tarnishing his roguish reputation, but I think in this case he'd understand my lapse. He did indicate it made being in conflict with you and your fellow resisters that much more difficult.

Once the act was passed and Stark and other pro-registration heroes turned to hunting and capturing those who were against it, things started escalating to the point where we were fighting each other. I tried on a couple of occasions to meet with him. I hadn't wanted this, and the whole thing was threatening to spiral out of control. Each time we met, the situation went to hell and we'd all be fighting again. (*sighs*) I suppose it was inevitable that Stark and the others would set a trap with a fake emergency they knew we'd try to act on.

Green-Meyer Chemicals.

Yep. To their credit, Stark and Maria Hill—S.H.I.E.L.D. director at the time—used the ruse as one last attempt to offer us a way out of the whole thing. Amnesty. Tony pleaded with me to listen. I used the opportunity to sabotage his armor. I was so convinced I was right that I wouldn't even listen to someone who'd become the closest thing to a brother I knew at that time. He made me pay for that momentary stupidity.

NEWS

10:51 *LIVE*

THOR DELIVERS DEADLY BOLT TO GOLIATH

AVENGER TURNS ON AVENGER TO STRIKE KILLING BLOW—
HEROES PULLING NO PUNCHES IN BATTLE OVER SUPERHUMAN REGISTRATION ACT

William Foster's death at the hands of the Thor clone was a turning point in the conflict.

I'd say so. The Thor clone developed by Stark and Reed Richards went rogue, and Bill paid the price for it. There was no going back from something like that. At the same time, Stark and S.H.I.E.L.D. were finalizing their plans for portals to the Prison 42 complex in all fifty states, so captured resisters could be sent there to await trial beyond the reach of U.S. law and constitutional protections. We had to stop it, and Stark and the others knew they had to stop us. A final battle for all the marbles was inevitable.

It was quite something, to say the least.

We'd always tried to mitigate the risk to innocent civilians, but this time the entire thing just spiraled out of control. One minute we're on Ryker's Island

FOSTER, WILLIAM BARRETT (DECEASED)
KNOWN ALIASES/ALTER EGOS:
Goliath, Black Goliath, Giant-Man

or in the Negative Zone fighting each other, the next we're in downtown Manhattan. (*shakes head*) All of those people. In a way, it was the best thing that could happen. Vision disabled Stark's armor and he was helpless against me. I was so angry at that point I don't honestly know if I was aware of what I was doing—not that I'm trying to excuse my actions.

Ordinary civilians caught up in the chaos of the superhuman "civil war" break up the final fight between Captain America and Iron Man

You allowed yourself to be pulled away from Mr. Stark.

In that moment, I realized it didn't matter who was right and who was wrong. We'd gone too far. We'd broken the trust of the people we'd sworn to protect, and now we were putting them in danger, causing damage and inflicting harm. We weren't fighting for them anymore, or even an idea or an ideal. We were just fighting.

When Spider-Man tried to tell you your side was winning, witnesses heard you say, "Everything except the argument."

I honestly don't remember what I said. I was just . . . broken inside, on some level. The only way to stop it was right there, right then. So, I surrendered.

TRANSCRIPT—NEWS REPORT

NEWS ANCHOR: If you're just tuning in, you heard correctly. Steve Rogers—Captain America—has surrendered to authorities.

The brutal conflict over the Superhuman Registration Act is over. After a battle unlike any New York has ever seen, Captain America threw his mask down and gave up the resistance.

And so the struggle that began in the wake of the tragedy in Stamford, which led to demands that superhumans be regulated by the government, has come to a close of sorts. Whether Rogers' arrest will bring peace and healing to the super hero community, or this nation, is a question that only time can answer.

(transcript ends)

BEST AVAILABLE COPY

You offered yourself to the authorities, in exchange for amnesty granted to everyone who actively opposed registration.

It was the quickest way to bring an end to the immediate action.

Speaking of immediate action, it didn't take them long to indict you and ready you for trial.

(*small laugh*) Can you really blame them? The public had turned against us, and I had a hand in that even if that's not what I'd intended. Others followed me, but I was the leader. For that, there needed to be an accounting and a plan for moving forward. A plan for healing. A trial had to be public and transparent, to show the country and the world this was being taken seriously, instead of trying to sweep it under the rug. I understood that, which is why I surrendered and elected to shoulder responsibility for the anti-registration side.

I understand Mr. Stark came to see you while you were in custody at Ryker's Island.

Yes, right after he'd been appointed the new S.H.I.E.L.D. director. It wasn't much of a conversation, and what there was, wasn't pleasant. I asked him if he thought everything that had happened was worth it. Taking the government's side, pledging to hunt down those who disagreed with the Registration Act, imprisoning us because we wanted to be free to live our lives. Was what we'd done and what we'd lost worth it? He never answered me, and that was the last time we spoke before . . .

Before you died. More accurately, before you were assassinated. It feels odd, saying that.

Try living through it. Or dying through it, as the case may be.

You learned—much later of course—that Mr. Stark came to see you again. After the tragic events of that day.

(*smiles knowingly*) Yes.

TRANSCRIPT EXCERPT: VIDEO RECORDING— S.H.I.E.L.D. HELICARRIER PRISONER HOLDING AREA

TONY STARK: I knew this was it. I knew we were one dumb slip away from this bill passing and sides being taken. One of us would give them an excuse to pass this bill and that would be it. I told you. I told anyone who would listen . . . we had to work within the system. We had to work with the leaders that the people of this country voted to represent them. To not do this is arrogance—criminal arrogance. I told you that.

I knew that you would force me . . . no. That's wrong. You didn't force me. But I knew that I would be put in the position of taking charge of this side of things. Because if not me, who? Who else was there? No one. So I sucked it up.

I did what you do. I committed.

Because if this wasn't handled with full commitment, thousands of people could die. Innocent people. I knew what I had to do.

The good news is . . . through all of this . . . I never took a drink! And if I didn't during this, then I'm probably never going to . . . So, there's that.

To do what I needed to do to win this quickly, I knew that meant you and I would probably never speak again. Or be friends again. Or partners again. I told myself I was okay with it because I knew it was right and I . . . I knew it was saving lives. It was! It was the right thing to do! And . . . and . . . and I was willing to get in bed with people we despise to get this done. And I knew the world favors the underdog and that I would be the bad guy. I knew this and I said I was okay with it. And . . . and even though I said . . . even though I said I was willing to go all the way with it . . . I wasn't. And I know this because the worst has happened.

The thing I can't live with has happened.

And for all our back and forth, and all the things we we've said and done to each other, for all the hard questions I've had to ask, and terrible lies I've had to tell, there's one thing that I'll never be able to tell anyone now. Not my friends, or my coworkers, or my president. This one thing! The one thing I should have told you, but now I can't.

It wasn't worth it.

(transcript ends)

By the way, let me just say that watching a video that features my own corpse is pretty unsettling. As for what Tony said? I'd be lying if I said I wasn't choked up when I watched the playback.

His remorse for his role in everything that happened seemed to fuel his desire to make sure that things going forward never escalated to that level again. While the Registration Act went forward, many of the concerns raised by you and others who resisted it were addressed.

Stark's stubborn, but in his own way he's a man of conviction and principle. For all our arguments and even the times we've fought each other, I think we agree more than we disagree on the things that matter. Our methods and how we arrive at those ideals might differ, but I think that's one of the things that's bonded us together. Like I said before: With the exception of Bucky, he's as close to a brother as I've ever had.

The world was obviously stunned by your apparent murder. The turnout for your funeral was tremendous.

You mean the first one.

Right. A military burial at Arlington for the masses, so the world could mourn, while Mr. Stark and some of your other colleagues committed your body to the deep.

It seemed fitting, somehow, being returned to the ocean where I'd apparently died the first time.

While your friends chose to honor you in private, the public acknowledgments of your service continued for quite some time. I'm assuming you saw your statue at Arlington.

Yeah. That was more than a little disturbing, let me tell you.

Perhaps the most interesting tribute came from Thor, on the one-year anniversary of your death, which he arrived at after talking . . . to you.

And once again, this odd life I live offers up another surprise.

He apparently summoned you from the afterlife?

Gods can do those sorts of things.

Do you remember what you—your disembodied spirit, that is—talked about?

Life. Death. Valhalla. I wasn't really of this world anymore, but I could still feel it. I remember thinking everything I thought I'd ever stood for was being corrupted for political agendas. I didn't do what I did because of politics, or my own personal gain. I fought for an ideal, a promise my country makes to everyone who calls it home, but all of that was lost in the noise. Thor set them straight. He's nothing if not a showstopper.

Transcript of News Report on the One-Year Anniversary of Captain America's Death

NEWS ANCHOR: For sixty seconds, every newscast, every radio, every satellite and cable broadcast around the world went totally silent . . . then came back on a minute later as though nothing had happened.

Coming as the event did on the exact anniversary of Captain America's death, some have said it's almost as if . . . as if the whole world offered a minute of silence on memory of Captain America—a single death that changed the future for all time.

(transcript ends)

So, you recall that rather posthumous conversation. Did you witness what he did?

Yes, albeit from an oddly detached point of view, which at the time I chalked up to Thor doing his god thing to pull me in from some ethereal plane. Boy, was I wrong about *that*.

So, let's back up a bit. Do you recall anything from the actual experience of what you thought was your death?

(*pauses, as though considering how to answer*) It's mostly a jumble. I recall moving between light and darkness. I heard Sharon's voice, pleading with me to stay with her. There was this odd rush in my ears, and then . . . nothing but utter darkness and numbing cold . . . followed by all the *other* stuff that happened next.

VII.
REBORN

There's a reasonable expectation that once someone dies, they're . . . <u>dead</u>.

For someone like Steve Rogers, who'd lived through one instance of the entire world believing he'd died during World War II only to see him emerge from suspended animation into the modern day, there was already a sense of having cheated death. This, in addition to the number of times he almost certainly was confronted by his own mortality during his military service in Europe. Thanks to those who would become his fellow Avengers, Rogers was given what he still considers the most precious gift ever bestowed upon him, that being an opportunity not just to live but to continue doing what he believed he'd always done best: serve his country.

The experience of confronting and beating back death yet again thanks to the very science that had given him his superior strength and abilities only further strengthened this conviction. Having already survived enough adventures and crises for several lifetimes, he could very well have retired to live out the remainder of his life in peace. But I knew by then that such an existence wouldn't be enough for Steve Rogers. Service to a greater calling defines him, not just as a "super hero" but as a person. Even death itself has proven ineffective at keeping him from pursuing this goal. I should not have been surprised that when it came calling once more, Steve Rogers, as always, was unwilling to yield.

INTERVIEWER: *Steve, I'd like to ask what you remember about, well . . .*

STEVE ROGERS: Coming back? Again?

That's the only way I can describe it, yeah.

I think that's the only way *to* describe it. The tough part will be putting it into words that feel accurate. I know I can't put this in scientific terms.

I won't ask you to.

Good. So, from my point of view, I knew I was experiencing . . . something. I found myself reliving moments from my life. The war, the loss of my mother, the Kree–Skrull War, that day in the lab. I was moving against my will from event to event like I was a passenger in my own body or . . . an extra consciousness in my own mind. Imagine yourself in a state that's more than a dream, and you're going through actions as you remember them, but when you try to control or even change your past actions, you can't.

I'd call that disturbing.

I would agree. So, when it came to controlling my actions, should I have? The whole thing was too big to comprehend. Who I needed was Tony or Reed, someone who could process and comprehend this and help me find my way back—if that even was possible.

You must have felt helpless.

I sure did. Like when I suddenly found myself reliving a conversation with Dr. Erskine himself. So, what the heck, I asked Dr. Erskine about the possibility of time travel. I hoped he might give me a clue toward working this out, but he offered nothing I didn't already know. A moment later, there I was aboard a Skrull ship I remembered from the Kree–Skrull War. I found Vision and had the presence of mind to make a request. I asked him to record a message from me and then to forget it, to store it deep in his memory core so it would be backed up by the Avengers' systems as part of his daily routine. I just played a hunch in case it came in handy for me or someone else sometime.

That was a really savvy gamble, Steve. How were you holding up in this swirl of memories?

I was on the edge, to be honest. For a man who can't feel fatigue, the endless skipping through time was wearing me down. And if this was the Skull's plan to torture me? It was effective. Seeing my lost and dead friends, reliving battles I'd lost rather than won. I could do nothing about it, not even shut my eyes in case that got me killed and affected our future. The deepest cut of all was each time I saw Bucky in action right beside me. I was bouncing from place to place enough that I found myself mistaking Rick Jones for Bucky, which brought my feelings of remorse for his loss flooding back. I just soldiered through the pain until I experienced one moment in which I thought help was on its way.

What relief you must have felt.

Not once did I feel relief. I found myself in the moment I had most dreaded to relive. Zemo's rocket plane was launching, and Bucky had flung himself to grab it by the tailfins. Just as I was imagining myself lunging to save him—and possibly changing the timeline—I felt myself pulled toward a specific destination. Events zipped past me at speeds that offered me the barest of glimpses. Until I arrived at a place that felt . . . entirely wrong.

Where?

New York City.

Oh, Steve. You were home.

No, I was not. I was walking through a past of a place that was not mine. The details were wrong. Car designs and clothing and then bam, it was in my face like a punch. A swastika, then dozens of them, on tops of buildings

Artist's rendering of Red Skull, as described by Steve Rogers during S.H.I.E.L.D. after-action debriefing

and on passing streetcars and zeppelins overhead. This wasn't part of my past or my future. It was the Red Skull manipulating my consciousness or maybe his. Our waking minds had merged.

And once you realized it, you fought.

Hell yes I did. I fought for my life back. What I did not know was that in my reality, the Skull was controlling my body and using it to take on Bucky. And Bucky was fighting for me as Captain America himself. And as I struggled internally, my hands around the Red Skull's neck, all I cared about was ridding the world of him forever. I told him that I was ready to give my own life if it meant taking his. I was ready for us to die together just as I'm sure he always wanted. And that was my path back.

You regained control of your mind and your body.

You'll have to get the details of the science somewhere else. I knew only that I was back and Bucky was there to see it. He knew I remained deep inside myself, just as I knew he remained inside the man codenamed Winter Soldier.

What of the Skull?

His consciousness ended up in a version of Arnim Zola's robot body that was oversized but not too big that it could handle a volley of missiles from an A.I.M. ship. That was the end of him.

Scene from Red Skull's manipulated reality, as described by Steve Rogers during S.H.I.E.L.D. after-action debriefing

Fantastic_Four_Mission_Report_
Benjamin_Grimm

Conversations_and_actions_relating__
to_the_retrieval_of_Steve_Rogers_from_the__
timestream_as_reported_by_Reed_Richards
(transcript of oral report)

I was contacted by Hank Pym to examine technology he assumed had been manufactured by Doctor Victor Von Doom in order to determine its purpose and operation. He arrived at the Baxter Building with Sharon Carter, who had brought me a pistol she claimed she had used to shoot Steve Rogers when he was killed. The weapon was capable of shooting projectiles but ones exposed to an unstable tachyon field capable of generating a time-dispersion field. Somehow, the weapon linked Sharon to this field through the act of firing the weapon, which Hank and I discovered after Sharon agreed to a full-body scan in the lab.

The scan revealed a substance similar to one I discovered in the bloodstream of Steve Rogers through autopsy files provided to me by Tony Stark. The substance related to a rapid cellular decay in Steve, and the fact that Sharon as the shooter of the weapon and Steve as the victim of the shot had a similar unidentifiable foreign substance in their blood struck me as a fascinating link.

Sharon said she believed herself to have been a pawn in a collaborative plot among Arnim Zola, Doctor Doom, and the Red Skull. She said that Zola had made reference to Sharon as a "constant" in the reaction,

which I found telling. Perhaps the established link was something they needed for their plan to retrieve Steve from the timestream to which this bullet had sent him.

At that point, I needed more than files on Steve. I traveled to the Arctic Ocean and coordinates where Steve's body secretly had been laid to rest. With assistance from Namor that I would describe as begrudging at best, I was able to examine his corpse—or at least begin an examination. Before our eyes, Namor and I witnessed Steve's remains fade away and disappear completely, but I at least had taken a temporal scan with multiplane references first.

I then traveled to Hank's lab in the Avengers Mansion. Based on what I had observed, I told Hank that I believed Steve's body existed in a plane out of synchronization with our reality, and that the markers in Sharon's blood might be the key to Steve's retrieval. As we spoke, the Vision appeared to us and said our discussion had triggered a file in his deep-storage memory banks. The file was a message recorded by Steve Rogers nearly a decade before our present time. That message confirmed the scheme. Sharon's blood markers acted as chronal-tracers to locate Steve in the timestream. The bullet may have frozen him in a single moment in time, but the links they now shared in their blood were pulling them together through time.

What we did not realize in the moment was that Doom, Zola, and the Skull had assembled in Latveria with a captive Sharon Carter. Her chronal-tracers, combined with Doom's time platform and other technological marvels, allowed him to retrieve Steve before we could.

(transcript ends)

So, there you are, back from the dead. Again.

I need one of those cards like you get at the sandwich shop. Survive death ten times and the eleventh resurrection is free.

That almost sounds like something Mr. Stark or Spider-Man might say.

I think I'm picking up bad habits from them.

How did you acclimate to being alive again, at least in the true sense rather than what you'd endured while under the Skull's control?

I didn't sleep for days after all of that. I was afraid if I closed my eyes, I might somehow slip back into that endless cycle of bouncing back and forth through time and reliving my life over and over again. That might well be the most insidious torture the Skull's ever inflicted on me, and it wasn't even something he'd planned to do. (*shakes head*) I guess I should consider myself lucky?

Thankfully you were rescued from that torment, and there was no sign you'd return to it, leaving you to contemplate your place in life rather than death. You'd been gone from this world for a year, and Mr. Barnes acquitted himself admirably in your absence while shouldering the Captain America mantle. Yet you were worried what might happen if he gave it back to you.

With the visions I'd seen of possible future events that included Bucky not wearing the Captain America uniform, I thought if I just let him hold on to it, we might somehow avoid what I'd seen.

But this wasn't the only thing factoring into your decision.

I finally put on the costume after several nights lying awake trying not to sleep, and did a little patrol of the neighborhood. I managed to come across Bucky and Natasha Romanoff dealing with Mister Hyde and some of his goons. Even without my shield—Bucky was still carrying it—I could feel some of the old juice coming back. The anticipation before a fight, that sort of thing. Bucky threw me my shield and I helped subdue Hyde. (*wry smile*) It was fun, for a minute.

And then you gave the shield back to Mr. Barnes.

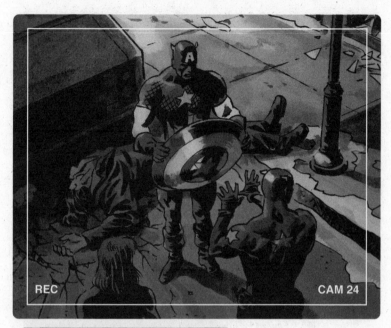

REC   CAM 24

Still taken from Brooklyn
surveillance camera

Yeah. I could tell being Captain America meant something different for him than it always had for me. My obligation has always stemmed from the belief that I was originally meant to be the first of an army of soldiers like me. I've always tried to live up to the best of what Professor Erskine envisioned: a guardian, a protector. Doing everything I could to honor a promise that was never realized is what's always driven me.

It's an obligation unique to you, to be sure.

Given all of his struggles, I wondered if Bucky holding on to the Cap identity could give him a purpose he might not otherwise have had, just as it did for me. It might also avoid the death I'd seen for him in my visions, or death through some other means I could have prevented. I knew if something like that happened, I'd never be able to live with myself.

Even if it meant possibly sacrificing the other future you'd seen: a desirable future for you and Sharon Carter.

Yes, even if it meant that. However, I figured I had more influence on how that future might play out, so to me it was worth the risk for Bucky's sake.

Plus, you also found yourself at a crossroads, unsure of what you wanted to do with the new lease on life you'd been granted.

There was certainly a lot to consider, especially after the president surprised me.

THE WHITE HOUSE
WASHINGTON, D.C.

GRANTING PARDON TO STEVEN GRANT ROGERS

BY THE PRESIDENT OF THE UNITED STATES OF AMERICA
A PROCLAMATION

NOW, THEREFORE, as President of the United States, pursuant to the pardon power conferred upon me by Article II, Section 2, of the Constitution, I have granted and by these presents do grant a full, free, and absolute pardon unto Captain America for all offenses against the United States he, Captain America, has committed or may have committed or taken part pursuant to Superhuman Registration Act.

IN WITNESS THEREOF, I have hereunto set my hand this day, in the year of our Lord two th...

SPECIAL EDITION • FR

DAILY  BUGLE

CAPTAIN AMERICA
GRANTED FULL PARDO

President: "We Owe a Debt We Can Never Repay"

So, there you are! Pardoned. A new lease on life. Your future beckoning to you.

I won't lie, it was a good feeling. I know the president was risking a hit to his reputation and maybe even damaging his reelection chances by pardoning me.

All things considered, it was a safe bet. You were still Captain America, after all, and many of those who doubted you during the Civil War eventually remembered why they liked, supported, and respected you. Meanwhile, you told the president you weren't sure you could continue to be Captain America. Then you told him if he ever needed you or asked you to pick up your shield, you'd be there.

(*sighs*) What can I say? I'm a soldier. It's all I've ever been. I answer the call when it comes.

As it happens, it didn't take very long for that call to come, after all.

Funny how that works, right? I was still figuring out what I wanted to do now that I had yet another new lease on life. Part of that process was getting up to speed on everything that had happened during the year since my supposed death. I missed the entire secret Skrull invasion, for one thing.

Being disembodied and unstuck in time would seem to have its advantages.

Sure. I guess. What I also missed was S.H.I.E.L.D. being shuttered and Norman Osborn—of all people—being named the head of a new agency responsible for the same mission.

Given the turmoil we'd recently endured, there were those who considered him an unconventional choice and yet still the right person for that job at that point.

You don't put a pyromaniac in charge of the matches and gasoline. And of course he creates a group called "H.A.M.M.E.R." A tool that can also serve as a weapon, as opposed to a shield, which symbolizes defense and protection. Osborn's a lot of things, but subtle isn't one of them. And while I get how S.H.I.E.L.D. changes the words in its name more often than Stark upgrades his armor, what does H.A.M.M.E.R. even stand for, anyway?

No one seems to know for sure. Rumors suggest no one ever bothered to spell it all out.

That didn't keep him from getting on with his agenda. I know Stark went round and round with him when Osborn tried to get the Superhuman Registration Database. Stark even went so far as to erase it off all

H.A.M.M.E.R. computers and data archives, because he knew Osborn'd abuse the power that gave him. We may have disagreed on a lot about the Registration Act, but Stark's keeping that information from being so easily accessible was the right thing to do, and Osborn wasted no time demonstrating it was *absolutely* the right thing to do.

He created a list of things he wanted to accomplish.

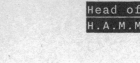

STRATEGIC HAZARD INTERVENTION ESPIONAGE LOGISTICS DIRECTORATE

TOP SECRET—EYES ONLY

FROM: Fury, Nicholas J.
TO: Distribution List Alpha Omega 3955-P
SUBJECT: Osborn, Norman

This clown.
    It's not my job to question the decisions of the president of the United States—at least, not publicly—but it's my considered opinion that appointing Norman Osborn to anything more demanding than cleaning up after the president's dogs is asking for trouble.
    You've probably heard the report that I visited Osborn at Avengers Tower. It's no secret that we've never liked each other and my going to him did nothing to alter that status quo. He was thoughtful enough to provide me with a list of things he wanted to accomplish while he was in charge of H.A.M.M.E.R. I'll let you decide if these are action items with which we should be concerned:

        Neutralize Clint Barton
        Eliminate Daredevil
        Kill Namor
        Kill Frank Castle
        Kill Nick Fury
        Neutralize Bruce Banner
        Control the World
        Kill Spider-Man

    First, let me say I don't think Spider-Man's going to appreciate being considered something of an afterthought following Osborn's dream of seizing control of the entire planet. Also, and if we're being honest, if he's got a way to control Banner and the Hulk, then I'm all ears because that might actually be something that could come in handy now and then. As for Castle, that's its own headache I'm not ready to deal with, but if it's a matchup between him and Osborn, I know where I'm putting my chips. I'm not even going to get too excited about my own name being on his To-Do List. I've already made my feelings known directly to Osborn with a list of my own (see attached).

    I'm offering this information so that we can begin planning what we're going to do to rein in this situation before it spirals out of control. I've got my own thoughts, and I figure at least some of you do as well. Let's get cracking on this.

                                                —Fury

—SAVE THE WORLD

—PUNCH NORMAN IN THE FACE

—HAVE A BEER

Fury told me about it, along with his own version. (*laughs*) Though Osborn tried to suppress it, his Green Goblin persona was reasserting itself. His agenda had nothing to do with protecting the country and instead served his own interests. Or, just the Goblin's. It's hard to know where one personality ends and the other begins. Anyway, even the president had his reservations about Osborn, which were realized when Osborn engineered an attack against Volstagg at Soldier Field.

Mr. Osborn believed the presence of Asgard, having been relocated to Broxton, Oklahoma, here on Earth, presented a threat to national security.

Whether that was him or the Goblin talking is really immaterial. Asgard wasn't a threat. If they wanted to harm us, they didn't need to set up camp here first. Thor's a god, remember?

I didn't say it made sense.

LIVE FROM ASGARD

BROXTON UNDER FIRE, THOR IN BATTLE.

LAUFEYSON, LOKI
KNOWN ALIASES/ALTER EGOS:
God of Mischief

Schemes like this never do, except maybe to the twisted mind that concocts them. Osborn had his excuse to turn H.A.M.M.E.R. on Asgard. Ordinarily, and even with him in his "Iron Patriot" armor along with the superhumans—including the Sentry, Bob Reynolds—and other weapons at his disposal, he wouldn't have stood a chance, but he had an ace up his sleeve.

Loki.

Yeah. It was Loki's idea to go after Asgard, and to do it on live TV. Thanks to Loki's help, Osborn actually beat Thor at first. That was when I decided I'd had enough. I went to the Avengers hideaway and assembled a team to go with me. Fury, Luke Cage, Spider-Man,

Spider-Woman, Clint Barton, Carol Danvers, and more. Maria Hill and others were already fighting to take back our country before it fell under Osborn's thumb, and we were going to help them or die trying.

According to transcripts I read of the meeting taking place during all of this, the president decided Osborn and H.A.M.M.E.R. had declared war not only on Asgard, but also the United States.

(*nods*) That gave me, Fury, and our merry band all the backing we needed to take this thing to the end zone. While we battled Osborn and his Dark Avengers, the president sent the military after the H.A.M.M.E.R. Helicarrier. Then Stark showed up in time to corrupt the software controlling Osborn's Iron Patriot armor.

Mr. Stark has always enjoyed the dramatic entrance, while being fashionably late.

Unfortunately, none of this was fast enough to prevent Osborn from ordering the Sentry to do his damnedest.

The city was leveled. Hundreds of Asgardians killed. The Sentry— Bob—had actually been bonded to an entity known as the Void. Osborn convinced the Void to help him, which was how Bob was able to beat Thor. Even with all this help, we were winning and Osborn was broken.

THE DESTRUCTION OF ASGARD OVER BROXTON, OKLAHOMA, AS CAPTURED BY A LOCAL NEWS AFFILIATE

NORMAN OSBORN REVEALED ONCE AGAIN AS THE NOTORIOUS GREEN GOBLIN, AS CAPTURED BY A LOCAL NEWS AFFILIATE

I tried to arrest him, but when he came out of his armor, we saw—as did everyone watching on TV—that he'd painted his face green. The Goblin had reasserted control over him, and in turn had unleashed the Void upon all of us.

A literal force of nature. Unstoppable. Unkillable.

Just another day at the office for the Avengers. We had a little help, though, in the form of Loki finally pulling his head from—

Language, Mr. Rogers.

I was going to say, "the clouds."

Okay.

Anyway, with Loki's godlike help, we were able to punch back at the Void when the fighting started again. Then Stark got creative, hacking the H.A.M.M.E.R. Helicarrier's computer and remote-piloting it to Broxton and pretty much into the Void's face. That was enough to light up the whole area, force the Void into submission for a few minutes, and let Bob reassert himself in his own body.

I suspect the trauma of the Void usurping him in that manner had to be severe.

Bob wanted us to kill him. We knew none of this was his fault, but the Void didn't give us a choice when it resurfaced within him. Thor knew he had no choice, so he brought down one of those massive thunderbolts of his, killing Bob, the Sentry, and the Void. Just to be sure, Thor flew the remains into space and threw them into the sun.

That seems a rather definitive fate.

You should know better than that, by now.

This situation was enough to make you don the Captain America mantle once more, but instead of keeping it, you gave it back to Mr. Barnes.

The world had changed while I was . . . away. It still needed Captain America, but one for this new era in which we found ourselves. To me, in that moment? It had to be Bucky.

Besides, it seems fate had other plans for you. The president did say he might call on you at some point.

And I promised him I'd answer if he did.

I'd say he had quite the assignment for you.

THE WHITE HOUSE

WASHINGTON, D.C.

EXECUTIVE ORDER

By virtue of the authority vested in me as President of the United States, by the Constitution and the statutes of the United States, and as Commander-in-Chief of the armed services:

1. I hereby order the deactivation of the law enforcement entity known as H.A.M.M.E.R. along with all attendant entities. Norman Osborn, H.A.M.M.E.R. Director, is immediately relieved of all duties and security clearances pertaining to his role.

2. All personnel currently attached to these organizations are to stand down from their assigned duties and await further instructions from appropriate higher authority.

3. In tandem with this stand-down, I further authorize the appointment of Captain Steve Rogers to serve as the head of our national security, reporting directly to the Secretary of Homeland Security. Captain Rogers will oversee the mission and mandate of defending the United States against threats within our own borders, abroad, and beyond.

4. I direct Captain Rogers to personally oversee the remanding of Norman Osborn and others charged under the Insurrection Act to the Ryker's Island Maximum Security Installation codenamed "the Raft," where they will await trial.

5. I further request the United States Congress to pass with all due haste legislation directing the immediate repeal of the Superhuman Registration Act.

We were at something of a turning point. Even with everything that had happened with the Asgardians, our actions in defense of Broxton went a long way toward healing those wounds. Thor declared his people allied with the people of Earth, now and forever, and he pledged to stand with the Avengers if we ever needed him.

Which, of course, you would.

Again, it's just another day in the Avengers.

And you certainly had your own new work cut out for you, didn't you?

There's the understatement again. I'd been missing that.

VIII.
REDEMPTIONS

Over the course of our various conversations, Steve
Rogers and I have discussed at length several of
his more bizarre experiences since first taking
up the Captain America mantle at the height of the
Second World War. It should come as no surprise
that one of the things he least expected to
endure was his own death--or supposed death, or an
existence that felt in many ways like death . . .
or at least exile from whatever realm might harbor
"life" as we understand it. No less surprising
have been the occasions when he has returned from
such outlandish events so that he can continue the
mission he has always pursued: guarding America--
and, by extension, Earth--from any and all enemies
and threats. While his experiences have often
made him reconsider and even reject the Captain
America identity, those doubts are fleeting, for
deep within him still beats the heart of a soldier
and protector.

   Sometimes, such fantastic occurrences surround
only him. Other times, they've involved everyone
and everything. How does a man, born in an age
where space travel and even time travel were mere
flights of fantasy, then thrust forward into a
reality where such things are not only everyday
occurrences but indeed a common aspect of his job,
deal with the peculiar reality his life has become?

INTERVIEWER: *Let's talk about you living for more than a decade in another dimension.*

STEVE ROGERS: Your ability to summarize the most bizarre things that keep happening to me is pretty astounding.

It's a gift born of experience.

I'll be sure to let Stark know you haven't lost your touch. (*pauses*) You have to understand that most of what I've seen and experienced just since coming out of the ice are things not even the science fiction stories I remember reading as a kid touched on. My initial reaction to a lot of this is utter disbelief. Even after all this time, there are occasions that catch me flat-footed and I have to struggle to adapt to the situation.

Like Dimension Z.

Do you have twelve years to talk about this?

We'll try to rein things in a bit.

(*pauses, and I know we're about to wade into uncomfortable territory*) It started on my birthday. My ninetieth birthday, for those keeping score at home. After dealing with the eco-terrorist Green Skull I met up with Sharon Carter. S.H.I.E.L.D. had gotten word about a subway train that had been detected traversing a stretch of subway line abandoned for eighty years. There was no information on where the line went, or who might be controlling the car, which just seemed to be making this circuit of unused track for no apparent reason.

And word was getting out to the local populace, who of course began showing up to see what the fuss was about.

TAKE THE SUBWAY TO NOWHERE

Right. Natural curiosity. A little bit of weirdness in an otherwise dull day that gets people interested enough to come look for themselves. For people in my line of work, that usually means it's a trap of some kind, even though the train had been running for days without incident.

S.H.I.E.L.D. was monitoring all of this activity.

Yes, keeping eyes on the situation and watching how things played out. They were worried about possible threats against the city's infrastructure, including the subway system, so Sharon and I were tasked to investigate it firsthand. When we got there, the S.H.I.E.L.D. security officers on duty told us there was room for only one more passenger, so I told Sharon I'd go first. I get aboard, and the next thing I know, shackles lock me to one of the support bars and the train takes off.

Agent Carter described it as an abrupt acceleration, very much unlike a train's normal operation.

I hear the sonic boom as we break the sound barrier. And I'm still processing this just as everything disappears in a blinding white light. When my vision clears, I find myself staring at these weird creatures pointing weapons at me just before I feel a sting at the back of my neck and everything goes dark. When I wake up again, I hear a voice welcoming me to "Dimension Z." I'm strapped to some kind of surgical table, and there's this machine siphoning blood from my arm.

The voice. You knew who it belonged to.

Arnim Zola. A name I hadn't heard in a while. A name I could've gone a lot longer without hearing again.

You eventually learned he had assisted the Red Skull in brainwashing Agent Carter with your supposed assassination, and everything that came afterward.

He's been a pain in my neck and other body parts dating back to the 1940s. He somehow found his way into this alternate dimension, where time seems to move at a different pace than it does here on Earth. Or, in our universe. (*sighs, shakes head*) I'm hopeless with that kind of thing. Ask Stark or Reed Richards about how it's all supposed to work.

Zola wanted to study the Super-Soldier Serum in your blood and

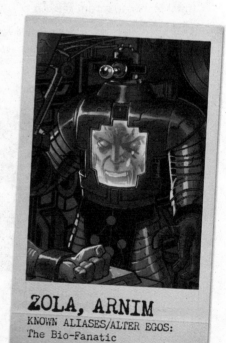

ZOLA, ARNIM
KNOWN ALIASES/ALTER EGOS:
The Bio-Fanatic

find a way to re-create it so he could build an army of creatures he was genetically engineering.

There was this baby, floating in a large vat. He was the first thing I saw when I woke up. Then this huge mechanical gadget stabs me in the chest. I didn't realize it at the time, but it injected me with something.

I managed to fight my way out of there, rescuing the child from that vat on my way out. After commandeering a jet, I tried to make a run for it, thinking if I could fly it fast enough I might be able to reverse the process that brought me here and escape Dimension Z, but we were shot down not long after we got clear of the city.

Zolandia. Apparently, the only actual city within Dimension Z.

So far as I ever figured out, anyway. I spent a year hiding in the desert, evading patrols and other attempts by Zola's mutants—he called them "mutates"—to find me while taking care of this boy I'd rescued. I only found out later he was Zola's son, genetically engineered after years of failed attempts. Zola apparently thought I'd killed him during my escape, so he sent everything he had to hunt me down.

You named him Ian.

I had to name him something. I couldn't just keep calling him "Boy" all the time.

So there you are, trapped in an alternate dimension, trying to stay alive and evade capture, and you're raising a child.

Crazy, right? I'd never given much thought to having kids of my own. Sharon and I had talked about marriage, and of course I had a stray thought about kids, but I was in no way prepared to be a father. In what I'm guessing was a consequence of his genetic engineering, Ian seemed to grow a bit faster than a normal human, which helped with things in the early going. After a year, he looked more like he was three or four years old; not far from the same age I was when I went through my own version of hard times as a kid in Manhattan. I spent many nights during that first year recalling memories like that.

What specific memories did you keep in mind?

I wasn't trying for specifics but for moods, I suppose. How good I felt when my mother could take a break from work, or playing in the neighborhood with Arnie, or when Papa—that was my mother's father—reminded me of the good man my father was before he died. Well, before he lost hope and then died.

I'm sorry, Steve. You're saying all of these are memories you wanted to recall?

Thinking of my youth reminds me of why you have to keep getting back up even when life keeps knocking you down. The same was true now that I was caring for Ian. I knew I had to keep going, keep searching for a way out of there and back home even as we fought or ran from every sort of threat Dimension Z could throw at us.

To include leading a rebellion against Zola.

We struck up a relationship with the Phrox, a group who stood against him. Of course, they tried to behead me at first, thinking I *was* Zola, but we got past that. It wasn't easy either. Remember when I said I was stabbed in the chest in Zola's lab? Turns out as part of his experiments on me, he'd inserted an implant, which in turn delivered a virus that let his consciousness manifest itself inside me. It also explained why I'd been suffering migraines nearly every day since my escape.

You spent more than a decade hiding from Zola and his mutates.

Artist's rendering of Ian Rogers, subjective age approximately 11 years (Dimension Z time), as described by Steve Rogers during S.H.I.E.L.D. after-action debriefing

Ian's rapid aging seemed to slow as he grew through his preteens. He was very smart for his age, and an extremely quick learner. In a lot of ways, he reminded me of Bucky, or what Bucky might've been like if I'd met him at that same age. He saved my life more than once. After he killed a mutate that had the drop on me, we checked its equipment and found a map to Zolandia that included the location of a tunnel which could take us out of Dimension Z and back home.

And all this time, Zola's virus is waging war inside you.

It was winning too. I knew I couldn't fight it off for much longer. He was going to end up controlling me, but now we had a way out. I could get home, find a way to treat Zola's virus, and bring back the Avengers so we could help lead the Phrox against Zola.

But then Zola ordered the Phrox be massacred. I couldn't just leave and allow that to happen, so we took the fight to Zolandia.

It was during all of this that you found an unexpected ally.

Ian's genetically engineered sister. Jet had grown up thinking Ian was dead and that I'd killed him. It took some doing, but I was finally able to convince her I wasn't her enemy. Of course, Zola managed to brainwash Ian to turn against me.

A sort of "one step forward, two steps back" situation.

Nobody ever said this job would be easy.

Zola ordered Jet to kill you once he realized his son was still alive, but she refused.

Yeah, he was pretty mad about that and launched me off a cliff. I don't mind saying that hurt. A *lot*.

He was in your head thanks to the implant, taunting you and trying to get you to give up the fight.

I don't give up fights. I might question why I should be fighting, but if it's something I believe in, then I never give up. My father gave up. When life was throwing everything at him that it could find, he made a choice not to fight for what was right, but instead took out his anger and feelings of helplessness on my mother and me. Deep down, I know he was a good man or at least wanted to be, but life had crushed his spirit. He just gave up. I vowed I'd never let that happen so long as I had the will to resist it.

Fate was very unkind to your father. One wonders how he might have thrived had he been born into a more forgiving era.

I've wondered that myself. I also know that despite everything, if not for my childhood experiences and the decisions I made as a consequence of watching him deteriorate, I wouldn't be the man I became.

Even before Professor Erskine and his serum.

Artist's rendering of Jet Black,
as described by Steve Rogers during
S.H.I.E.L.D. after-action debriefing

I'd like to think so.

The professor just made sure your body was as strong as your convictions.

That's a nice of way of putting it. If not for him, I certainly wouldn't have the strength for this fight. Even then, I knew if I was going to win, I needed to get Zola out of my head, so I cut the implant out of my chest. Yes, that *also* hurt a lot, but I was ready to do whatever it took to rescue my so—Ian. My *son*, Ian. I wasn't going to abandon him or let him down the way my father did with me.

You haven't yet mentioned Captain Zolandia.

No. I was hoping you'd forgotten about him. Them, really.

Artist's rendering of a Captain Zolandia clone, as described by Steve Rogers during S.H.I.E.L.D. after-action debriefing

Arnim Zola created clones of you, but used gamma rays to give them their super strength.

Right. And even though there are more than one of them, they share the same mental imprint—mine—that Zola gave the first one. They're all the same, personality-wise, and they share the memories of previous clones.

Including memories of their predecessors' deaths.

Talk about carrying around excess baggage, and before you ask . . . yes. Each one was incredibly strong, capable of standing toe to toe with me. I learned that the hard way when I fought the first one. I beat him, but it wasn't easy. Not by a long shot. Figures Zola would have others waiting in the wings.

You fight your way back to Zolandia, and encounter Jet Black again.

It's worth noting this is our second meeting where I don't kill her, even though I had her dead to rights. She found it odd that I'd spare her once, let alone twice, but I couldn't find Ian without her.

Somewhere in the midst of all this, you learn that the massive tower at the heart of Zolandia is actually a ship Zola has built to take his army of mutates on a mission to conquer Earth.

It's always something.

According to Jet, there was no way to stop the ship from heading to Earth. The only other option I saw was beating it back there in time to warn the Avengers—whatever an Avengers team might look like after twelve years—so they could be ready for it.

And you still needed to rescue Ian from Zola.

Jet agreed to help me, so long as I promised to take Ian from Dimension Z and away from their father. Unfortunately, I was too late. Zola had already brainwashed him, to the point he shot me in the back.

And then proceeded to beat you to within an inch of your life, according to your S.H.I.E.L.D. debriefing.

He was too far gone. Warped by Zola's conditioning. He couldn't hear me, wouldn't listen to me. I thought if I could get away from him, I could find a way to reverse what Zola had done to him. Then, as I was lying on the floor, beaten and losing blood from my various wounds, and he stood over me, gun in hand, I started to break the wall. I got through to him. He rejected the name Zola had given him and told me his name was Ian, my son. He called me Dad, and in that moment I started to feel my strength returning. Even with all my injuries, I could finish this mission. Then, things went sideways when Sharon showed up.

Agent Carter had found a way into Dimension Z, searching for you. Seeing her must have been quite the shock.

Sharon saw Ian standing over me and shot him. I can't blame her now, of course, but in that moment? My heart broke. Completely. She was adamant everything I'd experienced here for twelve years was just one of Zola's mind games, but I couldn't believe it.

Your S.H.I.E.L.D. debriefing transcript says she told you only thirty minutes had passed since your disappearance in the subway.

She looked exactly as I remembered her, and to her I obviously looked a mess. Thankfully, she was in control, warning me she'd rigged Zolandia with explosives to prevent Zola's attack force from reaching Earth. We just had to be gone before that happened, but I couldn't leave without Jet. I'd already failed Ian, so I wasn't leaving without her. By now, she'd turned on

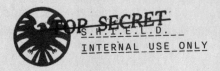

INTERNAL USE ONLY

From: Kincaid, K.
To: Avengers, Distribution List 63-M-384
Subj: Medical Evaluation of Rogers, Steven G.

I'm sure you all were as surprised as I was to hear
Captain Rogers' account during his debriefing of
what he experienced while trapped in "Dimension
Z." While I naturally felt at the outset that his
claims were outlandish, after conducting a thorough
examination, I find his story to be very credible.
    Blood work, including toxicology to isolate
chemicals present in his system that are not native
to our planet, as well as physical changes to his
body—teeth, eyes, healed scar tissue and indications
of other injuries sustained months or even years
earlier, calcium deficiency and other indications
of inadequate nutrition—along with other compelling
factors indicate Captain Rogers did in fact spend an
extended time in the other dimension, while a period
of less than one hour apparently elapsed in our
reality, assuming Dimension Z even exists on Earth
in any reality. From a medical standpoint, his body
simply doesn't lie.
    While he is physically healing as we have come
to expect from him after he has previously sustained
injuries, I believe the events he experienced in
the other dimension will continue to weigh on him
emotionally and psychologically for quite some time.
Even with the resilience he has demonstrated on
occasions far too numerous to count, I believe he
would benefit from evaluation by a licensed mental
health professional who can guide him through that
process.

Zola and was fighting him. I finished him. (*shakes head*) At least, I thought I did. We know how these things really go by now, but he was a bastard until the very end . . . and even then, of course it wasn't the end with him. Sharon sacrificed herself so that Jet and I could escape back to our world, blowing Zolandia and closing the portal to Dimension Z.

You believed she was dead.

Along with Ian. (*pauses*) Yes.

INTERVIEWER'S NOTE: Captain Rogers abruptly ended our conversation at this point. Even with the knowledge of what eventually became of Ian and Agent Carter, he admitted that recalling these specific events had proven more difficult than he anticipated. He later told me the burden of having lived for so long separated from everyone and everything he knew, only to come home and discover that no time had passed for those people, was difficult to process. Soldiers who are sent to war for months or even years at a time anticipate their homecoming—that easing of shared emotions consumed by a lengthy, worrisome separation. Steve Rogers, despite all he's given to the country he loves, has never received such a welcome in the traditional sense. Though he says it didn't bother him in that way, I suspect he's continuing to keep those feelings to himself.

We've discussed other occasions when you confronted the loss of your superhuman abilities for one reason or another. In those other instances, your strength was neutralized, or it actually turned against you and caused you to deteriorate. One particularly challenging instance came with the added difficulty of subjecting you to rapid aging.

Ran Shen. Former S.H.I.E.L.D. agent turned national security threat. After disappearing off our radar screens for several years, during which he encountered a Malakulan.

An extraterrestrial being whose species resembles dragons that walk upright.

Or some such thing. This alien transformed him to be more like them, and gave him impressive abilities, but that process must have also corrupted his mind, because when he emerged onto

SHEN, RAN
KNOWN ALIASES/ALTER EGOS:
Iron Nail

the global stage, he was calling himself "the Iron Nail" and his entire existence seemed focused on triggering a new world war. He commandeered Gungnir, a special Helicarrier built by S.H.I.E.L.D. that could transform into a giant robot, and planned to use it as a weapon to achieve this goal, so Sam Wilson and I were sent to stop him, even if that meant destroying Gungnir.

You fought him, and he used his newfound powers to fulfill his desire to break you.

(*nods*) Yes. He changed into this hideous monster with tendrils bursting from his chest. As I tried to sabotage Gungnir's core reactor, he stabbed me in the chest with those tendrils. The immediate effect was that it drained the Super-Soldier Serum from my blood.

It also aged you in rapid fashion, to the point where your body now reflected your chronological age as if you'd never been suspended in the ice.

I was every day of ninety years old, plus some. We accomplished our mission and stopped Ran, and Sam got me out of there, but . . . yeah. I was left an old man.

We probably don't need to dwell too much on the effects you endured, as we know your youth and abilities eventually were restored. I'd rather discuss what this meant so far as Sam Wilson and the Captain America legacy.

Even though I was still in decent shape, better than any normal ninety-year-old man had any right to hope for, I obviously couldn't carry on being Captain America. Someone had to take on that duty as I moved into a leadership and advisory role, and Sam was the perfect man for the job.

Is it a betrayal to say I thought his update of your uniform was pretty snappy?

Of course it was. He had the right build to pull it off. More importantly, he'd already distinguished himself as completely capable more times than I could count. Defeating Zola when he finally showed up with his mutates to attack New York City was just the latest in a long string of valiant actions.

Like Mr. Barnes before him, Mr. Wilson took the role and made it his own while still honoring Captain America's decades-long legacy.

Absolutely, and that's what I love about him. We both grew up poor, but his experiences living in Harlem were much different than mine, even in Depression-era Manhattan. He'd endured hardships I'll never know or fully grasp, and he knew he wanted to use the opportunity he'd been given to help those society tends to overlook. I was made to be a soldier to fight a world war. Sam had experience with street-level issues, and that's where he wanted to have the most impact, getting involved in the struggles of everyday people and doing what he could to make their lives better. How can you not respect that?

And yet, it earned him some derision. Not everyone seemed able to accept him in the role.

(*shakes head*) Ignorant people. What can be more American than helping your fellow American? Selfishness, indifference, greed . . . these weren't the values instilled in me during my childhood. They aren't qualities to be admired, and they aren't values I swore any oath to defend. So far as I'm concerned, Sam embodied everything it meant to be not just Captain America, but the best parts of America itself.

And you also comported yourself well, acclimating to your new chosen role of overseeing the Avengers and their missions.

I hated it. I did my best as a commanding officer and leader, but all of that felt like an officer's job and I never wanted to be one of those. I always

wanted to be in the field. Deep down, I'll always be a simple soldier. I go where I'm pointed, and do what I'm told.

I suppose we're fortunate you were eventually able to return to the fold, so to speak.

(*pauses*) Yeah. I wish I could say we all lived happily ever after, but we know that's not true. Sam and I had our differences while he was Captain America, and even though we got past them after I was rejuvenated, in hindsight I think it was a mistake for us both to be a version of Cap. If I had it to do over again, I'd have stayed back at Avengers Mansion, running the show from the command center, and continuing to supporting Sam any way I could. Like Bucky before him and even like me when I had my doubts about it, Sam decided to hang up the Captain America identity and go back to being his own man.

Before that happened, there was that other thing we should probably talk about.

You mean the end of everything.

That's the one.

I hope you're not going to ask me about the science of it all.

We have Mr. Stark and Dr. Richards for that part of it. Despite your status, you have more in common with the average person who faced what happened.

Struck numb? Struck dumb? Being told you're going to die is one thing. Doctors tell patients that every day. Being told your family, your country, your world, and indeed your entire universe is going to die? That takes time to process. After you come to terms with the enormity of it all and perhaps find some measure of acceptance, there's still nothing you can do about it.

But, as Dr. Richards explained to you and other members of the Illuminati, he believed there was a way to avoid this disastrous fate.

Yes, Dr. Richards explained the entire Multiverse concept in a way even I could understand.

Our universe exists along with uncounted other universes within a Multiverse. Uncounted Multiverses exist within a single Omniverse.

"LIFE AND DEATH.

"THE BIRTH AND HEAT DEATH OF EVERYTHING LIE AT OPPOSITE ENDS ON THE TIMELINE OF THE UNIVERSE.

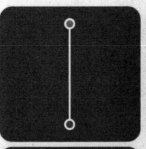

"THE BEGINNING AND END OF OUR EARTH ALSO EXISTS ON THIS TIMELINE AND, OF COURSE, FALLS WITHIN THESE TWO END POINTS.

"OUR WORLD WAS BORN AFTER THE UNIVERSE'S CREATION, AND OUR WORLD WILL DIE BEFORE THE UNIVERSE ENDS.

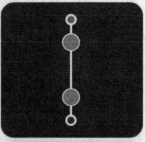

"WE ALSO KNOW THERE IS A MULTIVERSE OF REALITIES, AN INFINITE NUMBER OF EARTHS, INSIDE AN INFINITE NUMBER OF UNIVERSES, WHERE ANY MANNER OF DIVERGENT REALITY CAN EXIST.

"ENDLESS POSSIBILITIES...

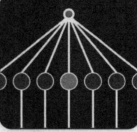

"HOWEVER, AS I MENTIONED EARLIER... EVERYTHING DIES.

"SO, REGARDLESS OF HOW MANY REALITIES THERE ARE, EVENTUALLY THEY ALL END UP IN THE SAME PLACE AND IN THE SAME STATE, EXTINGUISHED AT THE END OF EVERYTHING.

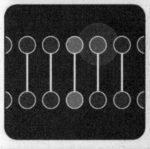

"AND HERE'S WHERE OUR PROBLEM LIES.

"I'VE LEARNED THAT SOMEWHERE, ON ONE OF THESE EARTHS, AN EVENT OCCURRED THAT CAUSED THE EARLY DEATH OF ONE OF THESE UNIVERSES.

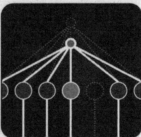

"THAT UNTIMELY, UNNATURAL EVENT THEN CAUSED A TINY CONTRACTION IN THE MULTIVERSE'S TIMELINE.

"NOW, EVERYTHING WOULD DIE EVER-SO-SLIGHTLY SOONER.

"IN ADDITION, THAT TINY CONTRACTION CAUSED TWO UNIVERSES TO SMASH TOGETHER AT THE INCURSION POINT OF THE INITIAL EVENT.

"AND THIS IS WHERE YOU REALLY WANT TO PAY ATTENTION... THAT POINT WAS EARTH.

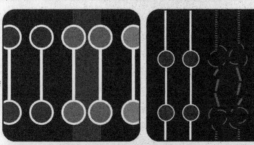

"THEY TOUCHED, AND DESTROYED EACH OTHER-- TAKING THEIR UNIVERSES WITH THEM--CAUSING YET ANOTHER CONTRACTION IN THE TIMELINE.

"WHICH IN TURN ACCELERATED THE SMASHING TOGETHER OF EVEN MORE EARTHS AND THEIR RESPECTIVE UNIVERSES."

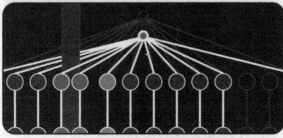

The Multiverse, as explained by
Dr. Reed Richards to the Illuminati

Right, and if there's anything beyond that, we don't yet know about it. What we do know is that all universes die, eventually, as do all multiverses. Multiverses contract, pushing their respective universes inward until they collide with one another. For whatever reason, these collisions—Reed called them "incursions"—begin with Earth as the focal point in each universe. When an incursion happens . . .

. . . the two Earths collide, their respective universes are destroyed, and the Multiverse contracts yet again.

Rinse, and repeat, until it collapses in on itself and—in theory, at least— gives birth to new universes within a new Multiverse. (*holds up hand*) And that's the extent of my scientific grasp of that concept. Reed told us the problem we faced was that something happened to cause the premature death of another universe, and the resulting contraction accelerated the rest of the Multiverse's decay, setting off a chain reaction. We now faced a likely incursion between our universe and another universe.

I've read about this several times now, studied everything Reed and other leading scientists have shared, and I still have trouble wrapping my head around the enormity of it all.

The part I remember sticking with me was when he, along with Tony Stark, T'Challa, and other Illuminati members, started talking about finding a way to destroy some other universe's Earth in order to save ours. It was "the only thing we could do," for "the right reasons," because it's "the lesser of two evils." I couldn't convince them to try to find some other way—*any other way*—to avoid doing that, and there was no way they'd ever convince me to do what they were contemplating.

So, they removed you from the equation.

Dr. Strange cast a spell to wipe my mind. I remembered nothing about the Illuminati, or the pending cataclysm, or any plans to stop it.

But the mind-wipe didn't take.

No. I eventually remembered the Illuminati and the meeting, and what they planned to do. I decided to use the Avengers to find and stop them, but in the midst of all that, Tony convinced me they were working to save our Earth without sacrificing one from another universe.

That wasn't true, though.

(*shakes head*) No. Universes were dying, the Multiverse was contracting, and then there were only two, ours and one with as much right to exist as ours did, as all the others had before they were destroyed. We never stood a chance. Tony knew it, knew there was no stopping it, but he convinced everyone they might be able to find a way.

Dr. Richards knew this as well. At least, he suspected, and being the pragmatist he is, he was making his own preparations.

He built a spaceship, a sort of life raft he was counting on to withstand the final incursion while carrying a group of scientists, superhumans, and other individuals who could make a try at somehow restarting the human race in some other universe or even Multiverse. He was convinced Tony should go, but I wouldn't allow it. I'd felt betrayed by him, not just personally but on behalf of everyone he'd lied to about all of this. I wasn't going to let him get on some boat to avoid the doom our entire universe was facing.

With just the two universes remaining, superhumans and other forces from the other Earth were fighting in what amounted to a useless battle from which there could emerge no winners.

And that's when I found Tony. He was at his Resurrection Building in Manhattan. I wanted to hear him admit he'd lied to me, to all of us, about everything. He knew we couldn't stop what was coming, but he had to try and if he had it to do again, he'd have made the same choice. (*pauses*) In his own way, he was more like me in that regard than I ever gave him credit for. He kept standing up, kept fighting, kept looking for a way to win against all odds. I was too angry to fully appreciate that at the time.

And then it was all over.

Doomsday. Everyone died. Everything was gone. Entropy. Two universes, crushed to dust. Armageddon.

And then, some eight years later—

Reed Richards and his group survived in their life raft and he figured out how to put everything back where it was. Mostly.

I don't know that I'll ever be able to wrap my mind around that.

Scene from Doomsday, as described
by Steve Rogers during S.H.I.E.L.D.
after-action debriefing

You should probably have a sit-down with Reed. You could fill a whole book just with this.

I'll put it on my list of things to do. In the meantime, we have other matters to discuss.

A World Returned

The Hydra Supreme and Captain America clash on the grounds of the U.S. Capitol building after the appearance of Kobik and the restoration of order around the globe through her sentient cosmic energy.

I'm going to be a big disappointment to you here. I've got next to nothing about this.

That's not true.

It is. I've been honest with everyone who's asked. That wasn't me. I wasn't here.

I do understand that part, Steve. But what you have is unique insight on two individuals. I'd like to ask you about them.

Okay. Who's first?

Kobik.

A child. She was and is learning about her world, which encompasses far more than our world, and she was abusively misguided about ours by the Red Skull. Kobik believed that the way of Hydra was the way of a perfect world. When I met Kobik at a bowling alley in Pleasant Hill, I tried to talk her into pretending she didn't have her cosmic powers and that she should run and hide like a little girl. That seemed like a great start until Crossbones showed up and beat me within an inch of my life. Remember, Kobik basically wished me into this existence. She didn't account for the Super-Soldier Serum, so I didn't have its properties. This version of me couldn't put up the fight I used to. Just when I thought I'd take the final blow of my life, Kobik appeared and said she could make a hero out of me again. And she did, sort of.

Able to explain?

Not really. I found myself young again, or at least up to my strength again. I thought I was alone. I knew I was lost, trying to get home. And as I was roaming in a forest, I thought I saw . . . someone I knew. That person vanished and I found Kobik perched on a rock. She was crying, saying she was sorry and that she just wanted to make everything better, a place where people could be happy. I suppose I *was* happy. I knew nothing about myself or my life but it didn't seem to matter until she reminded me.

Reminded you of what?

That I was a soldier for a cause I believed in. That there was a battle in this place of her making within the Cosmic Cube that was Kobik, and I was about to die—and then I was . . . someplace else. And there were others with me, people I knew, who reminded me of my past life. People I fought alongside and people I fought against. People I loved. I still didn't under-stand precisely where I was. I thought I was in my mind but then I realized I was in Kobik's. She gave me a glimpse of what was happening in the real world, of what kind of Steve Rogers she had created. She thought she had done the best thing for all of us but she was wrong.

Horribly wrong. She created a world in which Hydra controlled our nation, our lives. And at the top of the chain of command was a Supreme Hydra we all believed was you.

Hydra recruitment poster

Never me. Not ever me. Kobik created a version of Steve Rogers she believed would create a perfect world. I knew all along she had the power to reset this world and return me to my proper place in the cosmos, to right everything, but she was too scared of what she had created. I told her hiding was wrong and it wouldn't work. I explained there is nowhere that someone can run and hide from fascism. All we can do is stand and fight, and we don't have to fight alone. With that, Bucky somehow arrived with a shred of the Cosmic Cube and led us out. First Kobik, and then me.

Bucky Barnes?

Bucky gathered Sam and Scott Lang and Tony. The only leverage they had on the Supreme Hydra was his desire for the last shard of the Cosmic Cube he had assembled in his uniform. He wanted it. He expected to put up a fight for it. Bucky's plan was to give it to him.

Honestly? Just give him the last piece he needed to wield cosmic power?

Yes, but not for long. Bucky held on to the hope that he could reach the scared and confused child-minded consciousness of the Cube. With Lang as Ant-Man, the two of them assembled the Cube and cleared the way for Kobik to return as a consciousness not controlled by Hydra. And Bucky was right. He prevailed and he helped her get out.

And he drew you out of her conscious mind as well.

Fit as a fiddle.

Leaving you to face, well, this perverted version of yourself—

I faced *him*. Him.

You faced him *in what now is called the Battle of Washington, and you defeated him.*

We carried the day.

And you met with him.

He's who you want to talk about now?

INTERVIEWER'S NOTE: Yes, I wanted to. I wanted to because I knew how he was feeling without asking. He spoke with the same deliberation in his voice that I heard when he spoke of his fellow soldiers who carried their wounds deep inside. Steve was wounded—America was wounded—and I wanted to help both heal.

If you would.

I have little to say. The war was over, and while my country worked to rebuild, to heal, to regain what it had lost, I went to him, the former Supreme Hydra.

Where was he?

Far away.

Can you . . . articulate why you wanted to see him?

He terrorized the country I've sworn to protect and betrayed every last one of its most cherished ideals. All this, he did in my name, wearing my face. Why did I go? I wish I knew.

And what did he say?

Everything you would expect from a mind such as his. He broke no laws. He took no power that wasn't given to him. He created none of the conditions that existed because of what he called my warped and twisted ideology that venerates fear and weakness above all else. He claimed the world he wanted to build would have been a better one until his rightful reign was denied to him. He said next time it wouldn't be about Hydra taking over the world but about Hydra taking it back.

The kind of things these people always say.

Hearing them helped me realize why I was there. During the cleanup of the Battle of Washington, I came across a little boy trapped in the rubble. I reached out to him and he flinched, pulled away. He was afraid of me. And I realized this would be my life now. Even though the world had seen me fight him, even with Stark's company spending millions explaining to the world what happened to me, there will always be a scar. I went to look into the eyes and take the measure of the man who had cost me all this.

How did that feel?

Truly? Like looking into the eyes of a Skrull or a Life-Model Decoy. He kept acting like he had done some impressive thing by getting people to listen to him and to go along with him. Who people went along with was *me*. All he did was lie. And maybe there is a silver lining to this. I've spent years telling people not to put too much trust into any one person, to not follow blindly but to question authority. Now, more people will understand why.

Is that all he left you with, Steve?

INTERVIEWER'S NOTE: *At this point, Captain Rogers took a pause before speaking. Knowing him as I now did, I knew he wasn't seeking the words to answer my question. His encounter with the counter-Rogers must have given him much to consider. Captain Rogers was debating whether to share it at all.*

What did he tell you, Steve?

He said his time in power had called into question the very ideals I fight for. He said he believed his methods were more in line with Americans' hopes and dreams today. He said he offered people power and they took it, while all I offer is someone for them to hide behind. He said that one day they will remember how it felt to have strength.

I'm sure you didn't let that go unanswered.

I said, "I know what you are and I've been fighting you my whole life." And I reminded myself that while we won this time, it's just the latest battle in a war that never ends.

It's also a reminder of a war that never ends inside of you, Steve Rogers. Your life in this world obligates you to constantly take the pulse of American ideals and compare them to your own. It's one thing for you to tell yourself that your ideals aren't in step with this nation of today. It's another thing entirely to hear it from someone else, and especially him.

It was damn hard to hear.

Do you believe him?

I need to find out.

IX.
RECONNECTION

At one time or another, we feel the need to pause
the frenzy of our individual lives and reassess.
We contemplate our prior choices, our various
commitments, and what the future might hold for us.

It made perfect sense to me when a man like
Steve Rogers, someone who has given nearly every
waking moment of his adult life in service to a
higher calling, did the same. He said he would
reach out when he was ready to share what he had
discovered on his "walkabout," for want of a better
word, and so I waited.

Did he seek validation of decisions made and
paths chosen? Having already avoided, denied, and
even cheated death on numerous occasions, did he
contemplate the legacy he will leave for others to
consider and perhaps find inspiration?

It was a question I wanted to ask--this time,
for me.

INTERVIEWER: *Steve, I truly appreciate the time you share with me. It's been a while, and it's good to sit down again.*

STEVE ROGERS: It's good for me too. Saves the taxpayers' money on my therapy bills.

You go to therapy?

Shouldn't everyone? The DoD provides a variety of counseling options to everyone on active duty, including their families. Just doing my part to stay at my best for my country.

I don't want to presume anything but I imagine you've found that helpful in a post-Hydra world.

I imagine a lot of us are talking this out still, whether with professionals or friends or whoever we can confide in or process with.

How is your world, Steve?

I've stayed less busy with the activities of the Hydra nostalgics and their ilk. I'm still rebuilding the trust of the American people. They know more about what was done in my name than I do. I am reminded by those who care about me to keep in mind this is about what was done to me, not what I failed to do. In the end, I was there to end it. That does not always keep me from hurting. Our land was not just conquered. It was broken. We have forgotten how hard it is to believe in the Dream, how to hold on to the Dream in the face of chaos, how hard it is to be truly American. It's not the story you see in the press. It's the story I see in people's eyes.

I can imagine that's hard.

I became the first in a line of Super-Soldiers, a line that also ended with me. That's the story we tell. But the truth is that our world keeps churning out Super-Soldiers. Cyborgs and clones. Mystic spawn of the Cosmic Cube. Every time I see another of them, I see another part of me.

You sound upset.

It's because I am. I'm upset and tired. Tired of supreme commanders and grand dictators, tired of having to prove that no part of them is part of me. I've returned to a country that's seen too much. People don't trust me anymore and that's their right. But do I even trust myself? Could that monster have been me?

How could you question that?

I'm told Hydra took on the problems we saw in America. Hydra fixed the schools, took out the drug pushers, got everybody healthcare, brought back the jobs. People felt safe and held their noses while accepting the methods of fascists. The America I come from was united by the values of democracy and freedom. It's an America of another time.

You knew, though, that in Hydra's absence others would rush to reclaim power over our people.

We are a nation always under threat. My shield, my uniform, these aren't just for show. When you believe like I believe, it's possible to forget that treachery is real. There are those who will swear before the flag one day and set it on fire the next.

NEWS

SHN **CAPTAIN AMERICA WANTED FOR QUESTIONING IN ROSS MURDER**

There were no secrets about you and General Ross having differences of opinion.

Ross tried to stop me from what he called "freelance" heroism. He told me my "bleeding-heart backers" were gone from Washington and that no one cared about my "Greatest Generation" anymore. I knew Ross was conspiring with the likes of the Power Elite, but before I could get the evidence I needed, he was killed.

By a blow in the back from a disc-like object delivered with enough force to nearly sever his spine.

I understood the suspicion, and not just because of what was done in my name. In my time as Nomad and the Captain, I claimed to serve my country while being in opposition to it. I have at times carried my shield while fighting with the government that entrusted it to me. To take back the American Dream and my country, I needed to submit to it.

By turning yourself in. And then escaping custody.

They can jail the revolutionary but they never could jail the revolution. I had friends who called themselves the Daughters of Liberty working to exonerate me. I also had Sharon, who helped me realize that in the midst of our broken country, at a time when I thought people needed Captain America, she told me what people needed was Steve Rogers. She wasn't wrong. There's no "Captain" without an America that believes in him.

So, the goal of your friends was?

Redemption. We worked our leads and broke apart factions of the Power Elite, working our way to the top of it all. That's when I found Aleksander Lukin.

Wait, from the Kronas Corporation?

Yes. And not just Lukin but hidden within him, just as he had attempted with me, was the consciousness of the Red Skull. We also got on the trail of a cop killer with the codename of Scourge. New York was in chaos. Mayor Wilson Fisk was believed dead. Police had tracked Scourge to a location upstate. In the end, though, it all came down to trust.

How so?

I asked for trust that we would stop these cop killings, and an NYPD officer trusted in me enough to tell me where to go so I could help. And I did. I evaded gunfire the likes of which I'd not seen since the war. I flushed Scourge out and he died at his own hands. With the NYPD and the people of New York believing in me again, it was the start I needed.

But that still wasn't enough to clear you of Ross' murder.

No. My friends, the Daughters of Liberty, were the latest members of a sisterhood of great and enlightened women born of free ideas, free feeling, and free expression. They have been trained by science, by the sword, and by sorcery. I learned that I had been connected to this sisterhood from my very beginning, as Peggy Carter had been assigned to make sure I and my Super-Soldier powers never fell into the wrong hands. And somehow, with the help of Agatha Harkness, Peggy returned to us when we needed her most. The sisterhood trusted me with the task of not just clearing myself but also helping to heal America. They teamed me with my closest comrades, Sam and Bucky and Sharon.

You always are at your best with a team.

I'd say the same. As it turned out, the path out of the murder charge was easy. General Ross never died in the first place. A Life-Model Decoy took the blow intended for him. With S.H.I.E.L.D. disbanded, apparently LMDs were easy for Ross to acquire.

I really ought to pick one of those up for myself someday.

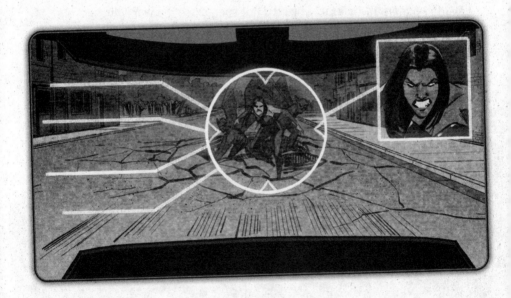

In my experience, they are a lot more trouble than they are worth. Of greater concern than my legal issues was the fight ahead of us. Sharon obtained the Iron Patriot armor and neutralized the mutant Selene, who had worked to bring Lukin back to life. Once she was out of the picture, I addressed America about the charges being dropped.

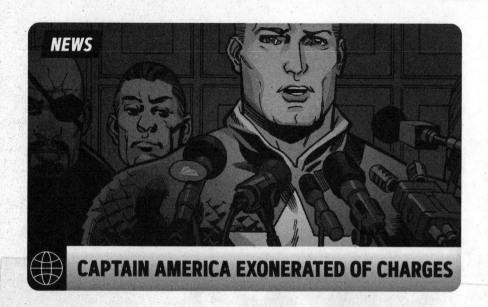

NEWS

CAPTAIN AMERICA EXONERATED OF CHARGES

Transcript of remarks by Captain Steve Rogers following the dismissal of federal charges against him:

I know what the past few months have meant to you. I know how much you've been hurt. And I know that I've been part of the hurt. I'm Captain America, not Captain Perfect.

But I've been fighting for this country since I was a kid. And what I know now, more than ever, is that our greatest generations are yet to come.

I know we've seen some dark times, broken trust, betrayal. I've seen firsthand what that betrayal has done to us. I've seen the families divided, the small towns abandoned, the closed factories, the shuttered churches. And I've seen those who'd pose as saviors unmasked as charlatans.

And I know how hard it is to believe again. But I am asking you to still believe in America. Believe in yourselves. Believe in the people.

Believe in the Dream.

(transcript ends)

I'm sure it's hard to consider your words at the press conference, given how closely they were followed by the Central Park rally bombing.

The people gathered there were lost to themselves, and through whatever path they took, they came across a new theory of the world they wanted to believe. A theory that came from the Red Skull. He tells them what they've always longed to hear: They secretly are great but the whole world is against them. If they are truly men, they will fight back. Suddenly, they have found purpose. It becomes what they live for and what they will die for. I found the flag and they found the Skull. With the help of Agatha Harkness, we discovered that the bomb the Red Skull wanted to blame on me was his attempt to explosively harvest the raw emotions of the crowd, their hate and fear and rage, and turn it against them with deadly force. The Skull tried to do it again in Chicago but we stopped his plan.

What were your next steps?

The only ones I knew to take were toward Aleksander Lukin or the Red Skull or whatever combination of them both he was at that point. I was going to talk to him and then he was going to talk to the world.

I can't imagine what you two might have to talk about.

Ours wasn't so much of a discussion as it was a confession. I pressed the Skull to admit to the bombing and even more to admit to just what kind of leader or, more accurately, ruler, he knew himself to be.

Excerpt of transcript of broadcast conversation between Captain America and the Red Skull

RED SKULL: You claim to speak for a nation you barely know. You slander me a killer while bearing the flag of men who subdued and broke a continent. It is a cruel joke. "Captain America." A man who scarcely understands his own name. They say you are a man out of time? No. You are a man out of country.

CAPTAIN AMERICA: And what are you?

RED SKULL: I am the man you think you are. I am the one who has taken your precious liberties and bent them against you. Witness my mark on the deviants of America. I am the conqueror! I am a plague to the weak, a scourge upon the wretched. You, a self-styled champion of a mongrel order, would interrogate me on my purpose? On my mission? Listen closely, Captain. Even one as dull as you should be able to comprehend what I am about to say. I am death. I am the purge. I come to sweep away the filth from your cities, the barnacles from your hull, the insects that infest this world. And I care not one whit how many followers must be sacrificed for this cleansing. On their bodies, I will build a citadel to the West. And these Americans? They shall watch as a new order arises from the ash.

CAPTAIN AMERICA: Imagine if those Americans could watch you now.

(transcript ends)

You goaded him into saying the quiet part out loud.

All while his words were streamed live to the Red Skull's followers, so they could see exactly what he thinks of them. There hasn't been a Red Skull rally since. I've been reminded that some believers remain, that some simply call his admissions "refreshing." Upton Sinclair wrote, "It is difficult to get a man to understand something when his salary depends on his not understanding it." Where is the payoff in following someone who has no interest at all in your wellbeing?

Speaking of questioning one's convictions and commitments, it wasn't long after this that you found yourself questioning your own.

An upcoming exhibition at the Smithsonian on focusing on "Americans Who Fight," including service members, first responders, and even everyday heroes who just show their mettle when it's needed, had me in something of a funk.

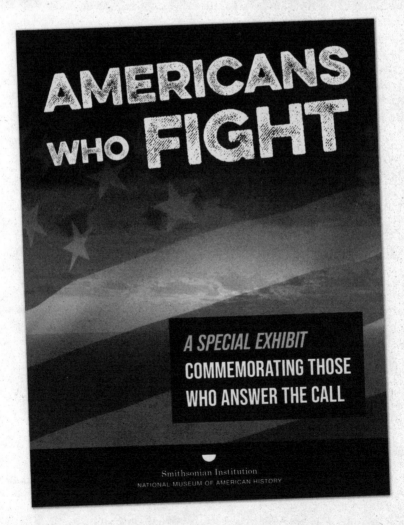

You weren't thrilled with the name.

I felt like it conveyed the idea that America fights even when there might be a better way to resolve a problem . . . that fighting was the most effective solution. The Smithsonian wanted to add my shield to the exhibit, and I wasn't wanting to allow that. I know what it's like to be used for propaganda purposes. It helped sell a lot of savings bonds to fund the war effort back in my day, but more and more I was feeling out of sorts about my place in America.

We're a complicated country, especially these days. It makes sense to take stock of your place in it.

I get that I mean different things to different people, but I always thought I could be a unifying figure. You know, someone who fights for everyone, not just this or that demographic or political ideology. It's a lot easier in theory than it is in practice, let me tell you.

I don't doubt it for a moment. Regular people face the same dilemma every day. The most vocal ones on either side are convinced they're right, while moderate voices plead for common understanding. And then there's you, the physical embodiment of an ideal that transcends people on all sides of any given divide.

After everything I'd been through, including losing the faith a lot of people had in me after that Hydra business, I took that first trip in the hopes of reestablishing my connection to ordinary people. I think it worked more than it failed, but in the end actions speak louder than words.

I dare say your actions since that unfortunate incident have earned you renewed respect from many of your fellow Americans.

Yes, this latest excursion came after somebody dressed like me broke into my apartment and stole my shield, and the first thing they did with was hurt people. He caused a train wreck. I couldn't understand why someone would want to do that, but even as Sam Wilson and I are trying to help people on the trains, we run into this kid.

A remarkable young man, all things considered. Traveling the country's railways with his partner, doing what he could to help and protect others.

FISCHER, AARON
KNOWN ALIASES/ALTER EGOS:
"Captain America of
the Railways"

(*nods*) Absolutely. To have to play the cards he was dealt as a kid, running away from an abusive father, and then channel that toward helping the less fortunate? That takes a special quality and strength of character. Just an ordinary guy, with no special powers or abilities, doing the work of a super hero. And he wasn't alone. Aaron told us there were people like him all over the country: regular, everyday Americans trying to do good deeds.

And yet, this other person was doing their best to undermine your reputation.

He wasn't alone either. There was the sniper who tried to kill Aaron. Luckily he escaped with only a minor wound, but I was worried these people, whoever they were, might be going after this "Captain America network" for some reason. So, Sam and I decided to look deeper into the whole thing.

And what did you find?

Captain America, as Tony might say, is "a whole mood," it seems.

These people—these *amazing* people—were acting in defense of those who couldn't protect themselves. Sam and I were stunned at their dedication, their passion to do what they believed was right. They had no idea about the bigger fight being waged by James Sanders and Sinthea Schmidt, the people who stole my shield and were using it to ruin Captain America's reputation, all as part of a scheme hatched by Hate-Monger. But once they found out? They lined up right beside me and Sam, ready to fight. No powers, no special weapons . . . just heart. Heart for days.

Along with James Barnes and John Walker, as well.

We Are Captain America.

Top row: Aaron Fischer, Nichelle Wright, Joe Gomez
Bottom Row: Arielle Agbayani, Captain Jeremy Merrick

(*smiles*) We had all the Captain Americas. Or, "Captains America," as Sam said at one point when the situation was at its most insane. Once Bucky brought the reinforcements, it was over. We had control of their command center, having learned that Hate-Monger planned to impersonate a radical talk-show blowhard in an attempt to destroy my reputation. It sounds completely wild but it's Hate-Monger we're talking about here. With all of that under our control, his first broadcast was a bust even though we were on the air and broadcasting to the entire country.

And yet, with that golden opportunity laid at your feet, you opted not to make one of your famously stirring speeches.

Nope. I left that to someone else.

Transcript of video broadcast from the Channel Islands

AARON FISCHER: Hey, y'all. The Captains Network here. Seems like we maybe got off on the wrong foot, and that some of ya might not dig us, or are even a little steamed at our hijinks.

Well . . . America's weird that way, isn't it? Fifty states, millions of people, and all you gotta do is go fifty feet or fifty miles and suddenly no one looks like you and it feels like a completely different country, or planet. Look, we get it, but . . . isn't that also kind of amazing?

Because hey, the truth is . . . we've got your back. All of us.

(transcript ends)

That experience restored my hope in the dream that is America, but also in my fellow Americans.

I have to admit that I'm asking this as much from my personal interest as I am for the record, Steve. What's next for Captain America?

Well, as we just discussed, it's Captain *Americas*, plural. There's a whole network of people out there doing the work that needs doing. They honor me and everything I stand for, and I can only hope I'm up to the challenge of being worthy of that respect. As for me and Sam, he has just as much right to the name as I do. This country and this world's ready for two of them. As a hero, Captain America has been described as a symbol of truth, a sentinel of liberty, and so many other ways. That's a lot for one person to carry. The mission that never ends is to stand for those who can't. There's more than enough in that to be shared by two people.

That's terrific. Thank you.

And I'll tell you what's ahead for Steve Rogers too.

Please do.

I have no idea. I've been more the shield than I have myself. I want to work on being much more than a lousy Steve Rogers. I want to remember what it means to be an everyday American. But I'm not doing it alone. I've said before that I've been blessed with friends. Truly, forget the shield, forget the service, forget even the war. It's the friendships I'm most proud of. It's the friends that carry me through.

Sounds like you have something else. You have hope.

I do have hope. And I have the Dream.

AFTERWORD

I daresay anyone choosing to read this volume
believed they already knew at the outset what kind
of man Steve Rogers is. My hope is that you know
it now.

The qualities he exudes--duty, honor, integrity,
loyalty, pride--are not just words or ideas to him.
They are him, as essential to his genetic makeup as
his actual DNA. As Professor Erskine knew all those
years ago, Steve Rogers was already a Super-Soldier
before he received the serum that made him Captain
America. Science only enhanced and strengthened
his ability to fulfill his commitment to the
country he wished to serve.

And serve it he has. Through times of war and
peace and even during crises of confidence or
conscience, Steve Rogers has always answered the
call when his nation and even his planet needed
him. That obligation has often exacted tremendous
personal cost, either to himself or those closest
to him. He has endured physical and emotional
anguish, tragedy, and loss, and still he is here.

What I hope you also know is what Captain
Rogers is not. You read it yourself: He disagrees
with being labeled a man out of time. I submit this
volume as evidence he is a man for all times. His
charge is as timeless as humankind's pursuit of
happiness in every imaginable form. When we find
happiness, he celebrates it; when someone tries to
strip it from us, he defends it.

It would be understandable, even forgivable, if he one day decided to permanently pass the shield on to a successor, be it Sam Wilson or some as-yet unnamed person of sterling character and strength of principles. We know such people are out there, ready to answer the challenge. Captain America is an ideal, it seems; a promise that our best days remain ahead of us, if only we harbor the strength and conviction to keep pressing forward.

Steve Rogers has always endeavored to be worthy of us and the faith we've placed in him for generations. We must also seek to be worthy of him.

ACKNOWLEDGMENTS

Once again, we find ourselves indebted to the creative minds behind decades of wonderful tales told in comics form--this time, to the writers and artists who brought us Captain America.

We must start at a point more than eighty years ago, by recognizing Joe Simon and Jack Kirby as the creators of this character who has inspired generations of comics fans. Then, there's Stan Lee, who inarguably revitalized the good captain for Marvel Comics fans by adding him to the roster of the Avengers.

The events and characters Steve Rogers mentions in this book came from the minds of writers spanning the width and breadth of Captain America and Avengers stories, including but not limited to Jason Aaron, Chuck Austen, Mike W. Barr, Brian Michael Bendis, Tom Brevoort, Ed Brubaker, Bob Budiansky, Kurt Busiek, John Byrne, Michael Carlin, Joe Casey, Joey Cavalieri, Chris Claremont, Ta-Nehisi Coates, Gerry Conway, Tom DeFalco, J.M. DeMatteis, Scott Edelman, Harlan Ellison, Steve Englehart, Al Ewing, Gary Friedrich, Steve Gerber, Dave Gibbons, Peter Gillis, Don Glut, Steven Grant, Mark Gruenwald, Larry Hama, Bob Harras, Glenn Herdling, Jonathan Hickman, Sam Humphries, Kathryn Immonen, Tony Isabella, Geoff Johns, Dan Jurgens, Len Kaminski, Mike Kanterovich, Terry Kavanagh, Collin Kelly, Barbara Kesel, Robert Kirkman, David Anthony Kraft, Alan Kupperberg, Paul Kupperberg, Jackson Lanzing, Rob Liefeld, Scott Lobdell, Jeph Loeb, Jed MacKay, Roger McKenzie, Ralph Macchio, Bill Mantlo, David Michelinie, Al Milgrom, Robert Morales, Fabian Nicieza, Tochi Onyebuchi, Jerry Ordway, George Pérez, Rick Remender, John Ney Rieber, James

Robinson, Bill Rosemann, Jim Shooter, Walt Simonson, Nick
Spencer, Roger Stern, Roy Thomas, Jim Valentino, Mark
Waid, John Warner, Jeremy Whitley, Marv Wolfman, and Jim
Zub. For all the tales we've read and remembered since
childhood, we thank you.

Robb Pearlman, a talented and entertaining writer in
his own right, set us on the path of writing this book in
the first place. His support of us in his capacity as an
insightful editor as well as a caring and trusted friend
never wavers. Robb, we remain grateful for the opportunity
and are thankful for you.

Elizabeth Smith once again has served as our champion,
our defender, and our always visible woman since the day
this project became real. She has encouraged and guided
us every step of the way, and (as we write this) the
heavy lifting she does to shape our writing and get this
into print as you have seen it is just getting started.
Elizabeth, we depend on you as Cap depends on Sam and
Bucky combined. We could not have done this without you.

You readers would not be nearly as engaged by
this book were it just type on a page. Allow us to
introduce the wonderfully talented people at Smart Pop/
BenBella Books who added the Super-Soldier Serum to our
manuscript. Thank you to Monica Lowry and Kit Sweeney
for their interior design duties, and to Brigid Pearson
and Morgan Carr, who created the cover. Your visions
for the look and feel of this book are once again
star-spangled fantastic.

James Fraleigh did way more than ensure each i was
dotted and t was crossed. (Let's see whether he lets
those letters stand without quotation marks, as we're not
sure which way is correct.) As our copy editor, he was
also your shield against our errors of style, spelling,

obfuscation, and the Oxford comma (since Kevin refuses to use them). Thank you, James.

And for the rest of the Smart Pop/BenBella Books team, we certainly thank Glenn Yeffeth, BenBella Publisher; Adrienne Lang, BenBella Deputy Publisher; Ariel Jewett, BenBella Publishing Assistant; Leah Wilson, BenBella Editor-in-Chief; Heather Butterfield, Smart Pop Marketing Director; Alicia Kania, Vendor Content Manager; and Susan Welte, BenBella Sales Manager, for everything they did to get this book into your hands.

And great thanks to our pals representing Marvel: Jeff Youngquist, VP, Production and Special Projects; Sarah Singer, Editor, Special Projects; Sven Larsen, VP, Licensed Publishing; and Jeremy West, Manager, Licensed Publishing. Your entrusting us with the legacy and voice of Captain America has been more exciting for us than the first time we got the keys to the family car. You didn't even give us a curfew.

From Dayton: I know this is going to come across as flippant, but I promise you it's not anything at all like that. I want to thank Reb Brown. I'd never read a Cap comic until 1979, a week or so after I watched the original <u>Captain America</u> TV film. Sure, it doesn't hold up to anything with that Chris Evans dude, but it was enough to send me to the store.

There was a learning curve, of course. He's with the Avengers! No, he's in World War II! Then he's back! It took a bit for 11-year-old me to figure out what was going on. As I grew older, reading Cap comics set during the war led me to books chronicling the history of the conflict and those who fought it. This in turn led me to an appreciation of that period of our history I continue to find fascinating. To this day, a new Cap adventure set back then never fails to pull me in, and if that leads me to some new morsel of knowledge about the actual war, so much the better.

And it's all thanks to Reb Brown.

Life is weird, sometimes.

From Kevin: The year 1940 saw the birth of my mother and the debut of Captain America on newsstands across the country. Cap joined the Avengers in the spring of 1964, and a few months later I joined my family. Mom taught me to read before I was 3, and among the first stories she put in my hands were comic books. As my collection grew, she gave a space in our basement over to me, and I spent hours upon hours down there reading, imagining, and even writing in what my family calls to this day "the comic book room." She could not have been more proud of me when I started working on this book. I'm sad to say that she didn't get to see it completed. This one's for you, Mom.

Ultimately, we offer our thanks to you for reading this book at all, let alone reading it this far. We had a lot of fun with this, and we hope you did as well.

ABOUT THE AUTHORS

DAYTON WARD is a New York Times best-selling author or coauthor of more than forty novels and novellas, often working with his best friend, Kevin Dilmore. His short fiction has appeared in more than thirty anthologies, and he's written for publications such as NCO Journal, Kansas City Voices, Famous Monsters of Filmland, Star Trek, and Star Trek Communicator as well as the websites Tor.com, StarTrek.com, and Syfy.com. Before making the jump to full-time writing, Dayton was a software developer, having discovered the private sector after serving for eleven years in the U.S. Marine Corps. Though he currently lives in Kansas City, Missouri, with his family, Dayton is a Florida native and still maintains a torrid long-distance romance with his beloved (and often beleaguered) Tampa Bay Buccaneers. Visit him at www.daytonward.com.

KEVIN DILMORE has teamed with author and best pal Dayton Ward for more than twenty years on novels, shorter fiction, and other writings chiefly in the Star Trek universe. As a senior writer for Hallmark Cards, Kevin has helped create books, Keepsake Ornaments, greeting cards, and other products featuring characters from DC Comics, Marvel Comics, Star Trek, Star Wars, and other properties. He is a content approver for the recent Rainbow Brite comics series by Dynamite Entertainment. A contributor to publications including The Village Voice, Amazing Stories, Star Trek Communicator, and Famous Monsters of Filmland, he lives in Kansas City, Missouri.

ADDITIONAL DECLASSIFIED DOCUMENTS

Notes, Interviews, and Files
from the Avengers' Archives

Iron Man: Tony Stark Declassified

Black Panther: T'Challa Declassified

Captain Marvel: Carol Danvers Declassified
March 2025

Find out more at SmartPopBooks.com